LOST GEOGRAPHY

Charlotte Bacon, born in 1965 and educated at Harvard and Columbia, teaches English at the University of New Hampshire in Durham. Her collection of stories, *A Private State*, was awarded the PEN/Hemingway Award for First Fiction in 1998.

LOST GEOGRAPHY

CHARLOTTE BACON

HarperCollins*Publishers*

HarperCollins*Publishers*
77–85 Fulham Palace Road,
Hammersmith, London W6 8JB

www.**fire**and**water**.com

This paperback edition 2000
1 3 5 7 9 8 6 4 2

A catalogue record for this book
is available from the British Library

ISBN 0 00 711315 3

Set in Walbaum

Printed and bound in Great Britain by
Clays Ltd, St Ives plc

FOR BRAD

 Contents

PART ONE

CROSSINGS

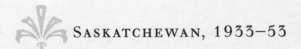# SASKATCHEWAN, 1933–53

One August morning, Margaret Evans opened the door of her clinic to find a tall, slight, sandy haired boy ranting about forest fires and cod. "Haul the nets in, man," he shouted in a dense Scottish accent when he saw her. "Haul them in!" Margaret, alone because the doctor was sick with flu, asked the boy's name. Martinson, the farmer who'd brought the fellow by, just shrugged; the Scot wouldn't answer. Too busy rambling about running from barns and horses in flames. As they spoke, the sick man slumped to the floor, worn to sleep or unconsciousness, Margaret did not know.

His fever was 104 degrees, high but not unmanageable, yet she was anxious. Just twenty, skills still bookish, she realized she not only was responsible for the young man's care but was, for the first time, going to strip a male to nakedness. As she sponged his chest with witch hazel, she noticed he was both thin and clean. Thin she expected; that was often so with workers on their way to British Columbia, where Margaret guessed he was headed. Few stayed in Saskatchewan, unless the mines up north lured them. But he didn't look like someone interested in tunnels and dynamite, secret ribbons of minerals. Too delicate in the wrists.

Clean, however, was a pleasant discovery. Filth often sat as thick as fur on the itinerants she and the doctor tended, men who smelled of liquor, sap, and old food. Her father encouraged her to become a nurse, saying, "You're good with the shoats, aren't you." How were people different from pigs? The answer was that pigs were cleaner. But this boy had recently bathed and smelled as sharp as willows. She turned then to his pants, easing them from his lower body, listening to the brief song of small change in a pocket. His legs were sinewed, veiled in tawny hair. When it came to his underwear, however, her confidence faltered. The squeamishness annoyed her. She'd grown up with animals. She had brothers.

She'd even felt the bulky outlines of a boy's crotch against her own, a night dizzy with fireflies last June, at a party to celebrate the end of her training. She'd drunk beer, her stockings were ruined on a bramble, and her mother was thin-lipped and silently appalled the week after. But Margaret had never pressed her hand to a man's bare hip, never even seen that swerve of bone, or watched, without a cluster of nurses and a clinical purpose, the mysterious creature sprouting between the legs. I am a nurse, she told herself, and smoothed down the skirt of her uniform. It was quite tender to see his equipment coiled in a soft, wrinkled C on its side in a nest of dark-red hair. There was nothing frightening about it—the hair was wilder, more disturbing—and she couldn't, as she swabbed him down, and inched on the bottom half of the pajamas, imagine why she'd been so silly.

He'd been quiet, breathing with the shallow intensity of high fever as she washed him, but now he began to mumble words she couldn't quite make out. She did hear quite clearly the rounded angles of his accent. Scottish farmers were as terse as the Finns, and even more committed drinkers than the Germans. Margaret's parents were English, a much milder race, it seemed to her, but she was born in Canada and had a rather tenuous sense of belonging to the island that had given her Christmas and a king. Her patient, then, radiated a kind of wan foreignness. The clinic wouldn't open until twelve, and for a few hours before other patients intruded, she daubed his forehead, leafed through her diagnostic texts, and listened.

She'd never heard a man, much less a Scot, talk so much. He began to speak more coherently, and she listened to threads of stories unwind from him. Streams of them, even, spilling in the same generous, rippled way that water did in a pond that had crested its limit. In the narrow bed, he spoke not only of fish and fire but of scones and knives, brothers and porridge, shipwrecks and anchors. "Don't be stupid, lad, the boom, the boom," he shouted at one point. Another time he sat straight up and said, "Pour them all another, I'll pay." That had made her laugh, even though he thrashed with fever. She sponged him down again and pulled up his sheets, waiting.

It was like a strange film, illicit and personal. Margaret loved the cinema, though she couldn't afford to go that often, and she wished she could sit in the darkened hall alone, instead of listening to Mavis Allen suck her caramels and to all the other irritations a crowd brought with it. She was sitting there, enjoying the sick man's strange theater, when he said, "Go on, now, fuck me." A ghastly thrill ran through her body. She went to tidy herself then and splash water on her face. He'd been with women. He looked young for that, but what did she know. "Men's drives," her mother had cagily called them the night Margaret went to a dance with one of Ole Anderson's broad, scrubbed sons. "Be careful of men's drives," her mother said, taking a kettle from the stove. Through the cone of steam, Mrs. Evans had given her a look that warned her daughter not to ask more.

Margaret had known what her mother meant. It was clear what was on Ronny Gilcreast's mind when he watched Coral Paddington cross the school yard, running not so much because she was late but because it gave her an excuse to bounce. The phrase had spread among the student nurses. "Men's drives," they'd say, slamming lockers as Mr. Pierce, a spindly anatomy professor, crabbed past, tugging his bow tie. But before the sick man loudly said, "Go on, now, fuck me," Margaret had not quite grasped the rough directness of men's drives and the feeling they awoke in her own body. It was after this she knew he would recover.

Early the next evening, Dr. Cross returned. He was a man with the red-netted cheeks of a drinker, and Margaret knew his bouts of flu were masks for hangovers. Polishing his spectacles, he listened attentively to Margaret's report. She'd taken thorough notes, knowing that despite or perhaps because of his attachment to gin, the doctor was cautious. It had been quiet at the clinic, the boy by far the most interesting case, partly since it wasn't clear what he suffered from.

Dr. Cross asked, "What's wrong with him, Miss Evans?"

"It doesn't seem to be meningitis or measles or scarlet fever," she said slowly. "He's not wheezing, so I'd rule out pneumonia." Dr. Cross listened, waiting, looking at her through his newly unsmudged glasses. He had told her when he took her on that he wanted a nurse who could think for herself, and though Margaret did not quite know if this quality was true of her, she'd said, "I'll look forward to that."

"I think," she said, gathering courage, "that it's a kind of influenza brought on by overwork." Despite the neatly documented maladies her medical texts described, most of what ailed the sick was unnamed, untraceable. She did not like this blurry aspect of nursing, but the doctor seemed satisfied, and they went in to inspect the young man.

He was fully awake, sitting up in bed. He had a cowlick, Margaret saw, and his collarbones pushed tight against his pale skin. What she noticed most, however, was that he looked a bit stunned. As if, Margaret later told him, he'd just realized he'd stepped into the wrong house.

What had given Davis Campbell this look of surprise was wondering how he had earned the luck to have such a pretty woman as his nurse. The brown sway of her hair, the smooth curve of her skin, the ringlessness of her marriage hand. It seemed miraculous to him. He was also aware that he was not wearing underwear and wondered if she had been responsible for its removal. How had his body had the good sense to get sick in the only town where he could have fallen into her care?

"Good evening. I am Dr. Cross. This is Nurse Evans. You

7

were brought here with a high fever. Do you know your name?" the man asked. Davis looked at the pair, in the trim whites of their work, waiting for his answer. He did know his name, which was something of a relief, because since waking, he'd been conscious that the fever had burned him empty. He'd lain in bed, listening to the voices in the room next door, looking at the play of twilight on the creamy walls. His fever, though much lower, still made his mind float a bit. He felt he might be some artifact they'd unearthed and were testing for its validity. He wanted to tell them, I'm not worth the effort. He was a curled leaf, a shriveled peg of corn, a pebble of nothing to be scuffed along in the dust. He had no idea how long he'd been in this room with its unvarnished nightstand. His gear wasn't visible and had probably been divided up by now among the other men he'd camped with. In short, it was clear that the two at the foot of the bed had no idea who he was.

So, for a variety of reasons, he did not answer at first. Davis knew he had a chance to become something larger than a wandering Scot, something that would make Nurse Evans widen her eyes with interest. But it was looking at her more closely that made him say, "Davis Campbell," the second time the doctor asked, rather impatiently. The lightest smile twitched at her mouth as she stood there, and it came to him that she had seen him, all of him, and the knowledge that her long pink fingers had touched his skin made it impossible to lie. It was something of a relief to be called back into the world.

During his week and a half of recovery, Margaret gave him books she thought he might enjoy. The history of the Anglican Church in Canada. A geological treatise on the Rockies.

At least he slept well, but he asked her after these two, "What if you brought something we could read out loud together?" The next day she shyly handed him Dickens.

"Have you read it?" she asked, and he knew how much he liked her when he lied and said no, he'd never had the pleasure of reading *Bleak House*. He'd loved it as a boy recovering from his first bad illness. At the age of thirteen, he fell in the ocean off his father's boat and was snagged from the water with the gaff, his body the color of plum jam. Like most fishermen his family knew, he and his brothers not only could not swim but did not believe in it. The sea wasn't recreation, it was a roof, a winch, a kettle, a resource. Swimming would have been like fraternizing with someone of the wrong religion, which they never had a chance to do, as everyone was Church of Scotland.

During Davis's convalescence, his mother slipped him books she'd ordered from the lending library. Kipling. A volume of Shelley. Wrapped in brown paper and with a sheet of parchment glued to the inside covers, stamped with dates and dotted with the feathery signatures of the women who'd read them before. They'd sprinkled their tea and scones on the pages, too, but after the first chapter of *Kim*, Davis barely noticed.

He grew stronger slowly and his mother kept bringing books. He read until his head ached. Stevenson, Scott, Shakespeare. Pirates, knights, castles, revenge. He'd had no idea. There was no describing how their pictures swam in front of his eyes. So when his brother said, "What do you want those for?" and kicked the bed steadily as he glared at the pile of books stacked on the blankets, Davis said nothing.

"Leave him be, John, and stop kicking the bed," their

mother said. When his brother left, Davis lay there. She said, lips pulled in as they always were when she was serious, "He's right, Davis, it's time to get out." And though she'd been the one to slip him the books, she also decided when his recovery was done. The power of mothers. Allowed to change their minds just like that. Her quick, chapped hands stripped the quilt from his thin legs and tossed him his clothes, yanking open the curtains as she left the room.

It really had been time to go back outside. He saw the buttery gold skin of the cows again and the crescent of the strand glittering in the high-summer sun. But something had changed. He would imagine now great East Indiamen anchored in the cove. He would see towering factories on the burn by the kirk. His mind shifted the landscape to suit itself, as if the weeks of stories he'd drunk in had leaked back out and dyed the village new colors.

His mother was the one who noticed. One morning she saw his mouth working as he stumbled to the house with the milk and she asked, "Saying your prayers?" Would it have been good to say yes? Davis was never entirely sure how his mother felt about God, though churchgoing was as much a part of her as the abrupt way she broke the thread when she finished sewing a button. A gesture worn into an indisputable fact of who she was.

"No, ma'am," he said, watching the froth of the hot milk give up a curl of steam in the cool morning.

"Then what?" she said, stopping in the doorframe to look at her youngest more closely. It was the type of light you couldn't lie in. Fog about to be burned clear. Light that ringed everything in a smudged halo.

"Poem," he said with the shame he'd felt when she caught him at six wetting his bed. Another quality of mothers: they saw you at your worst and then were competent and brisk.

"Which one?" she asked, her hands stilled on the broom. As if there were just a few from which he might choose. The milk staggered against the lip of the battered pail. He tried to move toward the house, but she stood there, solid as a post in the door.

"Sonnet," he managed to say. In his mind, he had the gorgeous words spilling. "Bare ruined choirs, where late the sweet birds sang."

She looked at him then. "Time for the books to be stowed, Davis," and she sounded sad. Had she been trying to protect him from wanting more than he should? It was a moment that taught him double living. He went on reading and borrowing and learning poems as he learned to nurse a whiskey, care for leaking boats, and stay upright on slippery decks. Then, four years later, having saved a tiny sum and read his way through every book in that part of coastal Scotland, he told his family he'd booked passage for Halifax.

But it didn't occur to Davis to tell Margaret much of this—no one had encouraged him to say what he had seen or heard—and instead he let her read to him nights when she got off duty and the doctor had gone off to drink and pore through his medical books. When smallpox snatched Esther's beauty, Margaret started to cry, and Davis was amazed to realize that something as slight as the edge of color marking her cheek could have the effect of weaving him into a town he'd so thoroughly intended to reject.

Arriving in Regina alone one dawn when the air was

already quilted with heat, he saw clearly that this barren place would not be where he'd settle. Davis found its stillness kept him from taking full breaths. Sitting at his campsite, he'd heard the sky's loud hum, as if bees were caught inside a low invisible hive. He'd realized he had a terrible headache.

He wandered into town in search of tea. In the first café he saw, with the edgy clarity of fever, the scars that wormed their way across the hands of the farmers, the droop of their lips as they slurped coffee from saucers. Faces and hands that spoke of a total resignation to labor. The tea arrived in a plump steel pot that reflected the men's faces, distorting them to unexpected cheer. Davis adjusted it so he didn't have to watch their cheeks pulled to smiles. In the grip of the second deep fever of his life, Davis saw his tea was shuddering and realized that it was because his hands held the cup and that they were shaking. Sweat bubbled his shirt to his back, and then he was aware only of another pair of hands, worked to the hardness of polished wood, hauling him into dust-rich wind.

She liked him. It was quite simple. His gray-blue eyes, the nose sharp as a weathervane, his quiet pleasure in her presence. But she knew nothing more about him than he'd arrived in Halifax a year before and was working his way across Canada. He was from a fishing family and didn't like the sea anymore. She nodded as if she understood, but she'd never seen the ocean and imagined it as something beautiful and murmuring, not as something to be avoided. She invited him one night, nearly done with the Dickens, to call her

Margaret, knowing as she did that it signaled an opening between them, a channel through which he could pass. It was late in August and the evening air would soon start creaking with cold. He was healthy enough to leave the clinic. It was time to decide if he was going to spend the winter in Regina or try to make it to the coast before the first blizzards.

Davis said, "Margaret. It's a pretty name," and placed a bookmark into the volume. "She's the patron saint of women in travail."

Horrified, she said, "Are your people Papist?"

"Worse," he said, "pagan." Men's drives. She smelled them then, when he smiled at her.

She puffed with being nursely, to distract herself. "Do you think you want to stay in Regina?" she asked, a pile of fresh linen in her arms, not looking at him.

"I'd try for a bit," said Davis, and she blushed with satisfaction, which she took care not to show him. The next morning, she mentioned casually to her father that the young Scot was feeling better and would be looking for work.

Mr. Evans met him in the café where Davis had first taken sick, and Margaret, doing errands that she allowed to steer her past the plate glass, saw her father's mouth move slowly as Davis, still pale from his time in bed, listened with a bend to his head.

At supper, her father reported he seemed solid enough and that Philip Hamilton needed a hand with late haying. "Where's he from?" Margaret's mother asked.

"Near the Hebrides. Got quite an accent," her father said. "Pass the potatoes, Margaret." So Davis stayed and word spread that he came on time and was not a drinker. He gathered the few scraps of work that were available, filling the holes left by sons driven to the mines or the coast by falling wheat prices.

Margaret would stand by the clinic's window and watch for him in town. Sometimes he strolled about with other hands, a scruffy collection of Ukrainians and Swedes, men whose English was as ragged as their clothes. Davis looked small next to them, fresher. Sometimes he was alone and she saw he was satisfied with his own company, playing with something in his mind. Once in a while, he would drop in at the clinic, holding his cap in his hands. They were shy with each other now that he was clothed and healthy. "Are you reading?" she asked once.

"Not much," he admitted. "No time. But you must have finished *Bleak House* by now?" Yet when she hinted she hadn't, Davis only commented, "That's a pity," and said that he had to leave. He confused her, and it made her more short-tempered at home. Her mother told her she was still in her father's house and to mind her ways, miss.

One night in October, Margaret returned from a difficult birth. Her mother greeted her and told her to bathe. Margaret was so exhausted that she first sat down on her bed, fingers wound round a shoelace but unable to tug. It had been the first baby for the couple. The father, a sweat-streaked Swede, had been drinking brandy and careened around the tiny house, flushed and swearing. The woman, too, was red in the face and lowing like a cow as she waddled around the crowded, smoky room. Whether her yelling came from pain or fury, Margaret and the doctor couldn't tell, because neither of the Swedes spoke much English.

Births. She'd attended fifteen or so since starting work, so that the infants, their parents, and the circumstances tended to blend together in an exciting, patchy tapestry of domed bellies slowly falling inward, cresting purple heads, pots of boiled water. But tonight, Margaret couldn't stop thinking about this particular woman's face. Stumbling about the room in the center of a contraction, the expectant mother looked ancient. But when her face uncramped from its scowl of pain, it was obvious she was very young. Her hair unraveled in fuzzed loops from its pigtails. A doll tilted on the bed. In the midst of the memory, Margaret heard her father mention her name in the kitchen. Then she heard her mother say, "that young man, the Scot," quite clearly. Standing, one shoe finally off, she edged toward the door to hear more.

Her father's paper rustled. Her mother clanked the cutlery about. "He's penniless," her father said.

"So are we nearly, Robert," said her mother, in a tone that managed to make the comment not a rebuke but a sad and obvious statement of fact. Margaret slipped the other shoe from her foot and went even nearer. It mattered what they thought, it startled her to discover. Her studies, her work at the clinic, the self-sufficiency the doctor demanded, all that had led her to quite a sharp picture of herself as someone modern. But she wouldn't be interested in Davis if they said she shouldn't be. She was horrified; it meant her body and imagination could pull her toward men. Yet if her parents said no, she'd tell him so, then go off to make sure the doctor was well supplied with tongue depressors.

But her father said, "He's good with horses, Hamilton said," and that was all. Her mother said, "He's got manners," and so with nine words, Margaret knew she could tie together what her body, mind, and family told her: that Davis was acceptable.

She went to bathe, carrying a vision of the tilt in Davis's profile, the clean lengths of his fingers. But even after she'd washed herself for the third time since the birth, it was the woman's face that came back most often and tried to edge itself on Davis's. As she tried to sleep that night, Margaret saw both her prospective lover's tall forehead and the taut circle of the woman's mouth as the baby, sheathed in red, finally squirmed from her body.

The pictures wouldn't quite overlap. Davis wouldn't put her in such pain; his equipment hadn't seemed at all dangerous. The narrowest part of her mind said that kind of terrible birth only happened to people who hadn't prepared. When it came time, she would read the latest medical information and be amply ready. In her version, she was wrapped in sterile sheets and a shiny range of tools clinked usefully. Certainly no drunken husband staggering about. Margaret tried to imagine herself in the act of giving birth and saw a tent cloaking her lower body, her face straining a bit, a veil of perspiration on her brow that a gowned nurse would politely wipe off. She would manage it.

That fall, Davis noticed that Margaret angled to see him about town. She would pop into the bakery for tea with a friend from nursing school, greet him at Martin's as she badgered the shopkeeper for a few dollars' more credit. She was good at getting her way. The economy of her nature became even clearer to him than her burnished prettiness. He liked her decisive way of walking, as if measuring off precise distances in her polished shoes. She hung in his mind, a vision of cheekbones and hazel eyes, even during the long days he spent in other people's barns, learning about pigs, tractors, and the gear of the landlocked. He treated the knowledge in a slightly amused way, as if he wouldn't let it change something essential in him. At night, listening to the snores of the men in the bunkhouse, he wondered, Why here? with the raggedness of a breath, a tide. Why here?

One November afternoon, after repairing fences at Hamilton's place, he was drinking coffee at the café where he'd fallen ill. Hamilton had paid him early, with a sack of beets and a quarter pound of sugar, because the first large storm of the year was gathering in the north. "Get back to town," Hamilton said, "and stay warm. If it's bad, don't come for a few days." Davis looked at the man limping back to his farmhouse, which his wife had packed with canned vegetables and cured meat, and Davis envied those laden shelves and the deep sufficiency of marriage. Mrs. Hamilton was no beauty, but she had almond-shaped eyes and made pastry crust that melted in flakes of gold on the tongue. That could be enough, Davis found himself thinking.

He trudged back to town, the wind pushing at him like a teasing hand, and found himself the only man at the café. Blowing on his stiff fingers, Davis drank hot water that was mostly chicory. He watched, along with Meryl the waitress, as the storm came gusting in. "Get your long underwear out, boy," she said as she poured him more and then lumbered back to her stool and cigarettes at the counter.

Meryl, for all her bulk, toughness, and frizzled red hair,

wouldn't have minded slipping the long johns on her customers herself, Davis guessed. She lived above the café and Davis imagined her in a flannel robe, knobbed feet in a tub of hot water, reading cheap novels and smoking. No one knew where she was from or why she stayed here. He wondered what she had hoped for as a girl. Something lighter, not so greasy, he expected.

The air quivered, blackened, and the storm was upon them. A wide eddy of snow spun down the street and seemed to pull the blizzard behind it, skidding, shimmering, like a flock of fiercely white and tiny birds. Gray figures walked thickly down the street, hands clapped on skulls to anchor hats.

"Sounds bad," Meryl said, and straightened out her newspaper. "Your first big blow in Regina, isn't it?"

Davis said it was and wondered how a storm here compared to one in Ontario. Canada had introduced him to this kind of cold, cold so strong it cracked leather, trees, and brick. In Scotland, he'd known gales and fog, but those were passing moods compared to Canadian winter. Hands cupping his mug, Davis thought it was odd that Canada hadn't chilled him. Instead, his year of traveling from Halifax out west had encouraged the birth of a darker, warmer thread of character. Davis had the impression he'd spoken another language during his months here. That he'd used words whose shapes were unfocused and heavy in his memory, the way dreams slackened speech. Words about liquor, women, money, and cards. Smoky, bruised, well shuffled.

As he made his way across Québec and Manitoba, he cut timber, laid track, and once fought a forest fire that leapt its windbreak and ran like a malicious, redheaded child from one house to the next. Within an hour, the town was destroyed. Davis coughed phlegm dotted with black stars for weeks. The charred boards of the house frames and the numbed quiet of the townspeople were all that was left. No one had cried, which seemed normal to him. Afterward, he went off with the other men who'd fought the blaze to buy his first woman.

He'd been ashamed of the crescents of grime under his nails on the woman's generous, brown-tipped breasts. Instead, he looked at the coins sitting on small bills worn to the thinness of vellum. It had triggered something in him—the silver change on the soft cash. He'd watched it as his hips pumped against the woman's. She kept yielding, opening wider, while the thin mattress bucked. The pine bedstead smacked the plaster wall, and a mist of white speckled her hair. He thrust into the tight, damp tunnel of her body and listened to the clink of change as the bed hit the nightstand and jostled nickels and dimes.

"Hey, boy," the woman said, suddenly awake to the scene and what it cost. "Go easy." Just as she spoke, he felt the surge in his groin and heard but did not see the quick, silver rain of change falling to the floor. Before he left, she scraped the money up and piled it neatly on the table. Covered up and quiet, the woman smoked and did not smile at him from the bed.

"Thank you," he said as if she were a pretty cashier at a restaurant, but she was silent. The plaster still dusted her hair. She was not much older than he was, he saw. Brunette, full-lipped, she had looked smudged and more grown-up in the vague light. He saw a bruise on her arm, the size and color of a greengage plum. She saw him looking, said, "You

19

didn't do it," and ground out her cigarette. He left quickly, jamming on his cap. He'd known that. The bruise was old.

It startled him, the precision of that memory, how clearly he could see the mottled edge of the bruise. He knew, too, he'd never tell anyone about it, tucked away like a secret letter. He stared out at the street as shopkeepers switched off their lights. People were going home. He smelled the crumbled earth on the beets and thought he should head back to the boardinghouse himself.

Then he saw someone slip on the sidewalk, scattering an afternoon's shopping. He darted out to help, the cold like a vigorous hug around his body, not knowing if the person who had fallen was a man or a woman, his feet already sliding in the dry snow. It was Margaret, and somehow he smelled her before he even saw her clearly. Something freshly laundered that the wind couldn't whip entirely away.

She looked up and said with shy briskness, "Hello, Davis, what a mess I've made. Lend a hand with the bags, will you?" and so as the storm stiffened their hair to white and bit through their gloves, they gathered the contents of Margaret's spilled packages. She shook the snow from her shoulders, straightened her coat. He pointed with his bluntly mittened hand to the café and she nodded. Meryl looked up when they entered and ushered in a wall of wind. "Pie, Margaret?" she asked. So as Meryl fed them pie neither wanted, their hats and eyebrows dripped cool puddles of melted snow on the tabletop. "We're a sight, Davis," Margaret said, glancing at him, embarrassed perhaps that her hair had gone so tousled.

"But it suits you, Margaret," he said, surprising himself, and after that they couldn't speak.

They courted through the sternest part of the year, through an unusually snowbound fall and deep into the cold palm of the winter. Davis rose at dawn to work whatever job was on the docket. He learned to scrape the frogs of skinny horses. To patch the windiest seams of a barn with scrap wood and tar paper. In the midst of mucking out someone's Herefords, the smell of their winter shagginess and their breath of sour hay filling his nose, he would wonder again how it was that he'd wound up here, preparing, it seemed, to marry a farmer's daughter in the center of the broadest, stillest land he'd ever seen.

Once he'd announced he was leaving Scotland, his father and brothers had neatly, quickly excised him from their talk and activities. A spot of mold on bread. A stray thread from a pant leg. He wasn't even asked to repair nets. His mother was the only one to ask, "What are you going to do?"

He'd been waiting so long for someone to inquire, but when the moment came, all he could say was "Fish, I suppose." It was all he knew how to do, in any case. He would follow the fish.

Then she said, "Why?"

That was a question he hadn't anticipated, and his silence gathered awkwardly in the smoky kitchen. He also knew she took his quiet as a slight. He looked around the room. The only dab of color was a maroon strip of Turkish carpet, a gift from an uncle who lived on the mainland, a merchant who'd been to London and brought back artifacts from his trip to prove he'd really been. It was faded now, and as Davis looked at it he thought he could not stand to watch it grow dingier year after year. Of course he did not tell his mother that. "To seek my fortune, ma'am," he said.

But she hadn't smiled. Instead, she wiped her hands on the apron and said, "God loves action more than talk." Her words had stayed with him the whole voyage, and he'd wondered if his mother had grown secretly closer to God the way he had to books during the four years he laid his quiet plans. He wondered, the whole rocking, horrible trip, what else he did not know about his mother.

Like all the women Davis had known in Scotland, she was gray-faced with thrift. It wasn't even disappointment in her lot. She had nothing to compare it to. But perhaps that was why she thought the books were dangerous. They had helped him imagine foreign countries as somehow lusher and more vivid than anything he'd seen. With women who were somehow rosier, less sapped.

Nova Scotia in 1931, however, looked like home, just larger, with more pubs. Even the cobblestones spoke the same way, announcing baldly who came home when and how drunk. In many ways, it was also worse. The Depression had boarded most shop windows, low tents of seaweed cloaked the moorings. The women were even more drawn than his mothers and aunts, more rattled by the men's drinking.

Davis could have endured all that. He didn't know how else to live. But what he hadn't expected was a sudden revulsion at the smell of ocean. It had waited for the span of the entire uncomfortable journey to hit him. He'd lain below most of the time, feeling or getting sick, his pockets lumpy with a tiny set of the sonnets and his wad of cash. But he didn't think to blame the sea. It was just a weak stomach, bad food, all the change. His hatred of the ocean's stink struck the second week he was there, at dawn while watching men bring in the catch. The salty wool of the wet sweaters, the blood on the gills. Billows of odor that made his gut slide and his eyes blur. It was everywhere. In pubs, his clothes, the hair of the whey-colored children.

The woman who ran the boardinghouse where he was staying said, "Write your mother. Tell her you're among the living." He did not. Instead, he spent money on whiskey, letting its sour lethargy glue him to benches. He stared at a button hanging by its last thread and peered through the yellow haze of the liquor at the weathered ribs of boats in dry dock. Roaming the piers again one daybreak, he saw the brown bodies of cod straining at the twined diamonds of the net. He heard the careless slap of water on pilings, and something drained, then flooded his mind. He did not need the coast, the humid cold, the stink of scales. That night in the pub, listening to the scrape of stools on sawdust and the thick anxious talk, looking at crumpled hands cupping pints, he decided to head west. Past fish. None of the writers he'd read knew Canada, so he didn't know what to expect. But he liked the picture his mind devised: miles of green forest, silken lengths of river, and, beyond the water and pines, something dry, empty, open.

The land did not look as he'd imagined, but somehow he was starting to grow used to its cold flatness. As he walked or hitched from farm to farm, he realized everyone in Regina thought he would marry Margaret, from the men in the boardinghouse to Margaret's father, even though he'd paid for nursing school as insurance against poverty. Davis recognized the way rumor spread in small places. It traveled like a cloud, gathering specks of dirt, darkening rooms. But whispered talk made him feel at home, hanging in the air like weather.

What surprised him, then, was Margaret's directness. Rumor, from his experience, worked slowly, came toward its target obliquely. They were drinking muddy tea at the bakery a week before Christmas. Yeast and warmth filled the room. They were here to exchange gifts. "So you know people are talking, Davis," she said. "About your intentions."

The night before, she'd let him kiss her, once, quite deeply, but just once. He'd left her on the porch at her father's house, aware of the crack that had opened in the curtains, and needed to walk about in the icy wind for half an hour before he could stand going back to his room. From a kiss to intentions.

The part of his mind that spoke of jagged mountains and rough nights with sooty men went to sleep then. All he could see was this young nurse with velvet skin and a tidy walk. He smelled the cinnamon rolls plumping in the bakery's ovens and felt something in him rise. "My intentions are serious," he said. "No doubt of that." He had no idea if this was entirely true.

"Well, then," she said, "that's fine," and she finished her cup of tea. She passed him his gift, as if they'd just settled an account, which, in a way, Davis thought, they had.

She gave him a new pair of boots with specially reinforced soles. Despite the other customers and the baker, Davis leaned over to unlace his old shoes and slip on the new. They fit perfectly. "Thank you, Margaret," he said. "I'll think of you every time I walk across a barnyard." The boots would last years.

"You can exchange them at Martin's if the size isn't right," she said, inspecting. "Walk a bit and see if they pinch." The bossiness of nurses. He obeyed. They felt made for him. How had she known his size, he asked.

"Good eye," she said. She'd watched enough horses shod. She'd dressed brothers, held blistered feet. He felt safe suddenly. A woman who saw things in their correct proportions. He realized then he'd come close to meaning it about his intentions being serious, and he let himself look more closely at her brown curls and imagine his hands pulling through them, lock by lock.

"Now it's your turn," he said, and watched her become motionless as a spooked quail when she saw the gloves nestled in tissue paper. They were fine-grained leather and lined with rabbit fur. "Davis," she said. "These must have cost the earth," which of course they had, but he hadn't cared. He watched her pretty hands slide into the gloves' warm sleekness and his whole body tightened with desire. Someone behind the counter dropped a tray of rolls and swore, and they jumped, suddenly noticing how close together they'd leaned their heads.

The wedding was simple and took place in the beginning of March, with winter still lying heavily about. Margaret's mother had pressed her best tablecloth. But throughout the ceremony, Davis found his eye pulled to the low ridges that lingered in the white fabric: Mrs. Evans's iron hadn't quite been able to steam away the months the linen had spent folded in the cupboard. Mr. Evans coughed at random intervals in the service, and Margaret's brothers shuffled their enormous feet, sending up a sea of creaks. The women, by contrast, were primly still, stark points of lace handkerchiefs peeking from their sleeves, as if to make up for the restless men. Margaret was too brilliant to look at. He'd glimpsed her, an arm in silk, the crown of her rich hair, and that was all he could manage. He did let himself breathe her in: a freshly rosy scent mixed with something like nutmeg. Even when invited at the end of the ceremony to kiss her, he only dared a quick scrape of dry lip against dry lip. My wife, Davis thought, and the word rolled oddly in his mind. A ball bearing on a tilted floor. My wife, he'd think, and the silver sphere of the word would roll to another corner.

The reception featured Mr. Evans's stash of whiskey and a roast beef. The men got quietly and thoroughly drunk and the women gossiped with hushed, fierce efficiency. Davis and Margaret stood to the side of the table that held the food, all of it brown except for a pot of mustard and the earthy glow of sweet potatoes. It seemed to be his and Margaret's job to slice the wedges of mince pie and make sure spoons were on saucers. It was good to have something to do, to smile and be polite to the thirty guests, all of whom looked rather proud but ill at ease in their best suits and dresses. "Welcome to Regina," several said, as if Davis had just arrived instead of having been there the better part of a year. Their stance was clear: they thought Davis was doing well for himself, marrying an Evans, and an educated one at that. A bit presumptuous. But what with the Depression, who knew how the world was changing. They, however, in their clean, uncomfortable clothes and rigid manners, would do their best in the face of chaos, brought on, naturally, by the States.

"Quite a step you've taken, Mr. Campbell," said Mrs. Althorp, in a flat tone he knew he was meant to take two ways. She appointed herself gentry because her husband was the banker.

"Indeed," said Davis. No one seemed to know quite what to

do with him. Mrs. Althorp was being as rude as she dared, and the Evanses were only gruffly polite. His father-in-law had clapped him roughly on the back but said nothing, and Margaret's mother had been too flustered with the pies and the guests' coats to add more than a hurried congratulations. It made him wonder how his parents would have responded. "You're too poor, Davis, to go thinking about a wife," his mother might have said. He'd only just written her about Margaret, and his previous letters had been spare, the letters of someone husbanding energy. She would have enjoyed helping with the preparations, however. She would have baked better mince pie. But what was done was done, and as he thought that, he looked at Margaret's hand and could imagine it as ridged and pale as the tablecloth in thirty years. All the guests were served by then and had their heads deep in their plates, forks clicking china. Davis layered beef and potatoes on a dish for Margaret, which she took shyly from him. "Here, love, eat up," he said, though what he wanted was to talk about his mother, and the sounds she made while bustling in the kitchen before dawn: careful clangings at the stove and whispers to the cat. Neither he nor Margaret could eat, and as the guests started to finish their food and shrug themselves back into their wraps, he began to let himself imagine not his mother, not his wife's hands in thirty years, but Margaret's shoulders as they currently existed. He envisioned them as round and positive as apples.

They were staying the night at the Prince Albert and caught a ride into town with Ole Anderson and his wife. Ole was ruddy and boisterous with whiskey and he let Frieda drive. "Come on now, we've got to get these chickens to bed," he crowed, and the last guests had tittered, though Davis noticed that Margaret's parents hadn't smiled. Ole kept it up in the car. "Don't embarrass them, you old goat," Frieda said calmly as she shifted gears. Margaret and Davis were bundled in the back seat, waiting for the feeble heater to croak to life, and Davis was conscious of Frieda's broad tolerance of Ole's tipsiness and his blunt ease with his proud, red-haired wife. They made marriage seem long, known, and comfortable, a wide bed. The bed at the Prince Albert, however, was the largest, whitest bed he'd ever seen. The first sight of it struck them both dumb.

Then Margaret put down her suitcase and started to talk of bald necessities. The rise in the cost of kerosene. The gingham on sale for curtains at Martin's.

"Go get changed, dear," he said. So she'd gone, dragging the heavy case. He sat on the bed, listening to the squeak of taps, the flow of water in the sink. Bouncing to test the firmness of the mattress, he noticed the sheets were rather scratchy. He loosened his tie. He'd never spent the night in such a fancy place. He hadn't realized that luxury, even the mild kind implied by a thick carpet, could make him uneasy. He began to whistle.

Margaret came out, wrapped in a padded dressing gown that obscured her form as effectively as a horse blanket. She's frightened, Davis thought as she sat at the dressing table, her hairbrush in hand. He sat on the bed, smiling at her. "Come over, Margaret." But she wouldn't. She blushed patchily, maybe still spinning a bit with the liquor her mother had slipped her at the reception. Otherwise, he could never account for what she said next, which was "No, you come here."

28

So he had. "I want you to take off your jacket," she said, putting the hairbrush down. He did. "Now the tie," she said. Each time, she carefully folded the garment he removed, all while she sat wrapped in her dressing gown, blushing and smiling. Now and then, she made sure the shade behind her was still firmly pulled down. It was hypnotizing. He couldn't say no, but he couldn't go nearer this giggling woman, either.

Having stripped him to his shorts, she looked down and, finally losing her composure said, "Oh God, Davis, it won't fit." It was then he was able to go to her, unwind the dressing gown, and carry her to bed. She was wearing a pink negligée with complicated buttons he ignored and instead gently eased the filmy thing off her, revealing the rich curves of her body. He lay beside her and traced with the tip of a finger the edges of her arms and breasts and face, eventually helping them both to realize that everything, in fact, did fit.

They moved to a house fairly close to the Evans's farm, which the tenant farmer had abandoned to move to Calgary. Davis worked there and at her parents' place, and Margaret rescued the house from its tattered state. She felt happier, she acknowledged, working at home, in near silence, than in the bustle of the clinic. The doctor was drinking more and more. It seemed a good decision to settle into married life. She and Davis broke the routine of daily chores with the fierce heat their bodies raised in one another. Margaret would wake exhausted sometimes, still shaking some mornings. Only after anchoring her hair in a knot at her neck could she tackle the business of the day. She'd had no idea this could be part of life. No wonder women never really talked about marriage. There was no explaining it. It was an initiation, and easier to think about alone, with a garden to tend and windowsills to scrub.

But that summer, she found her focus narrowing, and wasn't sure if she liked it or not. A jam turned bitter could bring her to tears. The progress of a segmented ant across the counter could hold her rapt. She began to stare at herself in the cloudy rectangle of mirror above the dresser. I could be on the moon, she told her reflection, and had a terrible moment when she saw herself as the full, pitted planet, rising ghostly and un-tethered in the sky. She began saving everything, as a way to make sure she stayed busy enough to keep that sort of non-sense from happening again. Boxes with bits of string too small to use. Tins of bent needles, all labeled in the handwrit-ing that had earned her such praise as a nurse.

Then she became pregnant. She'd known the moment the baby found its hold in her belly. It was a steaming August night, the wheat burned gold in the fields. The windows were open and wind domed the white curtains. She hadn't said anything to Davis, mostly as a matter of habit, but she knew for sure when the next morning the coffee sat darkly in her stomach when usually she welcomed its bright jolt.

It was a relief, really. It was what she felt she ought to be doing, and the rich pulse of her instincts seemed to dispel the thickening of her vision since she'd married. She began lay-ering the house in preparation. Pregnancy quickened her fin-gers, which flew across wool, fabric, thread, stitching up a year's worth of clothing for the baby she knew to be a boy. Her industry disturbed Davis. "It's a baby we're getting ready for, Margaret, not a siege," he chided. But she couldn't help it, she wanted to tell him. There was something live and supple being woven in her body and it released in her this profound need to stitch, paint, and clean. She pulled out her old medical texts and consulted with a new doctor in town on a monthly basis. "For the love of Pete, it's just a baby," her mother said. "Other people have had them, you know."

"But I haven't," Margaret protested, hemming the last satin inch on a coverlet. She imagined the birth as she sewed and saw the baby, perfectly pink, swimming gently from her body. Then one night, she dreamed that she was in labor and that her parents and Davis stood around her. They were in a clearing fringed in evergreens. Margaret stood on the hard ground, squeezing and straining, her legs splayed until she felt something finally slide to the earth. "Is it a boy?" she cried.

But there was an embarrassed hush from the spectators, and instead of a baby, her mother showed her that all she'd given birth to was a hand, a man's white hand. Perfectly clean, with a curl of hair on its back, the stump neatly sealed. They looked terrifically disappointed that all she had managed to grow was this one limb, an extremity at that. And instead of grief, Margaret felt shame. How could she have labored that hard for a mere hand? With expressions she couldn't quite read, her parents and Davis wrapped her in a blanket, tucked the hand against her chest, and slipped her inside a hollow log. Then they nosed her and the hand into a roiling river whose presence she had just noticed. She woke with a start, a band of sweat dampening her hair. Davis slept tranquilly beside her. He had the sweetest of sleeps, and besides, she didn't want to rouse him for this strangeness. "Expecting women have fancies," he might say. "Sleep, Margaret, for God's sake. There's chores to do." She hadn't been able to, though, until near sunrise, because the sense of having been caught passing in unfinished work was as unsavory on her tongue as brine. It won't be like that, she promised herself. It will go well.

The birth was quite different from any of the possibilities she'd concocted when it occurred that April. Margaret woke at dawn to a lurch of pain deep in her belly. She said nothing to Davis, who lay long and still next to her, as she knew first babies were slow to come. She also wanted to wrap the moment's newness to herself, and she lay there on her side, feeling the ache wrap itself around her womb and then release. It wasn't an experience to translate. So Davis had gone to work that pretty morning, telling her he'd be back for dinner. The labor, however, had proceeded with an unrelenting force, and at 9:17, her fingers probing the murky sink for teaspoons, Margaret's waters broke.

She waddled as fast as she could to the nearest neighbor, arms cradling her stomach, shouting at the baby not to come too fast. "Don't, don't," she shouted at it, and horrified herself that the first sound her baby might hear was its mother's voice panicked, unstrung, furious. Clouds were growing bulky and dark at the horizon. It was raining hard by the time she reached the Andersons a half mile away. Frieda had taken one look at her and shouted to Ole in the barn, "I'm going to town with Margaret Campbell." Still in her apron, the older woman had driven with violent precision to Regina as the storm gathered force, muttering in Swedish, probably swearing, as Margaret felt the baby start its rough journey through her body.

It had been that which she'd found so awful, the utter inability to do anything but yield to this insistent pressure.

She'd leaked everywhere. Milk, urine, and worse, and in Ole's truck. "I am so sorry, Frieda," she said.

Frieda, steering around a curve, not looking at anything but the road, said, "No one told you did they?"

No one had said a word of anything that didn't ring with practicalities. Booties knitted. Crib borrowed. No one had mentioned stretch marks, which Margaret had thought were a rash until the doctor had told her otherwise. Her medical books hadn't discussed something as minor as this and were also vague about pain. What else hadn't she been told?

Though it seemed to start quickly, once she was at the clinic, the labor stalled, lasted hours, a back labor they called it. Margaret, who had been kicked by Black Angus, deeply scratched by barbed wire, had her wind knocked clean from her lungs and her body jarred by falling from hay ricks, had never felt anything so shattering. Davis arrived with her parents, his pants fringed in mud, hair plastered to his skull by rain, bursting without asking into the room. "Margaret," he kept saying, dripping a wide puddle on the floor.

"This hurts, Davis," she shouted, "this is bloody awful. No one said it would hurt so bloody much." And she went on, raving at him as he twisted his hat to a ruin. She had no idea how much she had to say to him, and how fiery it was. How much wilder she was than the Swedish girl she'd disparaged. As rain glazed the windows, the nurse said tartly, "Mind your language, Mrs. Campbell, and push." Shit-smeared, pop-eyed, she howled louder, feeling along with the pain of the labor that she'd dented forever some version Davis had of her. All along, the story she'd told about herself had been only partly right.

Later, the slight, damp weight of her daughter in her arms,

her body pulsing in echoing ripples of pain, as if the baby were a stone and her body a lake, Margaret kept repeating to herself, "I'm a mother." Davis, gray in the face, came to kneel beside her bed and traced a finger across the baby's wild-strawberry mouth, and she began to weep. She realized, watching Davis explore his daughter, how quickly anger flowed to love and back, restless and beyond her grasp. Yet when Davis asked, "What is it, Margaret?" she could only shake her head. A girl, not a boy, but whole at least, not that paltry hand.

She marked her pregnancy and Hilda's birth as the start of the silence between them. Nail, rope, tea, hay: words so solid they were practically tools, that was the kind of language they most used once the baby was born. Partly they hadn't time to talk. Partly it was that they lived sparsely and used everything, even words, as if they had to be hoarded, like matches. But they grew quiet, too, because they became better at reading signs and gestures—the speed of a knife scraped on a plate, the curve of a particular sigh. Words came to feel inexact. The bend of Davis's neck as he washed himself for dinner told Margaret all she needed to know.

It seemed to Margaret that there were days they had done entirely without speech. Coming back to the house during a blizzard before the war, she remembered prying layers of clothing from Davis's back that had frozen to the stiffness of wood from hours outside tracking a lost part of a herd. A shroud of mist rose from their stooped bodies and they knew without speaking when to unwind a scarf or crouch down to ease off a boot whose toe had split in the cold. The animals were dead when they found them. She saw the hummocked mounds of snow first and tugged on the line that tied Davis's horse to hers, a single yank that meant it was time to turn around.

It was the late 1930s that brought this slow, quiet braiding of their lives. Two more children, Jem two years after Hilda, then Stuart, six years after that. Parcels of acreage acquired from neighbors selling out, brothers who moved on, her mother dying. Land and babies, requiring equal degrees of nurturing and guesswork. Then, just as they'd crawled out of the biblically bad times of the Depression, had come the Germans with their pretensions, tanks, and hateful ways. Davis had badly wanted to go. Margaret watched the flickering moods in his face as men gathered at Martin's to talk about the Battle of Britain. His Scottish memories swam up in him again, and he wrote his ancient mother more often, brooded more obviously in the evenings. He could have earned a deferment, thanks to a roof fall that dislocated his right shoulder. The joint kept floating out of its socket, releasing when he least expected. A man with a rum gun hand couldn't be any use. Though it panicked her slightly to see war tug at her husband so, she knew he had to be the one to say he'd never do for soldiering.

When he finally admitted that he'd been officially found unfit, she said, "There's lots of ways to be useful," proud of the patience she'd learned with him. But she hadn't expected he'd take her remark as license to buy the wireless. "It'll be good for the children to hear what's going on," Davis protested, clutching the huge walnut beast to his chest as he picked it up from the back of the truck. She didn't like the contraption, its disruptive crackle, its waste of electricity. The children teased her for calling it "the box." But the word "wireless" or, even worse, the vaguely European-sounding "radio" stayed too long on the tongue.

What she liked were the Sunday sermons given by a minister called Peverly, in a voice of calm roughness. "While the earth remaineth, seedtime and harvest, cold and heat, and summer and winter, and day and night shall not cease," he would say, and Margaret would feel comforted. Yes, comforted. Despite her father's death in 1941 and the war's ugly stain on the decade. By 1953, Margaret looked around Regina and her own life and found it intact. She and Davis were living on six hundred acres of farmland that supported in relative comfort cows, crops, and three tall, self-contained children. It seemed miraculous to Margaret that she and her husband had been allowed to survive with such matter-of-factness. Despite the bombs. Despite the camps. As if God or whatever controlled the flow of days had placed its hand between this part of Canada and bad luck worse than debt and locusts. She didn't stop long to think about this; she didn't have the time. She was pleased when she occasionally realized that she couldn't spare an hour to moon in a mirror or examine the patterned ridges in her nails for meanings and deficiencies.

Margaret granted herself only the mildest of lapses from vigilance. This August night was one of them, a dinner in town to toast, belatedly, their twentieth anniversary and a harvest that looked promising. Preparing tonight for the excursion to the Prince Albert, where they always went to celebrate, Margaret felt the keenness of her good fortune. It was like glimpsing the first green flare in the wheat, the half-smile of her youngest just as he went to sleep. She did not linger on it. It was bad form to parade happiness. It might hurt those less lucky. And it might, if acknowledged, be spirited away. By whom or how, she couldn't say, but it seemed safer to keep her contentment delicately veiled.

Margaret walked to the kitchen to say goodbye to the children. Their daughter, Hilda, spooned out soup for herself and her two younger brothers. They all glanced up. The hot bowls released three skeins of steam through which they stared politely at their mother.

It was her new dress, the first store-bought one since her father's funeral. Dark blue with emerald satin trim at the hem, wrists, and collar, as if a narrow river of green were edging a navy field. Her hair was curled and her cheeks were bright, as if she'd used rouge, which of course she hadn't. In the trumpet-yellow sunset slanting through the window, feet planted on the swirls in the linoleum, Margaret let herself feel proud.

"Good night," she told her family. "We'll be back by eleven." She kissed Stuart. Jem said, "You smell nice, Mum," which she used as an excuse to kiss him, too, though at sixteen he now avoided contact with anything that smacked of affection or frills. The practical, sharp-edged ways of men had begun to pull at him, and Davis led him steadily toward the farm, as if he couldn't imagine another fate for his boy. Jem didn't seem to mind, which mostly pleased Margaret. It was as if he'd gotten used to the bit and settled young to sobriety. Jem appeared born to farm. He had his grandfather's square build, huge hands, and instinctive ease with a tractor's engine.

Hilda, at eighteen, was more complicated. The girl was as pale and nervous as the twitch of skin on warming milk. She'd just graduated from Grade 13 this summer and was trying to decide what to do next. She didn't date boys, not for want of attention, but out of some deep shyness. She was good with a needle, Hilda, and bookish like her father, but said she'd rather die of shame than stand up in front of a classroom of children. Even going to town caused her to ravage her cuticles, and if they let her she'd stay in the truck.

Margaret and Davis barely mentioned their daughter's awkwardness. They didn't quite have the words anymore to say how Hilda's sudden moods upset their sense of balance. Life on a farm was busy enough without the queer twist in the air their daughter's tempers brought to the house. Her slight oddity pained them with its suggestion that Hilda, whose face and body were so much a twining of their own, should prove to have ideas beyond their experience. How could a child so clearly theirs be so foreign? Davis hinted that she needed more friends. Margaret sighed and suggested it might all be linked to the curse. But tonight, Margaret pushed Hilda's tense, oval face resolutely from her mind. She closed the window, as if the brisk smack of the sash on the sill could seal off worry from the rest of the evening.

Davis sat on the front porch and listened to Margaret talking to the children. Hilda disturbed him, too, though he thought he understood something of his daughter's troubles. While it embarrassed him to have a child who hadn't the grace to appreciate the ease she had, he saw in his eldest his own confusion of desires as a young man. If she were a boy, he'd pack her off to the Yukon. As it was, he hoped to send her to secretarial school in Regina. Some work with her mind and daily contact with others her age would chase away her bashfulness. He also knew that he pulled this tone of assurance over his worry like sheets and blankets over his cold and tired body. He didn't in truth know what to do about Hilda and so he said little to his wife. The same tone he used to soothe Margaret's fears about all they owed at the bank. They'd manage, he tried to convince her.

Against the tall blue screen of the sky, words were nothing, Davis thought, surprising himself at the picture he'd just imagined, letters spelling "wire," "barn," "heifer," spiraling black and tiny across the air like just-born flies. The heat today had pressed him hard. Warmth arrived in curving shimmers from the fields. His head ached slightly. His fresh shirt collar itched, and he wished Margaret would hurry.

He listened to the boys hoot insults at each other in the kitchen. Margaret's humming filtered from their bedroom as she tapped about in her heels. Two sounds so known it didn't even take a moment to place them. As knit into his day as the rumble of his own digestion or the combine's sputter. In this life Margaret had helped him to start, he never felt adrift: he was deeply necessary to his world. But it was also true that the smell of fish, even trout, still made him wince. He was glad to live so unequivocally away from the ocean. Still, he felt awkward about the dreams he had of lives he might have lived if he'd made it to the other side of the country. "Ungrateful," he said, in a voice not quite his and not quite Margaret's.

"Davis," Margaret called, "come say goodbye to the children." In the kitchen, he saw she was too self-conscious to have him see her in the new dress alone. She needed the shield of the kids' squabbling. But he couldn't concentrate on

Margaret's dark-blue radiance, because they were staring now at him. Stuart said, "Dad, you've got your tie on."

Twice a year, they glimpsed him in this tie and jacket, hair slicked in rows precise as those that scored his wheat fields. He looked suddenly as serious as the minister or doctor, someone of power and difficult news, so he used warnings they would find familiar. "Help your sister with the dishes, boys. Hildy, don't scratch records."

But as he ruffled the boys' hair, all he could think about was his wife, who looked fresh and citified tonight, as if she'd never worked a farm. Her hands, worn to leather, hid in gloves. She could never have been the woman to whom he'd made love as a river rushed past. She loved to sleep with him outdoors, under open skies. Rivers and streams were the only bodies of water he could tolerate. You could hear and see their impatience and tell where they were headed. In land so resolutely flat, it gave the eye a welcome bit of texture to hook to. They'd always loved those evenings by the creek, and Margaret claimed the boys had been conceived by the Waskana.

"You look lovely," he told her when they got to the truck, and she smiled. He steered around the deepest depressions in the driveway, the footprints of last year's rains. Watching the chaotic erosion of the road, he felt this old thought wander across his mind: What might have happened if he'd become ill in Manitoba or Alberta? What if he had made his way to B.C.? Would he ever have gotten used to the scent of ocean again? Did the Pacific smell different from the Atlantic? Would he have married, had children? Owed so much money to the bank?

Davis looked at his wife now, her hands gripping the pocketbook whose clasp she had just polished. In the tiger-lily light of sunset, Davis wanted to let his wife know that he was really quite glad he had stayed. Instead, he said, "We should order more feed."

Margaret nodded and said, "Yes, the price is supposed to go up next month," and that was all. She wouldn't want to hear more, he thought. The new dress had helped, though it had taken time to convince her it was worth fifteen dollars. She'd looked at the bills on the kitchen table as if they were insects that might sting. "Davis! Don't be daft!" Finally, he had had to take the money and tuck it into her apron pocket, coming within range of her wonderful, new-bread smell.

He loved how Margaret's body couldn't help itself, insisting on its calm abundance even under a firmly knotted apron. But aprons made him think of his mother. They'd written more during the war, sometimes as often as once a week, until she died last year. He had saved none of her letters, but apparently she had collected all of his. A brother sent them back after she was buried. They arrived in a crackling stack, bound in a red velvet ribbon. After unpacking them, he sat and stroked the fabric's soft nap for some time and then stowed the whole delicate lot away, unread. Eventually, he threw them out, remembering too clearly how his desire to show her he had made the right decision kept him from saying how much he'd craved her milky tea and scones.

Davis wanted to tell Margaret about these odd spills of association his brain sometimes followed, from money to aprons to velvet, but he supposed she'd find it unseemly in him. Abruptly she turned off the radio, because the station's signal wavered. "Almost there," she said, and Davis nodded, shifting to a lower gear to comply with the speed limit.

He knew his wife had never liked the radio. It was bad enough they had one in the house, but when they got the new truck, Davis, without telling Margaret, asked the dealer to add this feature. He liked the way sound decorated the edges of the hours he had to spend driving across the land. He'd discovered during his years in Regina a keen yearning for music of all kinds, from marches to sonatas, swing to opera. It struck him as he stopped to park in front of the Prince Albert that he had exchanged one secret life for another. While he gave up smoking and drinking when he settled here, another set of yearnings had taken their place. It was that amplitude of feeling in Hilda which frightened Margaret, although more and more Davis guessed where his daughter had acquired the trait.

How could he have impressed upon his sensible wife that he and Hilda needed lovely things? Small sensual pleasures swayed him still: stroking the patch of skin on the underside of Margaret's wrist. Currying the hocks of a horse to satin. Letting hot bread, butter, and honey shimmer on his tongue. When he was first married and realized the bright ripeness of Margaret's body he had nearly wept, but hadn't because he knew that speaking aloud his weakness for the sheen of her breasts and the alertness of her nipples would shame her. It was something he never told her, though he supposed she knew how much he loved to touch her still.

As he got out of the car and felt the first drops of the summer storm on his face, he wondered what she would think of his anniversary present. She always chose practical gifts. Handkerchiefs. A nice bit of hardware. She liked that sort of present, too. A handy tool for the garden. A new iron, but not even that—Margaret still preferred the old-fashioned ones you heated on the cookstove. Easing open his wife's door, he wondered if he'd made a mistake. It was lingerie he'd bought her, peach silk, from a catalogue and sent to a post-office box in town. He'd seen the catalogue in a newsstand by the train station, where it was sold as a lurid magazine. He had the package in the truck and decided to give it to her after supper. The rain was coming steadily now and there was a strange curl to the wind. Looking at the tidy, compact woman with whom he had lived for twenty years, Davis felt unexpectedly at sea.

Margaret smiled at her husband through the picture window: he'd shooed her inside as he went to find a parking spot. He was still sandy-haired and tall, with none of the stoop most farmers got. A handsome man, especially in his tie and dress shirt, shrugging his jacket into place and trying to skirt the raindrops. But he looked distracted now, pulled away from their night out in the way he thought she couldn't follow. It was the face he wore when he listened to music or sneaked off to read on a Sunday afternoon.

She learned to think of these as his quiet times, and although she preferred the terse company of farm life to solitude, she understood he needed somewhere separate. In fact, as Davis opened the door and crossed the floor to their table, Margaret thought that she now resisted time spent alone. It made her feel uprooted, vaguely aware of questions she had, as if some unwelcome piece of self might surprise her with its demands.

Davis sat down and said, "Turning into quite a storm out there." She nodded, and they were both silent, gathering their impressions of the restaurant and how it had changed since they last visited. She looked about the room as the fan sliced the air into slightly cooler strips. A candle sheathed in a faceted globe made the glass and cutlery sparkle in diamond points.

"Just a moment," Davis said, and walked off toward the bar. She could tell he was ordering liquor, an extravagance they allowed themselves this one night a year. She suspected it would be red wine, to go with the steak he knew she always ate. She tried to look at him as if she'd never seen him, a trick she couldn't play somewhere as everyday as the farm. But history as thick as theirs wasn't a coat you just hung up, and she couldn't imagine him as anyone but who he was. Davis, her husband. As if to insist on the inescapability of who she was, she caught a glimpse of herself in a tarnished mirror. Even in the tender light, her face and its long lines surprised her. She'd felt so new in this bright dress. She saw that Davis, too, looked worn in a way she'd not noticed in a long time. His hands, which he'd so abruptly decided would not be the hands of a fisherman, could be the hands of any man who worked. Calloused, scrubbed red for the event of town, the hands of the man who had hauled him into her clinic.

Davis sat down next to his wife, noticed the cozy bloom of her scent, and picked up the menu. "We've got a treat coming," he told her, and saw that she was somewhere else. It wouldn't be wise to ask where. It never was. She always pretended her mind didn't stray, that she had no fanciful turns of thought. To give her privacy, he focused on his choices for the night. Like Margaret, he always selected sirloin, but tonight the possibilities swam in front of him.

The lone waiter, a man named Edgar, came to take their order, and Davis noticed he had grown older. The jowl under Edgar's chin had spread, the hair fringing his freckled crown had further dwindled. Did his hand shake as he wrote down Margaret's request in his curly waiter's alphabet? She decided as always on sirloin, baked potato, and vegetable of the day. Davis, searching down the list, saw a new item, lasagna, and asked for that. "Lasagna?" Margaret queried. "What's that?" Edgar explained the concoction, which had reassuring ingredients wrapped inside its foreign name: tomatoes, cheese, and hamburger. Margaret eyed Davis, though, as if he might be getting ill.

"Sometimes nice to try something new," he told her, and spread his napkin in his lap. As they always did, they waited for their food without talking, watching others drink, laugh, and eat. Davis wondered if Margaret was thinking as he was of their wedding night here, a grand choice for the time that had caused talk. People hadn't taken honeymoons in those days, and only now, in these fatter times, did couples venture to the coast or to Banff, as if gorgeous natural scenery provided a proper introduction to married life.

He glanced at her now, flushed with the memory of that evening's discoveries, and saw her studying a couple in the other corner. It was a marvel to him, Margaret's ability to

enjoy sensual pleasures and then to get up and make breakfast, slaughter chickens, tend sick children. It was as if a
piece of her clicked on at night, then just as suddenly turned
off, like the refrigerator they had recently bought. "Davis,
we can't afford it," she cried, but it would make her life easier
and so he had gotten the contraption. Davis suspected that
Margaret's frugal ways, which masked themselves as virtue,
were actually a reflex against pleasure. Maybe she frightened
herself. They never talked about the rich and wanton happiness they found in each other's body.

Even now, Davis thought, as Edgar arrived with their
wine. Margaret turned to him and said, surprising him a little, "How lovely." They toasted each other, the clink a small
sound in the sleepy restaurant. What would really be lovely,
Davis realized, was this: Margaret agreeing to steal upstairs
right now to make love in one of the high-ceilinged rooms.
But he couldn't even ask her. She'd fear that people would
notice. He took a larger sip of wine.

Margaret had been wondering not if the couple in the corner
were married but if they were happy. They might be. The girl
was a tall young Scandinavian or German; he might be
French. They glanced at one another a bit uncertainly. He
poured her water with a certain care. Happy. It was a term she
didn't use much. She much preferred words like "finished,"
"sewn," and "stacked." Words with edge and heft, not "happy"
with its cheerful insubstantialness. Maybe it was the wine that
made her think about these matters, not even because it made

her giddy, but because it was something she linked to Davis, to his love of tastes and textures. He thought she didn't recognize how much he enjoyed the smell of a just-mown field or a good roast beef. She turned to him then and said, "Let's go."

He looked startled, which she liked. "Where?" he asked, after another sip of wine.

"Out by the Waskana," she said. It was a miracle that no more babies had been born to them. They were never careful in this part of life, especially not by the long gray swell of the creek, where when they were younger they had flattened the grasses and come home reeking of water and mud.

"But it's raining," Davis said, prolonging the issue, enjoying it, Margaret could see.

"There's the truck, Davis," she said, laughing a bit. She imagined the truck parked where all the teenagers nosed their cars, their steamy old bodies generating just as much heat as the girls' and boys'. But no one would be out tonight. It was raining, a week night. They'd be safe there.

"And what about your dress?" Davis asked. He smiled back at her.

"We'll be careful," she whispered.

"And dinner?" he asked, folding his napkin.

"We'll just tell Edgar we had to leave," Margaret announced with sudden determination. But it occurred to her, too, that part of her brisk resolve to go and make love like a careless girl by a wide river came from not wanting to stay alone with the problem of happiness. She wouldn't know what to say exactly if someone inquired if she was happy. How did you measure something so vague? Of course she was happy, she'd probably say crossly if one of the children asked. Now, have you fed the pullets?

The storm had deepened, a heavy soak, which Davis knew they needed. But he wished it were peaceful weather. He wanted to have his wife remove his faded finery, piece by piece, and then unzip her new dress and unfasten all her stiff and complicated underwear and see her shining naked in the night. Still, even in a cramped truck with its large gearshift, it would be enough. It sufficed to know they had abandoned expectations, confused and even irritated Edgar. It felt lavish, and suddenly everything held a glow of luxury. The fluted curves of the steering wheel. The fan shape the wipers revealed as they peeled away the rain. The pretty length of his wife's thigh. This was celebration, he thought. This was good.

Margaret, letting her body graze her husband's, liking the anticipatory tingle spreading through her, wondered suddenly about the children. It seemed strange she would never know if they had inherited this terrible capacity for pleasure that belonged to her and Davis. She would never know if they would have the same bountiful luck in partners. You don't know really what you've given your children, she wanted to say to Davis. You just don't know.

It was these separate moods that shaped their last moments. Davis's tempered joy, Margaret's wonder at the mystery of heritage. The truck, through no fault of their own, suddenly spun into the bridge that spanned the Waskana outside Regina. Later, no one would be able to reconstruct the accident, to say exactly what went wrong. The truck's nose slammed into the one rail that ran the length of the bridge and plunged in a heavy arc into the swift, deep water. Although neither of them knew how to swim, it wouldn't have mattered anyway. They were caught too long. The air ran out too fast. The farmers and mechanics who discussed the mystery the next morning did so quietly. No one wanted to think about how much time they must have had. Enough to realize they would die. Enough to say something.

Under a sky shorn of clouds, the mechanics towed the truck from the mud. It stood on the bank, water sluicing from its dented sides, and for a minute, none of the rescuers approached it. Margaret and Davis Campbell would be inside, a farmer and his wife, people with children. They recognized the truck, some even knew how much Davis had paid for it. Too much, they said, as Davis hadn't liked to bargain. But it was as if the spectators wanted to delay the events that would unwind from the deaths, as if those consequences had not already begun. Something about the bodies and the faces, their wetness, their refusal to shake themselves clean and stand up, would make the accident real, irrevocable. When the door was pried open, Margaret and Davis were found bundled in separate corners of the cab, he with his head thrown back, she with her lovely hair in corkscrewed lengths shielding her face. Then they noticed that Davis and Margaret must have clutched at each other before the river pushed them apart. They each held in their fist a ragged scrap of the other's clothes. He had his fingers clenched around a piece of fabric from her sleeve, she was holding a black strip of his jacket. It disturbed the spectators, this sign that it would not be possible to imagine the deaths as watery sleep. But they had to wait until rigor mortis passed for the grips to relax. There was no removing the torn bits of cloth: the fingers would have broken if they tried.

PART TWO

ANGLES AND EDGES

Saskatchewan and Toronto, 1953–61

In the three months after her parents died, Hilda encountered the idea that life could unravel before you in a matter of days and that, even more odd, you could hasten and, at times, enjoy its unraveling. It had started with certain discoveries about Davis and Margaret and involved as well Dr. Robbins, the man who told Hilda and her brothers of their parents' death in Waskana Creek. The doctor was a rather startling man for Regina, with his flamboyant ties and a certain casualness with money. It was said he had a touch for easy deliveries and limbs mauled in farm machinery. His nurse, Flora Parker, adored him and spread word of his inspired diagnoses throughout town. However, the morning they arrived to tell the three Campbell children that their parents had drowned, they both looked less confident than reputation rumored them to be. Dr. Robbins mopped at his neck with a melon-colored handkerchief, while the nurse dabbed at the wing of her nostril with a piece of delicate linen that looked too girlish against her chapped fist. "Hilda, boys, it's about your parents," he began. They were standing in the yard, the sun already high and unvarnished.

There'd been an accident, the doctor explained, looking slightly sideways at a cluster of martins scissoring past. Their parents had drowned. In Waskana Creek, just at the outskirts of town. Jem made a rough and terrible sound in his throat. With his boot, Stuart traced a square in the dust, over and over. None of them wept, except Miss Parker, great tears coursing down her lumpy cheeks.

From that moment, Hilda's vision sharpened, as if shock unleashed an ability to discern other people's motives with perverse clarity. So she saw the hectic drama of Miss Parker's sympathy, her near-delight in the situation's ghastliness. The crumpling in Jem's face and the fact that the cluster of wrinkles between his eyes would harden to a knot in his later life. She knew, too, that Stuart was drawing a box for himself with his toe, a space in which to hide himself, a coffin or a corral, somewhere inviolable. She was a vase of sensation, holding the sharp stems of the news, the harsh eaves of the house, the border of marigolds, the chrome of the doctor's Nash. She found herself saying, "We're not selling the farm."

Dr. Robbins looked steadily at her for the first time and said, "Very good, Hilda, but that's not the first worry, is it?" His handkerchief had turned from melon to persimmon with sweat.

Flushing, Hilda said, "I suppose not. Will you be wanting

us to come with you, then?" Miss Parker gathered herself to briskness and said, "I'll help the chickens pack their things."

"But who'll take care of the animals?" Jem shouted suddenly. It was if he'd ripped a hole in the air. It was dangerous, such a leakage, and Hilda clamped it shut. "Don't worry, Jem," she said quickly. "The Andersons will fill in for a few days."

Then she steered the boys back to the house, followed by Miss Parker, whose undergarments gave off ominous creakings. That was another part of the change Hilda experienced after the announcement of her parents' death: sounds and smells acquired an angle and edge she'd never noticed before. Greens burned greener. The curves and shadows of lies cast their own peculiar shapes in the air. Even the slightest whiff of curdling in milk became clear. It turned into something of a curse to her, this ability to smell and hear truth even when she didn't want to. It grew tiring to be so alert.

She had a hard time finding the suitcase, which was stashed deep in a closet, as if to emphasize the difficulties of travel. It didn't take long to pack, because it was still summer, and the clothes were thin and cotton. Even with the boys' things, the bag was hardly filled, though Hilda saw that both Jem's and Stuart's trouser pockets were bulky with talismans that would lose power if revealed.

Hilda herself felt strangely calm, as if her heart were suddenly gone and she'd been left with only this body, a husk of muscle and bone. As if her heart were a kind of crusty anchor whose weight she'd never quite gauged and her body, which she'd assumed to be so much heavier, was as light and brittle as straw. The only thing that jarred her was the sight, in the indoor bathroom that her father loved, of her parents' tooth-brushes. The stiff bristles of the red (Davis's), the softer ones of the green (Margaret's) sat propped in the glass, weary sentinels. Hilda couldn't stop looking at them, the dented can of tooth powder, her hand sweaty on the china knob.

In the car, Hilda sat between her brothers. Dr. Robbins steered cautiously down the pocked driveway, worried for the low, expensive underbelly of the Nash. Jem balled himself into a corner. Stuart let Hilda hold his hand, but he, too, had turned himself away from her and pressed his face into the leather seat. Only Hilda looked out at the grazing land and the wheat fields, some high, some low, some shadowed with Black Angus, some not, and all of the expanse yellow. A wind had risen. Clouds were thickening in a gray band at the horizon. Where were their parents now? What had happened to the truck? She realized she didn't want to see the bodies. She didn't even want to let the idea of them near the edge of her mind.

"We'll go first to the house," the doctor said to the rearview mirror. He lived on the west side of town, in a generous Victorian house whose ceilings were webbed with cracks. They were given a guest room to share. "I'll be back in an hour. Settle in and wander wherever you like." He smiled and gave his ginger bangs a push that made them messier. "You're allowed to look in closets." Hilda and Jem colored and Stuart looked shocked. Their mother would have been appalled. But it was better to keep moving, they all seemed to discover. Stuart and Jem unearthed a collection of damaged model airplanes. The doctor's linen closet was full of unironed sheets. He had books on art that were crammed with pictures of naked blue and orange women. An empty birdcage whittled from oily wood stood in a room piled high with old issues of magazines. It all looked foreign, somehow, even though they were firmly here in Canada—parentless and without much money, Hilda suspected. Like the image of her parents' bodies, that idea was best left unexamined at a certain dark border of awareness.

Poking through the doctor's house was a good distraction from the grief that was just beginning to pluck at them. It hooked like a raspberry thorn in the back of a hand, grabbing at unpredictable moments. Hilda saw it happen to both boys: in the middle of scraping toast crumbs from the counter the next morning it froze Jem's cupped palm. She saw it shake him, glaze his eyes, and then release. Stuart was less adept at hiding his, and in the next two days, Hilda found him in the smallest places he could squeeze into: a crevice below the stairs, behind the horsehair sofa. Once, in his sleep, he crawled between the box spring and the mattress. Jem and Hilda hadn't wanted to wake him, flattened but breathing, obviously comfortable with pressure. They crouched beside him, marveling. "How did he do it?" Jem asked softly, and Hilda shook her head, wondering at the evenness of his breath as the coils pressed deeply into his skin. When they roused Stuart, he couldn't remember waking in the night. They stood there staring at the round indentations in the boy's side and back. "Like someone stamped a bunch of Coke bottle bottoms on you, Stu," Jem said. Stuart looked as if he'd survived some initiation, something out of one of Dr. Robbins's *National Geographic*s. He looked as if he belonged to another species.

It struck Hilda that that was what happened when you were an orphan: you suddenly belonged to another tribe.

People's mouths twisted when they spoke to you. They couldn't approach you without a loaf of bread or a jar of pickles, but their faces skittered away from yours. Your clothing should look even more sober and modest than usual, clean but well mended. Your hands were supposed to lie like dead doves in your lap and your eyes look blank and tear-filmed. The only ones not to make them feel this way were the sheriff, Peter Johnstone, and the doctor. The first day at the doctor's house, the policeman visited, bearing a cardboard box.

"No way to put this nicely, kids," he said. He was short and stout, with an equine face, long and elegant. "Bad luck, terrible luck. Any idea why they were heading to the creek?" Jem and Hilda shook their heads. It was the first sign that their parents were not quite the stalwart, predictable people they had seemed. The second lay in Johnstone's box. "Brought some things we found in the truck. You may want them, we didn't know," he said, a bit pink in the cheeks. What made him blush, as they discovered, was not the rope and torch and handbag they'd pulled from the wreck but the soggy packet of apricot panties.

"God," said Jem, holding them up after Johnstone had left. "What did they want with these?" They smelled now of mud and were streaked with river silt. "Maybe it was a present," Hilda said. "They didn't still—" Jem started to say, and Hilda said, "Sort of looks it, doesn't it?" Jem had put the panties down, and they looked at them on a coffee table stained with rings wet glasses had left. "At their age," Jem said wonderingly. "Oh shut up," Hilda said, and smacked his arm.

She wrapped the lingerie in a sheet from one of the American newspapers strewn about the house and threw it in the trash. What else hadn't they known about their parents, she wondered as she sniffed Dr. Robbins's smoky Chinese tea. What was he hiding? On the surface, he looked loose and open. She could nearly admire the way he could use two pots of jam at once and leave their sticky caps about the kitchen. He was rarely there during the three days they spent at his house, but they looked forward to seeing him, an untidy swirl of silky ties, cologne, and possibility. He looked at them directly, unlike the other adults who came by, neighbors and merchants whose sympathy was as bluntly seasoned as their casseroles. Everyone was cramped with embarrassment and fear of saying something that would make the children cry. But we won't, Hilda wanted to say, we don't do that. Past its initial prick, grief was slow and wide, a kind of terrible vine that wrapped around you. You could look up and suddenly you couldn't move, it was so tight. There was no shaping it.

As it turned out, grief was the one area of their lives that was flourishing. When Hilda went to see the banker, Mr. Althorp, he told her with dark glee that her parents had been up to their necks in debt. The new tractor. The refrigerator. The pair of horses and the indoor plumbing. "But weren't there good harvests?" Hilda said, not understanding how her father could seem so solid but actually live so intemperately. How had he allowed himself the luxury of silk panties when he owed thousands of dollars? How much had her mother known? How had she endured all the owing?

"Not good enough," he said. Hilda understood why her mother hated this man sipping his sweet coffee in their parlor. She remembered how Margaret had spent days before his visits baking and scrubbing and muttering under her breath about interest rates and venal men. "In fairness, Hilda, most farmers live like this. He wasn't unusual." Althorp picked up his paperweight, a scene of a Swiss village in winter, and shook it. "An auction's the answer, my girl. And the proceeds should be enough to cancel the debt. Tough spot of news, I know. You have family in Vancouver, isn't that so?" Yes, one uncle there and another in Flin Flon, neither particularly quick with offers of assistance. Althorp jiggled up another blizzard in his globe, obscuring the houses.

So they would lose the farm. Marrying a local boy wouldn't do it, or selling off small parcels. It would be gone. She saw, too, how this pleased the town man, whose crafty ways with law and money yet again proved his superiority to those with humbler skills and stronger bodies. She realized as well that she felt solid for the first time in three days, as if her heart had returned to its settled place. The snow was muffling the Swiss church and fir trees when she said, "Mum never liked you, Mr. Althorp, and I can see why." He spilled his coffee all over his desk and knocked the paperweight to the floor, where it rolled to rest below a radiator. Hilda left feeling happier than she had in some time.

It disturbed people, their not behaving correctly. Saying rude things to bankers. Not crying enough. Insisting on certain arrangements for the funeral with a practical fierceness children shouldn't have. They resisted their orphanhood. They resisted the pity and condescension that were their due. People didn't like it. They didn't get a chance to feel lucky at having escaped that particular fate.

At the service the next day, the townsfolk felt slightly appeased when Stuart gave way to sobs. The front panel of

Hilda's navy dress turned warm and wet with his tears. The sun was brassy and indifferent, the mourners uncomfortable in dark clothes that drank heat. Hilda couldn't listen to the minister and instead remembered how she hadn't wanted to hear details of the accident, hadn't gone to see the bridge the way Jem had. She couldn't hear more than "ripped out in the middle, girder busted right through" or see more than Jem seated on the doctor's sofa, his hands, suddenly larger, dangling between his bony knees. "Stop, Jem, enough," she'd said sharply, their mother in her voice, and he had risen as if he had an old man's joints.

They held the reception at the Andersons'. The hay harvest was under way and men were ruddy in the face and neck. Women patted at their temples. Her uncles stood to the side, talking with Althorp. Hilda could see their clotted hope that they not be legally tied to Margaret's children or this land. They'd escaped. Edward wore brighter clothes than Charles. He sold cars now and had a steepled handkerchief poking from his suit pocket. Charles mined zinc and had a gritty face, as if the element he worked in had soaked into his skin and changed its structure. Though both were family men, neither spoke of wives or children.

Hilda listened to the scratchy dance of gossip that circled round her as she poured tea and sliced peach pie. Stuart ate too much and was sick. She smoothed the back of his neck as he threw up, glad to retreat from the press of people, remembering how their mother had soothed them. Fevers and stomach upsets had pulled something gentler from Margaret than scrapes and fistfights had. She would talk then about being a nurse when she was young and how pretty her uniform had been. That she'd been able to spot a malingerer miles away. "Get it out, Stuart," Hilda said, and leaned her head against the toilet's cool tank.

As she cleaned dishes, Edward came to the kitchen to say, "Got a spot of business in town with Charles, kids. We'll be out later," which Hilda realized meant they were going to find a bar and get drunk.

Frieda Anderson said, "Spending the night alone there, Hilda?" Her hands stilled their scrubbing.

"They'll be back later," Hilda said, which they both knew was not quite accurate. Hilda watched the older woman, aware she was thinking about the extent of neighborly duties.

"Come fetch us if you need something," Frieda finally said.

Back in their yard, Hilda, Jem, and Stuart turned and looked back at the compact block of the Andersons' house. Smoke kinked from its stovepipe. Inside was the whole family. Sons visiting for the funeral, mother, father. They were abruptly unwilling to enter their own house and approached the barn first. The horses nickered as Jem came close, saying, "Good Dick and Princess, good horses," his hands slippery with oats. Stuart talked to each cow, holding the wide heads and rubbing the rings of skin around their horns until they blinked with pleasure. Hilda felt no corresponding urge of affection for the chickens, who seemed as impervious as ever.

Instead, she went back to the house, which surprised her with its sameness. But it was stuffy with trapped heat, which she released by prying open windows, upstairs and down. Except in the bedroom where her parents had slept. Doors slammed and creaked wide again as the wind scuttled about the rooms. Hilda stood listening in the kitchen and watched the sun go down low in the sky. Margaret would have hated all the dirt that was no doubt silting up in the curtains. But it was better than air with her mother's perfume still in it. Hilda didn't want the boys to smell it. When they came in from the barn, hay in their hair, she told them to clean up. "You're not Mum," Stuart said, hands balled to sudden fists. "You can't say when I wash."

Jem moved quickly, pinning Stuart's arm between his shoulder blades. "Don't you dare talk to Hil like that, weasel," Jem hissed as Stuart hopped and squealed.

"Stop it, Jem," Hilda cried. "Don't be such a bastard!"

That froze both of them, Hilda swearing. It surprised her, too. Jem released his brother. Stuart cupped his sore shoulder, muttered "Sorry, Hil," and slunk to the washroom. Hilda and Jem listened to water wheezing back through the pipes. House sounds, familiar as their own hands. Like the steam that banged through the downstairs radiator each winter, clanking them awake. "Prisoners trying to get out," Davis had called it, and Margaret would scold him for scaring Stuart. Hilda could hear her parents' voices, even smell potatoes frying as the heat of the stove burned a circle through the shag of frost on the windows. How long did memories last? Did they expire like medicines, get thick and unusable like old paint? How long would this keep happening? She noticed then she had twisted a dishcloth to rope.

Hilda filled the kettle and set it to boil. "We're going to lose the farm. You have to be nice to Stuart." She told Jem the ugly things that Althorp had said. They were to get the harvest in, then auction off the house, animals, and land. By November, he said, it all had to be done. "We have to decide what we want to do," said Hilda. Where they would live, she explained, with whom.

"Not the uncles," Stuart said, coming in, his hair combed to glossy rows.

Jem curled over the table and tipped the salt shaker. Four streams of white crystal made a tiny hill on the gingham cloth. He flattened the salt to a circle and dragged a fork through it. "You should leave, Hilda," he finally said.

"And go where?" she answered him. "And do what?" She was making them tea and cold chicken sandwiches for supper. Neighbors had brought roasted birds, tomatoes and marrows from their gardens. It's all they would eat for weeks, Hilda thought. Leftovers and handouts. And lucky to have it, Margaret would have said. The wind trudged through the kitchen and ruffled the tablecloth.

"I don't know," he admitted. "But Regina, it's not your place." They ate without talking, and between bites watched as Jem mixed pepper with salt and carved patterns in the gray lake.

That night, Stuart stayed with Hilda in her bed, and as he slept, breathing with the warm quickness of a small dog, she thought about what Jem had said. That there were places other than Regina that were better for her. Places where she might make friends. Places where she wouldn't turn into a woman married to a debt-riddled farmer.

Late that night, she heard the slap of the door on the jamb as her uncles came back. The refrigerator door eased open, some of the windows were pulled shut. They talked without worrying if they would wake Hilda and her brothers. Eventually, they made their uncertain ways to the washroom and then to the back porch, where she had a bed ready for them. Leaving had not improved them. She traced her finger around the edges of Stuart's ear and thought she could not stand the thought of anyone else hemming his trousers. But she could not sleep.

The next morning, Hilda rose before it was light. She fed the animals so the boys wouldn't have to, made coffee, could not sit still. Snores rattled from the porch. She was going to clean today and decided to start in the parlor. The sun slanted across one of the three prints that decorated the room: Westminster, Salisbury, and York Minster, matted in burgundy red. The stiff gray lace of their stonework had hovered in this room as long as she could remember. She had never liked them, and realized now that she resented how those prints were all that represented decoration in their home. As if color spoke of something large and ungovernable that Margaret had banished. Her father, she suspected, hungered for it more than her mother had.

Hilda beat the davenport, and dust plumed in beige veils. Margaret used to talk to it like a mortal enemy—"You think you're going to get the upper hand, but we'll see about that." She had faced off against it, and how stupid that had been. Dust was such a limp opponent. It made Hilda cry, alone in the room as the motes eased back toward the furniture. She wondered later if it was the clarity that the tears brought which made her notice that a web had fuzzed Westminster's glass. How Margaret would have hated that. She pulled a chair to the wall and took the picture down.

Hilda looked at the print, saw the hatched lines that wove together to suggest the spires and glass. It had been hard to make. There was artistry behind it, a sort she would never learn. She flipped the print and saw that the paper backing had been slit at the top and taped over. The kind of tape her father had used for temporary patches on a broken barn window. Hilda did not peel it away. In a house she felt she knew so well she could have found her way toward it by smell from the fields, here her father had matter-of-factly tucked whole threads of his life away. As if secrets were normal. Perhaps she was learning that they were. What had propelled Stuart between the box spring and the mattress? Why had Jem gone three times to look at the accident site and the ruined truck?

She went to wake her brothers. "Dad's stashed something," she whispered. "Don't wake the uncles." The boys' eyes were grainy with sleep, but they were quick and quiet as they came downstairs. "It's the church picture," Hilda explained. "It's got a pocket. You do it Jem."

He tore the paper away and they found that their father had secured money to make a neat blanket on the blank side of the cathedral. "Where'd he get this?" Jem whispered, counting. When had he put it here? It was leathery and smelled of copper. "Is it real?" Stuart asked, pulling a chair to reach for the other prints. But neither York nor Salisbury had anything hidden in it.

"Oh, it's real, Stu, that it is," said Jem, counting below his breath the way Frieda totted up stitches for a sweater. It amounted to a thousand dollars plus a bit extra. Hilda sat there, with a stack of it on her lap, leafing through the bills as if they might give her some odd disease you couldn't have in Canada. Like obvious luck. Like largesse. They decided he had done it when they'd had a good price on cattle about five years ago. "He must have hidden it from Mum," Jem said. Margaret would have made Davis pay ahead on the mortgage, they knew. "He was holding out on her," Hilda said. Even more simply, they couldn't believe he'd had the time to sneak in here and slice open the print to hide the cash. Evenings, he'd seemed too tired for more than the wireless. Where had he marshaled the energy for such craftiness?

Stuart said, "But you couldn't lie to Mum," and it was true, from their perspective. Margaret had a way of shaking out partial truths, skewed stories. But she hadn't been able to control Davis to the end. There had been ways he'd slipped past her, things he'd preserved for himself. Hilda had never thought of her parents as needing respite from each other, but it now seemed they must have. Intimacy and then distance. She had never realized that their marriage might be complicated.

"What do we do with it?" Stuart asked. "Does it mean we don't have to live with Uncle Edward?"

"Bloody hell," said Jem. "They can't see this. Where are we going to hide it?" They took a pillowcase, stuffed it full of the money, and tucked it behind Hilda's bedstead. The uncles wouldn't dare to enter a girl's room.

As she made the boys breakfast, they spoke softly to one another. "It's not enough for the land and the debts," Hilda said. "But what if we used it to go away, you know, run off, to Toronto or the States?" She split the yolks in the pan and let their gold heat to stiff yellow.

"Go," said Jem, testing the idea and pouring coffee. "We could, I suppose."

"Lower your voice. You'll wake them," Hilda said. "Eat while it's hot."

But Stuart was rigid at the table. "Why would we leave?" he said.

"Why not?" Hilda answered, listening to the ragged and separate breathing of the boys. "Dad was our age when he left. And he was alone. And he switched countries, crossed an ocean."

"We could, you know," Jem told his sister, slowly. "Stu, you could stay with the Andersons. They don't want to see us go with Ed and Charles. Did you see Mrs. A. looking at them? Way she looks at Ole when he gets into whiskey at the fair."

"We don't have to decide today," Hilda said, suddenly confused. The thought of Stuart not having anyone to make his lunch for school made her feel sick. Her mother would have been horrified. Her father, though, might have understood. He might have pushed them gently on. "I'll talk to Dr. Robbins," she told her brothers.

When their uncles wandered mid-morning to the kitchen, Hilda saw that Edward was wearing his fine if wrinkled clothes again. He drove a grand car, too. He cared rather too much about getting dirt on his spotless shoes. It was shameful that he minded after so many years on a farm. Was that what cities did to you? Made you worry about getting smudged and gave you a cagey look? He looked as if someone had unplugged him. A battery run dry. His brother, though not so prosperous, had the same emptied face. She fetched them coffee, made eggs and toast, and excused herself. She had errands in town, she said, and wanted to catch a ride with Ole if he was heading in. "Hilda," Edward said. "A question for you. Have you thought of where you and the boys are going to live?"

She had the advantage of sobriety and cleanliness, the cultivation of the moral edge so essential to relations between Protestants. "Uncle Ed, we'll not be coming out to the Coast or going to Flin Flon." Charles speared a slippery triangle of white.

Edward said, "Nice eggs, Hilda." He seemed relieved. She had never experienced her family as a burden. That he saw them as such was obvious. And it was also clear that the prospect of not being responsible for them was cajoling him out of his hangover. "We're hoping to live for a bit with the Andersons," she said. "Stay nearby. It's what Mum and Dad would have wanted." But who knows what they wanted? Nothing was clear now. She thought of the mound of cash under her bed. Charles's knife scraped the toast.

"We'll talk with Ole and Frieda and see what we can do," Charles said. "Ask if I can stop by this afternoon. That's a girl," he said, and leaned to flick a crumb from his trouser leg.

All the way in to town, bouncing on the seat of Ole's badly suspended truck, Hilda wondered when she would feel well again. She wondered what Dr. Robbins would say if she asked, which of course she never would. She was almost surprised to find him at home, but he was, bent over a sandwich—hard-boiled eggs, celery, mustard, and bacon. He seemed glad to see her and listened to the story about the money. The kitchen smelled of grease and the honey he was going to slather on another slice of bread for his dessert. She admired how he let himself eat what he liked. It seemed a great assertion of adulthood, the following of peculiar appetites.

He did not interrupt, just continued to crunch the nuggets of celery in the sandwich and watch her as his jaw moved. "What do the boys want?" he asked. She explained, and mentioned their hopes of the Andersons.

"And your uncles?" the doctor asked, preparing a pot of Lapsang Souchong for two. "They didn't seem to object," she told him. Ed had in fact mumbled something about leaving for Vancouver the next day or so. So instead of talking to a relation, here she was telling her story to another man she barely knew, a man she liked because of his glossy magazines and imported teas. She didn't even know where the money was from. Had her father perhaps stolen it? What else didn't they know about him? And despite it all, here was her body pulsing to be gone. Hilda felt dizzy and cradled her spinning head in the bowl of her arms.

She heard the scrape of Dr. Robbins's chair on the linoleum and felt his hands on her neck and hair. Soft, she thought. Town hands. "Poor girl," he said. "You just want to go and have an adventure, and all you can think about is how long you'll burn in hell for it." He laughed, and then she felt his lips on her nape, just where a curl began to kink. "Poor girl," he kept saying. "How old are you, pretty girl? Eighteen, and just," and then she was in his arms saying that yes he was right, just eighteen.

He'd done nothing more than kiss her and call her pretty girl, casually, as if he'd never had another role in her life. As if he hadn't been the man who'd given her shots, weighed her, bandaged her foot when Princess stepped on it. As if he hadn't been the man who, a week earlier, had told her that her parents had drowned. And she behaved, in returning his touch, as if it were the most obvious thing in the world to kiss the family doctor. As if she weren't parentless and without prospects. Even as she felt her lips on his and breathed in his spice up close, she wondered at this thought: the thinness of the fabric between who it was you thought you were and what it was you could actually do. When he stopped kissing her, it wasn't from sudden recollection of his station or his relationship to her, but because he had patients to see. "Two o'clock all of a sudden. Time to get back to the surgery. Old Flora will be stamping about," he said, and delicately shifted her off his lap. He lit a cigarette and said, "And as for you, Hilda, get the boys settled, then head out. Give yourself a deadline and go." He shrugged into his jacket and was gone, waggling his fingers and leaving the honey and bread untouched. As if the kisses had been the finish to his strange and hasty meal.

Hilda stood and walked slightly off kilter to the washroom. In the speckled mirror, she saw how his hands had disheveled her hair. She scraped her fingers through it and it only looked worse, which was hard to care about when you'd just had your first real kiss. All the heat that had sprouted in her. It was the first time she was sure Margaret could not have extracted the truth from her. Hilda washed the sandwich plate and screwed the cap back on the honey. Toronto, she decided. In Montréal you might have to speak French and that would be complicated. No one in Regina went to Toronto. She would find work. She would find men to kiss her. She would learn to smoke. She could see herself, silk-stockinged, a smile tickling the corner of her mouth, men glancing at her with a nod as she swished down a street where the lights glowed with the luster of pearls and cars throbbed with purpose. Funny, she thought, if Mum and Dad were alive, this would never have happened. I would never have known my head could work like this.

It was as if her mind were growing stormier. During harvest, Jem spent one day in the fields in a shirt of Davis's and it released their father's smell in the kitchen and made them all leaden with grief. The next morning, Hilda bundled all of Margaret's and Davis's clothing into old sheets. She walked to the Andersons' twice that day, great white sacks on her back, and told Frieda she could have what she wanted. Frieda was drying plates when Hilda knocked on the porch door. She could have asked what in the world are you doing, but didn't. She merely nodded as her towel rubbed the lip of Ole's coffee cup.

But Hilda put off other unpleasant chores in a fit of procrastination that Margaret would have chastised. There were the drawers and other closets to sort through. The house badly needed cleaning. The auctioneer was scheduled to come look at the place that Friday. A man of bizarre proportions named Sykes, all caved-in cheeks and billowing waistline. He'd seemed excited at the thought of Campbell land and property moving on to others.

The memory of his greedy face made Hilda red with a fury that allowed her finally to start. She swept, scrubbed, dusted, mopped. Her arms ached with walloping carpets in the yard. Hilda knew what she was doing: punishing herself for the bad luck that had fallen upon her family. For the imminent loss of the farm. Something stark to make amends for not being able to fend off adults with unseemly hungers. As she polished the only silver her mother had owned—a tea set scrolled with roses—Hilda imagined the horses balking as other farmers slipped other bridles over their heads, refusing to be led by hands they didn't know. She saw the chickens' squawk and fluster suddenly boxed into crates, ready for beheading near someone else's coop. She heard the plain rooms echo with the clomp of other people's boots. She imagined the whisper and rock of other people's parents at night when they thought no one was listening, the thump of bed on wall, the heavy sighs.

That was enough to send her to the drawers. Spoons seemed safe enough, their clanking familiar. But then she got to the backs of kitchen cabinets. Her head deep in the cool, webby dark, she saw a stack of small boxes. Behind the cast-iron pot she'd used for stews, Margaret had stashed small labeled containers of cardboard. Safety pins, said one. Another held pennies, green with copper crust. Hilda sat on the kitchen floor, fingers waking dull music from the coins, and said aloud, "Why did she do this?" The boxes were everywhere: behind the baking pans, below tea towels. Scraps of plaid and calico from ten years' worth of dressmaking. Buttons and ribbons from hats and shirts. All at layers just beyond where her children's fingers would have probed.

Hilda gathered the boxes to the middle of the table and sat there for a bit, a new shape to her mother gathering around the old one, adding an edge of strangeness. She must have spent hours doing this sort of thing, Hilda thought, fitting the top of a shoe box over frayed boot laces. But the question was why. Her heart bobbled oddly. It was a variety of panic, she realized, because her mother had seemed the most stable and known of people. A woman whose life could be shaken out like a sheet to dry and there it would swing in the bleaching wind. Instead, the boxes she found behind the pots in which their food had steamed spoke of something wily and sad. A secret river of feeling and worry.

That night, Hilda showed Jem the collection. "She was a good mum," Jem said, a bit wonderingly, and Hilda thought he meant that she was brave not revealing her concern, tucking it away like the threads of hair that always escaped her bobby pins. Hilda could see her now at the stove, one hand jabbing a lock back, the other fussing at a crock of soup. She had a headache which came from not weeping at the sight of the slanted hand that noted the boxes' precise contents.

Jem stayed home from school the next day so he could show Sykes the land after Hilda gave him a tour of the house. The auctioneer followed her, scribbling down the contents of each room on a yellow pad. He licked the pencil lead each time he made a fresh entry. He smacked up the biscuits she served him, as if he'd not eaten in days. "Rough luck for you young people," he kept saying. "Hate to see it go. But that's the way of evil in the world." Sykes belonged to some evangelical sect and was given to statements that vaguely implied your wickedness. When he'd gone Jem asked, "Do you think you could kill someone just by hating them long enough?" They had started to say things like this to each other in the weeks since their parents died. Heretical comments that wouldn't have come to mind before, much less been spoken aloud. "I saw an article about witches in the jungle at Dr. Robbins's that said you could," Hilda said.

But Sykes was very much alive when he sold their horses, cattle, davenport, silver, and even the prints the next Saturday. The first snow lay about the land in a grainy crust. Farmers came from miles around, but neighbors attended, too, people who had clutched their hats to their chests at the service, delivered stew, people who now would not look at them as they bent into the wind to load their trucks with saws and chairs, lanterns and pitchforks. Hilda had sent Stuart to spend the afternoon with Frieda. All they'd kept were Margaret's old boxes and Davis's money, and only because they'd hidden those away. "Shoelaces and a bit of cash," Jem muttered as he paced near the barn, waiting in a storm-heavy wind to see who would buy Dick and Princess.

They had supper at the Andersons', and it was quiet until Ole finally asked, "Who got the house?"

"Sykes's brother," Frieda said. He'd just married a second time and was bringing his shy, plump wife to slave for him. He had his brother's thin cheeks, wide belly, but no God. People said he worked horses until they died under him. People said the same thing had happened to the first wife.

Stuart poked at his beans and Frieda told him he could be excused if he liked. But the rest of them sat there as fat glazed on the ham. Hilda imagined Sykes's wife making curtains and stocking the pantry, Sykes cursing every stitch and jar of beets. They would make mistakes, Hilda thought, like growing tomatoes on the sunny side of the house; but the wind blew hardest there and weakened the plants. Sykes had a pack of low-slung dogs that howled and stole sheep and chickens. Ole offered to add a tumbler of whiskey to their coffee. Even Frieda accepted some. "You poor lambs," she said, and drank. It was the first liquor Hilda had ever tasted, and to her surprise, she liked the bright stripe of heat it woke in her throat. Ole clapped them on their shoulders and told them to get extra blankets. It would be a bad night.

Hilda was sleeping in the parlor, but even with a quilt wrapped around her, she shivered herself awake. It was no use. She pulled an armchair to the window and tried to peer at their house through the gloom. The storm had not quite hit, but twists of white whipped the glass from time to time. Then she saw the shadow against the already fallen snow. Someone was out there, moving across the road and toward their barn. She dressed quickly, throwing on over her own clothes whatever woolly things she found hanging on the kitchen pegs. There was no time to find a torch, she was just going to have to follow. She couldn't stand the thought of someone lurking there. That people had come openly to buy what had once been theirs was bad enough.

The wind forced her to walk with her head tucked low. There were too many prints crisscrossing the yard and she lost track of the shadow. By the time she got to the barn, she had no idea where the person had gone. She stood under its eave, near the wide door, in the lee of the wind. She was breathing hard, whether with fear or cold she could not quite tell. Then she saw it. In the kitchen. A tall orange bloom. A column of color inside the dark house. The front door opened and she saw Jem turn to toss a canister of kerosene into the yard. The fire made the muntins of the kitchen windows look for a moment like slender bones and the next second, the glass exploded. Heat and pressure pushed Jem stumbling into the night. His hair was spiked to quills. It was then he looked up and saw his sister.

"I had to do it," he yelled. "I couldn't let Sykes have it."

How she managed to hear this as the fire began to lick the rest of the house and spread, wind-fed, to the second story, Hilda did not know. Perhaps he never said it. But it was what he meant. She went to him and took off one of Ole's sweaters to wrap him in. The snow was coming down now, but the licking flames warmed the yard, cast an apron of heat and light onto the ground. The fire seemed to talk, Hilda remembered later, rollicking through the house, crackling and whuffing. She wanted to stay and watch until the roof collapsed. She wanted to stay and think why it was her heart soared when she saw that Jem had torched the house. She had a vision then of Davis laughing, a wide, rare laugh. Because he knew, as Margaret hadn't, that nothing lasted. That no matter how many papers they had filed at the bank or how many acres rattled with grain, no one was ever really home.

But they had to get back to the Andersons'. The storm was fastening itself to the fields, and they could barely see their way to the road, which would soon gather drifts. They could die like stupid cattle on the range. They held hands as they moved forward and thought of nothing but finding the road. The kerosene can Jem had retrieved banged against his outer leg. When they reached the Andersons' porch door, they saw Frieda in the kitchen, waiting. She had made them tea.

"Get in and take off those wet things." Hilda and Jem said nothing, snow sluicing off them in the kitchen's warmth. Frieda rose and shoved a log in the red mouth of the stove. "Make sure those clothes are dry by morning." She took the can from Jem, and they never saw it again. But neither of them could do anything except stand at the kitchen window and watch the hectic orange blur of the fire through the scrim of the storm. The wood in the stove sputtered. Their clothes steamed. They could not hear the house burn through the wind, which sang high and angry all night long.

The next day, Frieda told the Regina police that the children were home all night, that she'd woken with toothache and gone to check on them. She had pinned her hair in a severe braid to the top of her head. She wore a clean cardigan. She had sent Jem and Ole to check on fences at the farthest edge of their land. Why were they troubling such poor children, who'd lost everything in the last months? The police were polite and drank her strong coffee. As Frieda spoke to the two men, Hilda stood by the window and watched Stuart explore the ruins, the house like a big singed crow crowned with tufts of snow. He seemed tiny next to the exposed and smoking ruin. When the wind gusted, it sent the smell of charred, wet wood to the Andersons'. The snow had stopped near dawn. Stuart was sometimes hidden by a bank the plows had raised on the road. Hilda and Jem had been lucky that none of the drivers had seen them last night.

Frieda fed the police slices of lemon cake that made their cheeks shine. When they finally trundled off, Frieda said, "I am too old for lies," and just went upstairs. "Go get Stuart, then bring me tea and a sandwich in an hour and do not ever tell Ole I was napping," she told Hilda.

When Jem came back that night, raw in the face and blue in the lips, he sat with Hilda and drank cup after cup of coffee as Hilda told him what had happened. "We'll have to go. Not right away, but soon," said Jem. It was true. The police might decide to lay aside too detailed an inquiry, but Sykes would not and he was more dangerous. They agreed that

Stuart was probably safe and that Frieda would frighten Sykes after a bit. But it seemed clear that the two of them should quietly make the opportunity to leave.

"Jem," Hilda said, "I'm glad you did it."

Jem said nothing, but got up and rinsed his cup. "I think I'll try B.C.," he said. "I'd like to see the Pacific." Hilda peered out the window, although it was too dark to see their old house. Sykes had been out to inspect the damage and had spent the afternoon kicking shattered rafters and tossing blackened bits of floorboards into the drifts. His wife had stood nearby, wide and shivering, clutching her collar. "Hilda," Jem said, still at the sink, "it was beautiful, wasn't it?"

"Oh, it was, Jem," she told her brother, turning from the window. "It was."

The wind shifted again in the night and Hilda could smell the ashes from the parlor. That odor wouldn't leave for a long time, she suspected. She would know the stink of burned house wherever she found it. What was strange was how light it made her feel. And how oddly thrilling to have participated in something so drastic. She would never have thought herself capable of anything but the blunt actions of truth. She wondered as she lay there in Frieda's quilts what else she did not yet know about herself. She wondered if she would like the woman she was going to turn into.

Later in the week, Hilda rode to town with Ole and forty dollars of Davis's money folded to a tight rectangle in her pocket. She bought Frieda a blue straw hat that had a spray of lilies of the valley festooning its brim. At Martin's, she found a new oilskin for Jem and two pairs of shoes for Stuart. She got Ole a bottle of schnapps, which she would give to him privately. Everywhere she went, people were spiky with interest. "How awful about the house," they'd say, and Hilda agreed that it was terrible. "How long did it burn?" Philip Hamilton asked, tugging on gloves before going back outside. "I wouldn't know, Mr. Hamilton," Hilda said, looking straight at him. "We were fast asleep." Again, the thrill of the new self rang through her. She could have told him exactly when the roof sprang into flame and when the central beam had snapped. The kitchen clock had ticked above her head the whole damp, shivering night. She could feel the neighbors' caution with her as they pried for news, expressed regret, and disentangled themselves from her family's run of horrid luck. Hilda could see, as they buttoned coats or folded receipts in wallets, that they were sifting what she'd said. At her last stop in town, MacGregor's, she realized that these were the same people who would be relieved that she and Jem were leaving. They wouldn't mind it if most of the Campbells and their strange ways excised themselves from Regina. The thought struck her as she fingered a velvet skirt that cost five times what Margaret would ever have spent on store-bought clothes. And though she told herself she did not care what others thought, she bought for herself a sensible valise and not the lush skirt she yearned for. It was just that she didn't want to hand Molly Partridge, the cashier, such a fine scrap of gossip.

Just after Christmas, Frieda gave them a farewell supper of chipped beef, peas, and fresh bread. She invited Dr. Robbins and made Stuart give them a small goodbye speech. She had given the boy a Guernsey cow of his own to look after, and even let Ole get drunk. Jem was smoking, a new habit, and laughing, and Hilda realized how tall he'd suddenly become.

Dr. Robbins watched Hilda from across the table and gave her a kiss on both cheeks when he left. "Write me, Hilda dear," he said, waving from his car. "I will," she cried, waving back. They would try to meet back here for Easter.

And then the next morning, three of Frieda's sweaters stuffed into the top of her valise, Hilda found herself bundled into a second-class compartment on a train to Toronto. She tried to wave to her brothers and the Andersons, but the breath of the other passengers had misted the windows. She knew they were waving, that they would stay until her train pulled out of view. At least that's what she thought would happen.

What surprised Hilda most about the city was how much she missed the baldness of the Saskatchewan sky. Sky that openly revealed its threats, intentions, and good behavior. Here, buildings and hills interrupted the blue, which itself was slyer, more cloaked in mist, thanks to the lake. The light was altogether thicker. The cold had a mildness to it, that was true, and the wind blew less fiercely. It wasn't so much that Hilda found herself missing the farm, but that what had replaced it had routines of grimy boredom which she'd been sure existed only on the plains and in relation to crops and animals. This was the next thing she missed most: the being known and neatly socketed into a town, a landscape. In Regina, when people whispered about you, at least it meant they knew your name. After the accident and the fire, her family had earned some notoriety. Now her story dangled amid all the others here in this large place and even, as the months passed, lost heft and importance. "I'm an orphan and my brother burned down our house," she sometimes found herself wanting to confess to friendly-looking women on the TTC. But, being Canadian, she taught herself instead to work crosswords as the subway cars lurched downtown.

Since she didn't talk much to people, she wrote Stuart and Frieda every three days and received frequent letters about new stamps Stuart had found and how badly Sykes was doing on their land. Ole sometimes scribbled a note about the weather or the price of feed and added comments like "Mind your Ps and Qs." Now and then Jem sent on a skimpy bone of news. He was fishing, on salmon boats, and the money was good. He liked the water. He had good mates.

Hilda wrote back as if all she did was go to concerts and the cinema. She tossed in asides about ice skating at the rink outside the City Hall and the way the trees there were wrapped in colored lights. She never mentioned work, which was in a café off Queen Street, where students and a few rather seedy businessmen came for cheap meals. She had to wear a uniform, pink and itchy, and a white cap. It had been the first place she'd applied, and when the manager asked if she could deal with grumpy customers, she said, "On the farm I used to help to geld bulls," and he had tossed up his hands and said, "No need for anything so drastic, love, just don't let them boss you about." She even wished sometimes that the customers would summon the energy for testiness and be less dourly interested in newspapers and hash. She wished one of them would ask her to go ice skating. Instead, she went to the Royal Ontario

Museum on Sundays and obseved couples link arms more than she observed the gold-framed paintings.

She didn't write about the YWCA, either. What was there to say about the women who talked anxiously all night long in languages she did not understand? She would have liked to be friends, but their smiles were as thin as cracks in pottery and their faces spoke of being more at home somewhere far from Canada. Most of them came from somewhere warmer, former colonies, where they'd learned their old-fashioned, lilting English. Their clothes often weren't sturdy enough for winter, and once Hilda saw a young Indian woman start to weep while listening to a prediction of a cold snap on the wireless. Even the Canadian girls were hard to talk to, tight-lipped about what had pushed them to the city.

The only person to whom she showed something other than stoic cheer was Dr. Robbins. She had written him, as she'd promised, and was horrified to realize how much she counted on him to answer. Which he did, sporadically. It didn't even matter to her that he never really commented on her previous letters or seemed interested in her life. She needed to tell someone about the café. About the books she was reading—Conrad, Lawrence, and Jack London, books the librarian down the street from the Y recommended. His letters were mostly news about his patients that she assumed they wouldn't want shared. "Mr. Bell and Alex Snow at it again last Saturday. Mr. Bell's got a whopping black eye he's trying to blame on walking into a barn door." Thrilling, naughty, careless letters. He had never kissed her again, but the letters, with their breezy betrayals, hinted at some intimacy.

Hilda became more and more unguarded in her responses, relating dreams she'd had, telling him her concerns about Stuart. She worried that he would find her provincial and tried for a time to sound more streetwise. She cultivated sarcasm with her customers. Her tips grew smaller.

The doctor didn't like it either. "Stop pretending to be Barbara Stanwyck. It'll become a habit and you'll forget how to sound like yourself." In that same letter he mentioned he might be heading to Toronto in May for a conference. She did not like how he affected her from afar. His visit became all she could think about. She realized she would be ashamed to take tea with him at the Y. Besides, she was starting to mind the sobbing women curled around the telephones. All that damp homesickness.

In early March, she found a room in a widow's house off St. George. She had a bedroom and a small bath on the third floor and shared the kitchen with the woman, Mrs. Colgate. It was heavenly, the soft bed, the crispness of the curtains, the buying of her own sheets. It occurred to Hilda then that she might do something other than fill orders for steaks and sausage. It occurred to her that she might decorate her room a bit, something strictly forbidden at the Y. She let herself acquire small luxuries. A tiny vial of perfume. A kind of toothpaste she'd not tried before. She ate one night at a Greek restaurant and loved the bite of the feta cheese, its crumbly feel in her mouth, and the sinewed waltz of the waiters who darted about the small space and never dropped one of their battered trays.

Granting herself slight pleasures came gradually to feel more comfortable. She discovered there were things she liked and things she did not. Her favorite time of the week was Sunday morning. Leafing through the want ads, she drank her coffee and listened to the thread of Brahms seeping from Mrs. Colgate's room. It felt so grown-up, sitting there in the frosted winter light, the elegant music curling toward her ears. She circled possible jobs in red ink. She couldn't stomach the thought of Dr. Robbins seeing her uniform, which was giving her a rash, though she washed it often. Scooping up tips and scrubbing countertops did not reinforce her belief that she was suited to other work. But on Sundays, when she looked at the papers, everything felt possible. She was starting not to mind that she could float down the street and remain unknown. It was even preferable to exchanging polite talk with Althorp or watching Sykes building the stumpy replacement house. It was even starting to make her uncomfortable that customers knew her schedule and name now and that she remembered how they took their coffee. Worse, some of them had started to get glossy in the eye when they saw her tie on her apron. She circled a job at a travel agent's that asked for "girls who understood the necessity of good manners."

It was a small shop not far from the café. Betty's Custom Travel. Betty turned out to be Robert Truscott, an edgy blond fellow who said he had named the shop for his mum, who'd passed on a few years back. She'd loved adventure, he said. The Thousand Islands. Montréal. "My mum died recently," Hilda offered, and she saw him assess her with a bit more interest. "In an accident," she added, "with my dad." It was the first time she'd found being an orphan useful. He paid her more than she'd earned at the café, and the hours were better. She answered phones, taught herself to type when he was at lunch, and was polite, as promised, to the clients who came in to organize honeymoons and cruises. She spent a great deal of time unfolding and pasting up posters of bougainvillea dangling against whitewashed Greek houses. She was also responsible for arranging new displays in the window: sand spiked with toy umbrellas, a great paper sun stuck to the glass, specials to Florida. Sometimes Hilda let herself think how all this frivolous spending of money on vacations would have shocked her mother, and the thought both pleased and distressed her.

Still, this new life was not exactly what she had hoped. Hilda had allowed herself to think it all might be a bit more fun. She had the vague sense she was missing something important. Not men so much as the twinge of excitement that she got from reading books: a sense of the world's fullness, intricacy, dark patternings. She'd had it kissing the doctor, so part of it was men. He gave her a sense that life required stirring up, as if the most interesting things were lying at the bottom. But his was a muddy kind of excitement, not quite savory. Wasn't there something else? Walking to the subway one morning in March, past mothers bundling children onto school buses, she wondered how they became what they were. How did you go from being Hilda to being one of those lipsticked women who browned roasts on Sundays? And did she want to be so calm and careful? She imagined Dr. Robbins sitting across from her in her boardinghouse kitchen. "What do you want, Hilda? What makes you happy?" Or other sorts of questions asked only by people who were reckless with themselves and others. Walking down the sidewalk, past tidy cottages and gray mailboxes, Hilda thought about the idea of happy. She saw useless armfuls of cut flowers, bursts of lilies, puffed buds of wild roses. She saw silk scarves in extravagant prints against creamy skin.

But Mr. Truscott called her his "steady Western worker," which made Hilda forget being happy and feel instead like a draft horse, though she'd lost weight in the city. Still, he began to entrust more work to her, liking her tidy habits of filing and the fact he had seen so much more of the world than she had. "Oh, which is better, New York or Venice in June," he would sigh loudly to customers.

One afternoon in April, just as the city began to think about green and Hilda was doubting she would ever hear from Dr. Robbins, her employer introduced her to Mr. Delano. He was a large man with a pepper-colored mustache and a sloping belly. Large but delicate, and a shock of nut-brown hair. Mr. Delano was going to organize tours from their office for French and Italian tourists coming to Toronto this summer. The dollar was good against the franc and the lira, he said, and Mr. Truscott was expecting "hordes of Europeans, floods of them." Mr. Delano would guide them about the city and Hilda would provide "support as needed." She might even, Mr. Truscott said, take one of the tours herself.

To Hilda's ears, Mr. Delano spoke lovely French and Italian. He was often on the phone to people who lived in these countries, engaged in laughing conversations spiked with *si*'s and *ecco*'s. They sounded more like long gossipy chats than arrangements for the serious schedule of tours Mr. Truscott was expecting. She'd never met anyone so robustly un-Canadian, apart from the women at the Y, whom she hadn't managed to get to know. He had other interesting traits, such as predicting the weather through his sinuses, which he claimed were sensitive to shifts in humidity and pressure. He was a nice distraction, Mr. Armand Delano. April slipped to May. Hilda arranged an alpine scene for the shop window, with green felt fields, a toy train, and a cardboard Mont Blanc she made herself. "Looks just like Switzerland," Mr. Delano said kindly. He predicted warm, sunny weather for the week.

He was right. Mrs. Colgate was playing Chopin études now instead of Brahms. Hilda was thinking about a class at the university in the summer term. She was starting to feel she knew her way about. She had a place she bought groceries. A newspaper vendor. Small signs of belonging, like sharing the Sunday funnies with Mrs. Colgate on the porch now it was getting warmer. It jolted her slightly at the end of May to see a message waiting that said a Dr. Robbins was in town and would she please ring him. He was staying at a fancy place near the water and sounded delighted to hear from her. Would she like to have dinner the next night?

Hilda stayed late at work. Mr. Delano was making another set of his leisurely calls, and she listened to the hop and chirp of the languages he slid between and wondered if the skirt she was wearing was too long. *"Ciao, ciao,"* he sang into the receiver, and then looked at Hilda. "Truscott giving you too much to do? You're too young to stay so late at work. You should be out," he said with a sweep of his square hands, "enjoying life." As if life were a circus that had just rolled into town.

"I do enjoy myself," she told him. He had no idea what her life had been, much less what it was like now. She snapped a file cabinet closed rather more sharply than she intended.

"Not enough, I think, Hilda," he said, and wished her good night.

She thought about that, about how he had been able to see something buttoned tight in her. She hadn't known he was even looking. What he said about enjoyment kept creeping across her mind as she ate supper with Dr. Robbins. He looked much the same—floppy ginger hair, expensive clothes sloppily worn, at ease in the well-appointed dining room. Everything smelled of rich meat and perfume. A string quartet played moodily behind potfuls of palms. He'd already ordered wine, which he began to pour when he saw her coming through the door. Apparently, she had changed. "Hilda, you look lovely," he said, rising to pull her chair out. Older, he said. More mysterious, he added teasingly.

She rather needed the wine. The other diners were women in sleek suits, men with expensive polished shoes. Confident with silverware. The burgundy made her remember how she'd imagined happiness, as scarves and flowers. Low vases with rosebuds stood on each table, but brown nibbled the petals' edges. The women wore lengths of silk knotted at their throats, but it did not chase the shadows from their faces. Was she enjoying herself, Hilda wondered as she sipped the wine. Was this how people did it?

They talked of his patients. He said that his conference was rather a bore and that he was thinking of leaving Regina. She asked after Ole and Frieda and if he'd seen Stuart. It was odd to speak of these things that had been her life here in this paneled room with its jacketed waiters and velvet curtains. The wine helped to soften the conversation's pauses and oddnesses, but mostly it made her look at the doctor and to see how candlelight spooked hollows from his face. It also made her think of rather startling questions. "How old are you?" she asked.

"Thirty-one," he said, and poured her the last of the second bottle. The room was emptying. The quartet was packing its instruments. She saw a violin being snapped into its case and a waiter bend to tie his shoe. "What else would you like to know?"

Hilda thought for a moment. You could know certain things about people that land or animals could never tell you. You could know where they were born and the names of who had made them. You could know where they'd studied, traveled. Those things were traceable. Humans left tracks. But knowing all that didn't mean their motives weren't cloudy and vague. It didn't mean much, finally, the grasp on a birthday or the state of a bank account. "Do you want to sleep with me?" she asked, tired of how soupy the wine was making her head.

"Well, yes," the doctor said, wiping his mouth with the broad napkin, "that's rather the point, isn't it?"

She was glad she'd had such a good meal on him at least. He'd been rough, not quite kind about her never having made love with anyone before. "You kissed like you'd slept with a barnload of farm boys," he said sadly. But that was because I was kissing you, she wanted to tell him from the tangled sheets, where she sat propped on pillows and hurting rather a lot between her legs. At least she hadn't bled all over the place. They'd both been relieved at that. She realized abruptly that she did not want to be there with him anymore. That she did not like his smell. His hands and tongue. Her head ached and she stumbled a bit as she dressed. He watched her from the bed, lazing on his side. "Don't go, Hilda," he said in a voice that struck her as unconvinced.

"Good night, Dr. Robbins," she said, then realized she had never called him by his given name. "Good night, James," she added, and closed the door, glad that the carpeting masked the sound of her new heels. They made a racket on the pavement in the cool spring night. She walked the whole long way home, giving herself blisters. Serves me right, she thought as she put plasters on them. Her body throbbed. What did other women know that she did not? Why had it all made her so sad? She washed herself three times. How disappointed Margaret would have been.

She was rather useless at work the next day, but Mr. Truscott was off at a convention in Hamilton. Mr. Delano was in and insisted she drink a great deal of tea. Tactfully, he did not ask why she had such circles under her eyes. She wanted to say to him, "I tried enjoying myself last night, but it didn't quite seem to work." Instead, she drank the tea and changed the posters of Greece for ones depicting Spain. Spain was the new Greece, Mr. Truscott had explained. When she got home that evening, Mrs. Colgate hinted that it had been a late night for her, hadn't it, and Hilda apologized, saying it wouldn't happen again. "It's not that, dear," the older woman said, "it can happen as long as you're quiet. It's just that it should make you happier." Hilda had needed to go upstairs then and read three chapters of Dostoevsky to quiet her mind and push back memories of Dr. Robbins's indelicate hands. How could he have handled her like that when he had been so good with needles? No one else in town gave such painless inoculations.

Naturally, they did not correspond again, and Hilda heard from Frieda that he had moved to Alberta. A woman apparently, Frieda wrote. "Bit of a dark horse, our Dr. Robbins." Had Hilda seen him when he'd been east? Hilda never answered directly. She willed him out of her mind with work and books. Mr. Truscott was letting her handle hotels now. She was learning about train reservations and international flights. But her period did not come when she expected it. She thought that curdling rage might make the blood arrive, or doses of strong coffee. Saying she had a touch of the flu, she asked Mrs. Colgate for the name of a doctor.

When Hilda heard later in the week that she was indeed two months along, she left work early and went back to her room. She allowed herself to think briefly of Margaret. Just a glimpse of her mother's face. It was stern, horrified. She didn't even try to read. She lay in her narrow bed, through supper, and was staring at the ceiling, holding her stomach, wondering how it would stretch, when she heard a knock.

It was Mrs. Colgate saying that a Mr. Delano was downstairs. Would she see him? How had he known where she lived, Hilda wondered. Although it was July, she was cold, she realized, and put on a jacket to greet him. "Would you like a bite to eat?" he asked, as if he were in the habit of stopping by and taking her out. "Yes, it would do you good," he decided for them.

They went to the Greek restaurant that Hilda liked. "How

did you know where I lived?" she asked him over mous-saka.

"I asked Robert," he said. "I hope you don't mind."

She didn't mind, she realized. He had clean nails, but his palms were ridged with callus, which was surprising for a city man. "Do you work with your hands?" she asked him.

"I live over an antique shop and help the owner a bit lift-ing things, putting on new varnish, just chores," he said. "It's good to do something apart from talk all the time."

"Why do you speak French and Italian?" she asked. He explained that his mother was Québecoise and his father Italian and they didn't like the other's language so they moved to Toronto from Montréal as a compromise. They both hated English and forced their son to speak both their native tongues. They were dead now. So were her parents, Hilda said. The conversation lapsed then, and Hilda saw it was not the angled quiet the doctor had tried to muffle with wine but an easy one. The sort she had with Mrs. Colgate over the papers. Friendly. Respectful.

Mr. Delano took her out a few more times, always to a dif-ferent restaurant. He introduced her to chopsticks, to which she took naturally. Her appetite was huge. She was going to have to tell him soon. Mrs. Colgate, too, would notice. But what was odd was that during these dinners, she never thought of the pregnancy. Of the slow churn in her belly. Of the shame and worry that kept her rigidly awake. They walked afterward by the lake for the lick of a breeze through the heat. He never touched her. She did not invite it. It hung between them, this not touching, pleasantly. At work, too, they were cordial as always.

Over dumplings one night in August, however, she finally told him. She didn't quite know how she managed it—she avoided any direct statement—but she told him. That she was having a baby and that she didn't want to marry the father. He seemed willing to read the small clues she left. But he appeared to understand, sitting there with his hands steepling on the table. "You won't be able to stay at Mrs. Colgate's."

"Or at Mr. Truscott's," she said and realized how sad that would make her. The small competence gone.

"I think Truscott can be handled," Mr. Delano said. Then he asked if she would stay at an extra room at his flat. His brother had recently married and moved to London. It was small, but it would do. She could walk to work. When she was ready to have the baby, perhaps then she could go home. She looked at him. He was kind. He was not careless. He ran his tours for the French and Italians with great skill. He made them think Toronto a shiny place, full of vigor and freshness. They called afterward to say, in their complicated English, how much fun it had been. How fine Canada was.

"I barely know you," Hilda said, poking at her dumplings. The restaurant was almost empty and the waiters smoked listlessly, sad not to have to dodge and swear at one another. "I don't know how old you are." Her voice rose. "I don't know if you're a nice man," she said finally. "I can't tell anymore."

He walked her home then and said she should of course think things over, and if he could be of help, he would like to. He was scrupulously polite, but then he always was. "Good night," he said as she stood on the porch, beneath a bulb feathered with the pale bodies of moths. She watched him go. He stopped at the end of the walkway and called, "I am thirty-nine," then waved at her. She waved back. She couldn't help herself. It was what you did when someone was friendly. You waved back.

His was a bounteous sort of thoughtfulness. A small bouquet of cornflowers on her desk. An arrangement made with an evidently distressed Mr. Truscott, who told her to wear a ring. "I expected more from you, miss," he said, but with Mr. Delano about and bringing in so much business, he didn't say more. "He can't, you know," Armand told her. "Betty never told him who his dad was, did she?" It was also luck that it was a prosperous summer, and Truscott let himself take two weeks in Marbella, leaving her and Armand to manage on their own as sleepy August wound down.

Apart from her doctor, Hilda had told no one other than this warm, round man. She could feel him watching her as she helped elderly ladies sort through brochures, the baby stirring about below her loose dress. Within a month, she'd be showing. She would have to decide who else should know. The thought of Stuart learning the news appalled her. Frieda even more so. Mrs. Colgate might have guessed, but wished Hilda well the day she left, even giving her one of the Chopin records and asking her to come take tea whenever she liked.

Evenings, Hilda listened to the études on Armand's machine. She made baby clothes as the music played, working from patterns she bought at the wool store. She was saving money by not paying rent, which Armand would not accept. She began, although the baby would of course change everything, to feel safe. It was an orderly, rather spacious flat, with tall, narrow windows that looked over an alley. He tended his plants with great care and would have liked to have a cat, but the landlady forbade it. He was a great reader, and when he wasn't downstairs helping Mrs. Elders polish furniture or lift rugs, he was in his deep armchair, a stack of novels listing at his side. He would read passages aloud to her from time to time. They shared the cooking. They were discreet with the use of the single washroom. She hadn't slept better than this since she was a child. She would look at him sometimes, fingers twitching his mustache, eyes darting across the page of a book, and wonder at her strange luck. The baby would twist, the music would end, but she would still sit there, marveling.

He never touched her, though she came to realize he would like to. And what amazed her most, she did not reject the idea of being taken in by him or even touched. She wrote to Frieda, Stuart, and Jem as always, but never mentioned the baby. She did not know quite what she wanted to say. It was such a complicated event, this child, this discovery of Armand. It amazed her, too, that she did not let the memory of Margaret's stern face dissuade her from liking the ripeness her body blossomed into. From enjoying the sway and tumble of the baby inside her. Women glanced enviously at her on the street, men carved places on buses and sidewalks. Her doctor pronounced her blessed.

It was thanks to Armand, Hilda thought. There was nothing to be ashamed of, he implied. A misstep, but what wonderful luck. He never asked who the father was or what had happened. Did it matter? Look what it allowed to unfold. He brought her pastries soaked in nuts and honey. He gave her beads of Czech glass. She took to making sure his pants were properly hemmed and, in a gesture she knew she could not undo, to buffing his nails, which had a tendency to peel. They did so much of this in silence, without speaking large words or naming grand emotions, Hilda thought at times that she would burst. There was so much to say, wasn't there? But perhaps love lost its sheen when spoken. Perhaps, too, if they mentioned it, the spell would disturb itself, disperse. Besides, when something this lovely came your way, who was to question where it was from?

Sometimes he would show her Mrs. Elders's antiques. She loved the cool shop, its faceted decanters and elegant carpets. Did it matter that a beautiful rug had belonged to a bad man? Armand asked her late in October, as she floated across the shop, sloped and golden as a pear. Did the violence that the rug had witnessed make it any less beautifully woven and conceived? It survived, he reminded her, where often people did not.

"Things don't always survive," Hilda said. She told him then about Davis and Margaret's death, about Jem's burning down the house. "So that's why I came to Toronto." Slowly, she told him more, because he neither insisted on knowing nor seemed revolted. They sat in the shop, the lights in the street slowly going out. It was easier to talk in this dark, unfamiliar place. She even told him about the panties. And eventually about Dr. Robbins. He came to her then, sitting in an old rocking chair, and pulled her to her feet and gently put his arms around her. Their bellies got in the way, which made them laugh. They stood there quietly among the cabinets and tea sets and Victorian mirrors and held each other.

They began to use the shop as a place to talk. Upstairs was for cooking and reading, sleeping and chores. Here, they told each other stories. She heard about his parents and their terrible feuds. Weeks of silence broken only by thrown glass and doors shivering in their jambs. His grandmother who lost her mind and wandered with one shoe about the winter streets. One night he had to carry her home in his arms in a blizzard. Hilda imagined the stories hanging there, like the flare of a cigarette spelling a name in the night. They would sit until the glow and smoke fell away and then realize they were tired. Upstairs, he insisted she drink milk before she slept. Bones, he said, don't neglect the bones. "Don't lecture," Hilda said, finishing the glass. "It doesn't suit you."

When he asked her to marry him in January, a month before she was due, she said yes with no hesitation, the baby dipping its head with what Hilda wanted to think of as consent. They signed papers at City Hall, had lunch at the Royal York as a gift from Truscott, and walked carefully back through the cold to the flat, where they made love for the first time. "Have to follow the proper order of things, sometimes," Hilda said. "No such thing as proper order," he said. "There's just what happens. If there'd been proper order, none of this would have happened, would it?" He took her great roundness in his hands and soothed her. How awkward it was, how they enjoyed themselves. They woke to a great snowstorm and lay the whole day in bed, a cloud of warmth inside a cloud of cold.

She gave birth to Danielle February 10. A perfect baby girl, with a shock of red hair to remind them of Dr. Robbins's ginger hair, but everything else came straight from Davis. The long tilted eyes, the shape of the face. It astonished Hilda how that made her weep. Her father sprung to life in a baby. She had to tell Frieda and her brothers. She couldn't have stood their not knowing this rich twist of luck: Armand and this baby, both herself and her grandfather. "Quite a life you're having," Frieda wrote back. "Ole and I are happy for you." She sent a quilt for the child and Stuart added a p.s. of congratulations to Frieda's letter. From Jem all she got was a note that said, "Glad we did it, aren't you, Hil?" She was. She was decidedly glad.

She went back to work three months after the baby was born, thanks to a renewal in her friendship with Mrs. Colgate. The older woman was able to look after Danielle during the day, and Hilda was glad to know someone who'd handled croup and colic. It gave her time to concentrate on the agency. Truscott was shuttling more of the responsibility to her. Flights were becoming slightly cheaper. People were jetting off to odd spots. Hilda spoke with people from Air India all the time. Goa. Tahiti. The posters were getting more and more tropical. Mr. Truscott was always going off to test some tour or other, and now and again would ask Hilda if she had thoughts of vacations abroad. But she didn't. She had Danielle, Armand, work, the antiques shop. It was lovely as it was. She'd done her traveling, she thought. She'd landed just where she needed to be, she realized as she booked flights and canceled reservations. People traveled out of restlessness, and here she was, content as a cat in a warm barn. Holding Danielle's bright heat in the rocking chair, listening to Armand laugh at something he was reading, the lamplight golden in the room, she would shiver with her good fortune.

That they could not have more children was something of a disappointment. But it allowed them time to spend with

Danielle, who was quick and fiery. A fierce child, whose red hair tilted to dark blond in her first year and whose eyes remained dark blue. Truscott sold them the agency a few years later, and when Mrs. Elders died in 1960, she left them the antiques shop. There were friends to entertain, Armand's friends, cheerful people given to long, loud evenings that made everyone muzzy in the head the next morning. There were the shops to manage. They rented cottages by lakes and even bought a car, a convertible that made their hair wild and made Danielle crow with pleasure. Toronto grew livelier with the dispersal of the Commonwealth. Hilda started arranging tickets for men and women who were going back to families and their former countries, not only Canadians rooting out the exotic. One person's fantasy was another person's hometown, she learned. She herself had no desire to go back to Saskatchewan. Stuart was at university in Alberta, Jem had bought a boat, Frieda and Ole had given their farm to one of their sons and moved to town. More and more, Hilda could not quite remember what the farm looked like, though its skies and dawns sometimes filtered through her dreams. She asked Stuart and Jem for photos, but only Stuart sent one. He looked stiff in his coat and tie and wore glasses. He said he had Christian friends now and was leading his life for God. He said God would forgive her for her sins. They'd found their answers, Hilda thought, all of them. Sea and silence for Jem, strict belief for Stuart, a redefined family and work for her. It could have been so much worse. But then one night Armand did not come home and it did become worse.

He died of a heart attack on his way back from Christmas

shopping. After spending rather a lot at Eaton's, he'd lumbered back to the subway with his packages, and just as the train roared into the station, he'd collapsed on the platform. The police had come to tell her, and when she'd seen their uniforms past the chain she'd known the bad news they brought. They had with them the presents he had bought for her and Danielle. Perfect choices, as always, presents that impressed not so much with their cost but because they showed how well you were known. That your tastes and interests mattered. A crossword dictionary for Hilda and a lovely scarf to match her red wool coat. Stacks of books and a paint set for Danielle, in bags gone soggy with melted snow.

Danielle could not understand where he was. She kept running to the door when someone knocked to see if he was there. He was coming back, wasn't he, so why was everyone crying? The days after Armand's death, the flat was filled with friends and colleagues who would step over the threshold, see Armand's African violets glowing under their purple tube, and begin to weep. Hilda tried to explain. "Darling, Armand is dead and he can't come back. He has gone. He loved us, but he has gone." Which Hilda could see made no sense to her child, to whom love meant precisely that you did not go, that you could be counted on to stay.

Later, Hilda could barely remember the next six terrible months. She dressed Danielle for school. She sold the car and the antiques shop, managed the agency, and moved to an apartment that Armand never would have dreamed of living in: all white paint and angles. The weather was astonishingly mild until it flowered into powerful summer heat and storms that made the parks and gardens as lush as jungles. Hilda wanted nothing more, however, than to wither, and woke once to find she had ripped open the feather pillow in her sleep. She lay there in their huge bed—they had needed its deep softness—and felt the feathers drift back upon her arms and neck. Danielle slept with her most nights, and it was only the pressure of the child's body at her hip and shoulder, the quick beats of her breathing, that made Hilda rise, dress, cook.

But the bitterness was in its way more dangerous than the grief. The fury of deprivation, not just once, but twice. She wanted to write and ask Stuart what his fine God thought of that, but she knew the answer. That she'd sinned and was being punished. But there'd been no sin with Armand. Her anger made the coffee boil to tar. She was burning food and it made her think of the orange flames that ate their old farmhouse. Anger crimped her generosity, and a woman at the travel agency told her it was too unpleasant to work there. Mrs. Colgate said gently, "Hilda, it was no one's fault." That checked her, the widow's cautious voice. It was true. There was no reason for pain. It simply was. There was nothing for it but to move ahead. It's what her mother would have done, Hilda thought. Then she realized it was what she had always done herself.

With that in mind, Hilda woke one July morning, and though the sky was as gray and dense as felt, Hilda told Danielle they were going to the beach. "We'll get out of this heat, Danny," she said, and the child seemed glad. All summer, people had talked about the temperature. Everyone kept mopping themselves, walking limply down the sidewalks, and glancing dolorously at thermometers in front of banks. "Where are we going?" Danielle asked. "To Lake Muskoka," Hilda said, and felt glad for the word. Lake. Just saying it sounded cool and deep. And it was a trip. They hadn't left the city since Armand's death. She had let everything but her anger shrink in those months: energy, hope, the ability to move.

Even their old bathing suits didn't fit, so they stopped first at Eaton's. Hilda's costume was navy blue, Danielle's green with tiny white dots. Their hair danced when they opened the windows of the car they'd borrowed from Mrs. Colgate, a sensible hardtop. The wind stung their cheeks and gave them the impression of coolness. It let Hilda feel she would manage there in the water. She did not know how to swim. Armand had begged to teach her, and she'd relented just before Christmas, promising that this summer she would learn. Right now, she wasn't quite sure what she was going to do with Danielle at the edge of the lake. But it wasn't until she was in the changing rooms with their clanging doors and the smack of rubber shoes on concrete that she grew frightened. Hilda turned her back as she changed, sliding one limb out of her clothing at a time. When she was done, she said, "God, it's more revealing than I thought it would be," and tugged at the skirt, hoping it would sit lower on her body. No one had seen it since Armand, and she wondered when anyone ever would again.

But once they were outside, all she saw was the lake, the entire shimmering plate of it, a sheet of rippling blue. Hilda was talking out loud as she led Danielle through the crowd flopped on its bright towels. "Might be a bit cold at first," she said, her hold tightening. "Mind you don't step on that boy's bucket, Danielle." They walked past the striped umbrellas pitched at odd angles in the sand. They smelled the bake of reddening skin. Hilda saw the whole families. The way a man's body slouched against his wife's as he slathered cream on the hump of her freckled shoulder. She guessed Danielle saw it, too, and pulled her daughter a bit more crisply along, the water suddenly looking more attractive than it had.

Then they were there, facing the bright expanse, which somehow grew smaller when the waves lapped at their toes, and she couldn't concentrate on anything but the cool water, the grains of sand, and the tickle of sensation climbing her ankles. Hilda gave Danielle's back a slight prod and said quite gently, "Go on in, Danny. It'll feel lovely." So Danielle had waded in until the water was past her knees. She and her mother watched boys plunging through waves farther out, howling and whipping seal-black hair off their faces when they emerged from a dive. Hilda had stilled herself at the lake's edge, watching Danielle move forward.

Danielle stopped, as if sensing a test, as if she would be asked her alphabet or her colors. But she seemed to realize, too, that it was a darker one than that. "Go on Danny. It won't eat you," Hilda said. Her daughter's face appeared to say, But you're wrong, Mum. It can. There was appetite there. It wasn't quiet. Still, Hilda stood there in her suit, arms on her hips.

"No, Mum," Danielle said. And she sat down. The water came up to her chin and stained her suit a dark green. Then Hilda was there, also sitting down. "Smart girl," she said, and pulled Danielle onto her lap, feeling her daughter's damp warm suit and, inside, that double thump of her heart, wondering what had let her risk her child's safety this way. How could she have? The waves ruffled them. The boys splashed past, rope-armed and fierce-eyed. Their immersion had made them hungry and somehow stronger. Hilda and Danielle pulled up sand from the bottom and let it fall in golden clumps back to the water, where it sifted in a milky pool around their legs. They listened to the croak of gulls, and when they got chilly, they stood and went to warm themselves. By the end of the day, Hilda had walked in with Danielle on her hip to the point where her waist was covered. That was what they both liked best, their arms around each other, the tang of salt the heat produced on their skins, and the steadiness of Hilda's breathing. There they forgot that the families on the beach had something in their wholeness that let them swim with confidence. "It was a good day, wasn't it?" Hilda said on the way back to the car. "Did you have a good day, Danny?" she asked, shaking out the towels and feeling the sand prick her feet.

Danielle didn't answer, absorbed in the way the parking lot's tar had heated into black bubbles. Hilda bundled her daughter into their car and strapped her in with the safety belt. Then she felt it: seeing Danielle with pink cheeks and heavy eyes, smelling the rich grease of beach food and her own sun-warmed skin. A flare of pleasure. Enough, she thought. That's all I'll expect. That's all I'll need. It will have to be enough. It was so dangerous to ask for more.

PART THREE

MAPPING HOME

 Toronto, 1962–73

When Danielle was seven and classmates first
made her pay for not having a father, this is
what her mother said: "Tell them he's away,
then punch their lights out."

"Even girls?" asked Danielle, whose hand quieted, then
tightened around the handle of her mug of cocoa.

"Even girls—just not in the face. They cry too hard if you
hit their faces," Hilda explained as she leafed through
brochures that featured tanned women propping beach balls
on lean hips. "Pastel cube of cement for a hotel and lots of
rum and sunburn. Strange sort of vacation." Hilda lit a cigarette. Since she had sold Armand's antiques shop soon after
he died, she worked now only on ferrying her customers
about the globe. "Can you do it?" she asked, looking glumly
at palms the printer had turned a startling blue-green.

"Punch them?" Danielle asked. "I think so."

"Don't just think it, Dan, do it." She shuffled the brochures into a neat stack. "Where should we send Mrs. Gladstone and her sister, my girl?"

"The same place they went last time, the place with the fans and verandahs and the nice waiters," Danielle said, and wiped off the chocolate mustache with the back of her hand.

The surprise of a thin, blond girl's ridge of milky knuckles in their noses had silenced the jeers. That Danielle could postpone the actual fight until after school and so escape detention was even more admirable. She could have had friends if she dared. But when Danielle read books about knights and castles, what she understood best were moats, portcullises.

The afternoon Danielle first came home breathing hard and diamond-eyed, Hilda said gently, "Had to sock someone today, Dan?" Then she helped Danielle cough out the story to say who it had been—Eddie Fitzpatrick, a real snotbrain—and what she'd done—shin kicks and a hard smack on the lip. "I'm sure his mother loves him, snotbrain or not. Who won, Danny? Was it you?" And when Danielle started to smile instead of hiccup, Hilda said, "Good girl. Remember, no biting. Fair's fair."

Sometimes her mother would offer tips. "Never go further than you have to. You know when they give up." It was true. Jeremy Edwards, rather tall for Grade 2, had looked as if he was dangerous, but the punch to his ear had crumpled him somehow. You had to scan the way their faces folded and their shoulders hunched to know. They were softer than she thought they'd be.

It gave her an odd feeling, this success with her fists. She was fast, she had good timing. She knew when they thought they had her trapped and she waited for their slackness. They never expected that a girl would want to punch so hard. But she did. When she felt her balled hand slam into a jawbone, a small sun of pleasure burned in her chest. Take that, said the cartoon characters, and that. Danielle didn't know what "that" was, but it was something large, to do with Armand dying, Hilda's loneliness, their new flat in Yorkville, which was always too quiet and too neat.

In her mother's white kitchen, she would drink her cocoa and Hilda would cut carrots and ask questions. The vegetables sang as they struck the hot pan. "Did he bleed? Where?" Those afternoons, when the light's color might swoop from padded gray to yellow straw, she and her mother spoke coolly about violence. It was talk that calmed her nerves and made Danielle feel both at home and deeply strange. Around them, the smells of Hilda's good and solid food would rise in a cloud of oil, meat, mild spice. "You look like you've grown three inches," Hilda said, making sure a scratch on Danielle's hand was scrubbed clean. She felt she had, but not only from her successful driving back of the boys. They had left her alone after the first week or two. It was the pelt she developed while ignoring the taunts from the girls that served her better. She pressed that part of her day to a dark pocket in her mind, barely admitting it to herself, much less her mother.

At school, she let herself be absorbed into the dry symmetries of study, its neatly allocated periods and subjects, the cleanness of the boundaries on maps. Its traceable, knowable histories. Its precisions thrilled her. But study did not answer the questions of who her father was—from which her mother, with her martial strategies, had effectively distracted her. It hadn't been Armand, she knew now. He was always Armand, not Papa or Dad, and he had brought to her a bearish love, without the sternness of a father's attention. Nor did she think it was her mother's new business partner, Edward Ellman, a tall stick of a man who wore round glasses. Danielle would stare at Hilda as she cooked those afternoons, the planes of muscle and bone shifting below her sensible dress as she reduced onions and parsnips to a manageable size, and say to herself, If Mum turns on the gas now, I will ask her who he is. If the steam is the exact shape of a mushroom when she lifts the lid from the pan, I will ask her. But the steam would curl into an arched cat or open-jawed fish and the pilot would die instead of light. And even if the coincidence had happened, Danielle was not sure she would have asked.

The answer might have ugly consequences, for all she knew. Life might get swampy where it now had the steady footing of packed snow. She knew she had Hilda. Instead, it seemed wise to watch other people's fathers, to get a sense both of how she was lucky and of how she had missed out. Spring Saturdays, when her mother had to mind the agency, she wandered their neighborhood and stood to the side as men descended into the engines of cars and talked of gaskets and pistons with casual warmth, emerging from these encounters with grease-slicked fingers and shiny faces. They invited their sons in for a look round the black vines of tubing, and the boys looked pleased at what they saw. Later, lounging on the curved bonnets, ringed in tobacco smoke, palming long-neck bottles of beer, they were happy being men. "Hi, girly," they might say in a friendly way if they noticed her, which they usually did not.

She also saw them steering lawnmowers in yards the size of carpets, their socks fringed in damp grass, a staticky radio that broadcast the Blue Jays dangling from the handle. They were less relaxed then, stuck so bluntly between chores and baseball. A woman would call to them sometimes from a window and they would answer in small, angled words. No, yes, soon, later. And they were least at ease on summer evenings, when, spruced up and combed, they gripped their wives by the elbow and walked down the pavement, on the brink of mingling with other clean people. It made their eyes slide off to the side, to see who was looking.

From watching them, Danielle thought a father might be useful for teaching you about mowers and tools, drinking beer and the avoidance of parties. Hilda, though, was on good terms with hammers and pliers, they borrowed Mr. Ellman's car when they needed one, and they didn't have a lawn. Men seemed most content when alone, like the bearded student she'd seen reading poetry in the nearest tea shop or the old fellow on the bicycle, his dog in a basket in the front, wheeling slowly down St. Clair. They also seemed happy in clumps or on teams. Women seemed to cramp them somehow, make their mouths worry. She allowed herself to be convinced that they were not essential.

For years, she and Hilda behaved as if this were so, except for their interactions with Mr. Ellman, who ate occasional meals with them—the food got slightly more complicated when he came, but otherwise life was exactly the same. He'd arrived on the scene when Danielle was eight. "Who is he?" Danielle asked Hilda after he'd taken his first meal with them. Hilda answered "A business associate" so readily that Danielle knew her mother had prepared the response in advance. And he was partly that; he helped arrange charter flights, a chore Hilda hated. A tall man, hair like old thatch, bones sharp as pieces of straw, he was as dry and precise as Armand had been round and easy. He squired Hilda to concerts, and once in a while they all went to the movies, which Danielle disliked because people might think they were a family. But Hilda said she wasn't going to marry him, and Danielle believed her, because she often talked about him in the same tone reserved for difficult clients or taxes. So there he sat on the brink of their lives, a cloudy man, for all his crispness.

Mr. Ellman liked history and would quiz Danielle on the succession of prime ministers. Tricky keeping all those Mackenzies straight, but she'd been memorizing tiny islands and capitals of tropical countries since she was small and could manage the names of a few sour, muttonchopped men. When she thought back on her childhood, that was how she saw it: a bright bowl of light at Hilda's table, her schoolbooks strewn about, talking with her mother about clients, neighbors, weather. The air beyond the bowl could change, grow bright then dark, scud with clouds or grow clear. Sometimes an old memory of Armand and his deep belly edged through. Sometimes a dream that she was lost in Armand's antiques shop arrived, a dream that had her clanking in the dark against cold chandeliers and crystal. Sometimes Mr. Ellman perched there, or a school friend. But the essential was Hilda, that table, the teakettle, that light.

Then, around Grade 8, the atmosphere grew stormy again. Eddies of whispers came to her about Hilda. From girls again, naturally. Clots of them talking about mothers and jobs and arrangements, turning to stare down Danielle as she passed in the hall. A few weeks later Eileen Carstairs broke from the pack and hissed, "Your mother is a whore," in the stairwell. Danielle was so surprised, and it had been so long since she'd needed to fight anyone, she forgot to wait until after school. She grabbed Eileen by the neck and smacked her head on the banister, opening a gash in the pale girl's forehead. That turned out to be a rash action. Detention descended heavily. Hilda had to miss work and come to school to speak with concerned administrators. Miss Engel, her rather loopy homeroom teacher, said, "Danielle, violence is never the answer." Letters of rather stinting apology were written to Eileen and the plump and teary Carstairs parents.

"Animal," Eileen shouted at recess after she returned to school, her lumpy bandage glistening. "Ape!" Fortunately, Eileen was pimply and curried favor with teachers and could not rouse her classmates to join in a general shunning. Danielle had recently acquired a vague shine that seemed to shift the way air smelled around her. Boys held themselves at new angles from her body, as if figuring out the shortest distance between them and her skin. So the relentless inequities of popularity asserted themselves and school became quite normal again.

Hilda pressed to find out exactly why she'd done it. "Bad form going after a pecked chicken, Danny. Eileen Carstairs isn't worth an afternoon of detention, much less six weeks." But Danielle, having learned from Hilda how to erect subtle barriers to questions, only mumbled that she'd been in a bad mood and Eileen was rather a simp, wasn't she. "Don't pick on people half your size, mental or otherwise," Hilda ordered, and Danielle obeyed.

But it ate at her. Hilda as a whore. Danielle knew the meaning, of course, she'd seen them from the bus, on Yonge between Bloor and Queen. They were thin and scrappy, pale, sort of like Eileen Carstairs actually, leaning over to talk to men in cars streaming rooster tails of exhaust. Typically, when she'd asked her mother who those women were, Hilda had glanced out and said openly—it was late and the bus nearly empty—"They're whores. They sell their bodies to men. Hard life, that." The picture did not match Hilda, who did an excellent impersonation of a Canadian housewife. Her hair was neatly bobbed. She wore aprons and clucked in the market at the outrageous price for lamb. Her kitchen shone with the fierce gloss of one appalled at the thought of dust or germs skimming her sink and stove. More significantly, everyone they knew—from neighbors to shopkeepers—treated her like a Canadian housewife, regular as boots.

But Danielle knew better than to invest total faith in Hilda's public persona. Hilda smoked and drank, first off, though not in front of anyone but Danielle and Mr. Ellman. That she worked, hard and unapologetically, also set her apart. Even more, it was how she worked that marked her difference, barking at tour operators, attending conferences, relentlessly professional. She had expertise. Not just opinions about hydrangeas and wool but training. Hilda had a man's rich competence, but how did that make her a whore?

Was it just that she did not seem like other women, so they gave her a name that implied her separateness from regular life? Hilda had a solid weight at her center that Danielle had not experienced in other mothers, who were looser, damper than Hilda. These women were sad, but in a rather fluttery fashion, not like Hilda's sadness, which was the color and temperature of stone. Deeply wedged. Her mother could be friendly, she was certainly attentive. But from Danielle's occasional forays, reconnaissance missions, really, into classmates' homes, she saw that some women offered a lighter, more quilted warmth. They fussed over bruises and scrapes. They spent time plucking dead carnations from centerpieces. They didn't bash pots around when cleaning them, cigarettes anchored in their mouths. They even took their children to skating shows instead of auctions, where seedy men went dark and fixed in the eyes when broken old tables were brought to the block and hands and cards flew up and down in obedience to the auctioneer's staccato code. It was the one activity Hilda engaged in that connected her to Armand, and that alone made Danielle nervous. Apart from a few pieces of furniture and glass, her mother had so resolutely swept the large, affectionate man out of their lives. But what was worse was that sometimes it was Hilda who got that fixed look in the drafty auction hall, who hungered for the carpet or lamp or china plate. Who hunched forward in her seat and let her hands dangle like a man's between her legs. Who cared about nothing but the acquisition. Who forgot she had made Danielle and was responsible for her. There were moments that fall and winter when Danielle tripped on the fact that from time to time she really did not like her mother.

One January dusk that year, an evening so cold it seemed milled from lead, Danielle headed to the agency as usual, a bit taken aback because she was almost looking forward to it. Although her feelings about her mother, her mother's work, and Mr. Ellman were complicated, the window's small gold glow offered easy, acceptable comfort. It was the only shop with a light on in the street; everyone else appeared to have closed early for the night. Danielle counted off the steps from Queen, a habit from deep childhood. One hundred and twenty-one was what it took. Inside, another habit would assert itself, drinking cocoa with her mother from a cup she had chosen. Cracked Meissen or Dresden, something precious and flawed, the few reminders of Armand she had saved. Danielle would wash it and look closely to see how real porcelain aged—in tiny fissures that merely emphasized the perfection of the cup's curves. Danielle loved how the gilt at the lip faded in and out of brightness, like the view of a river from a train.

She was slightly earlier than usual. Miss Engel had dismissed them with fifteen minutes to spare in the last period. Winter clearly flummoxed the young teacher; her hands were chapped, her boots weren't quite sturdy enough. She was from balmy Vancouver, and this was her first Ontario winter. In the middle of the grammar lesson that rounded out the day, she had slammed the textbook shut and announced, "Class, you may leave now." They had sat there, caught in the passive voice, a construction of which they should clearly be wary, rather stunned at this fit of fancy. Miss Engel was giving in to the passive voice. They resented it a little. School had patterns they'd been taught were inflexible, and this departure struck them as unseemly.

But Miss Engel was bizarre. Once, during Canadian literature, she'd said, "Nothing important has ever been written in this country," and made them listen to records that featured high, sad women's voices and delicate guitars. "Is that singer a Canadian, Miss Engel?" Marie Poncelet asked. "No, thank God," said Miss Engel, which quieted them again. She'd grown dreamy, even hummed along, and not noticed that Edward Morrison had taken advantage of her inattention to smash another bruise into spindly Newton Larrabee's upper arm. Sometimes she would talk about bombings in Vietnam in a way that made her face break into a bit of a sweat and then pass around newspaper photographs of petite Asian men and large American tanks, all of them fringed in palm trees. The same sort of palms as in Hilda's brochures, which Danielle found disturbing, as it meant that palm trees could be a setting for war as well as rum and punch. But she did not bring this insight to Miss Engel, who really didn't make a lot of sense sometimes, as was the case today, with this sudden announcement that the school day was over.

So they sat there for a moment, not even shuffling their feet. Danielle became aware of a thread of cold seeping in from under the window's heavy, peeling sash. "Really?" Charlie Green finally asked. "Really," Miss Engel said wearily, holding her forehead in her hands. She sat that way as they shoveled books and pencil cases into satchels and wound scarves around their ears.

Danielle did not tell her mother about Miss Engel's eccentricities, and she suspected that the other students didn't either. They knew a good thing when they saw it. She was kind, forgetful, and passionate on certain strange and forbidden topics such as violence, women, and money. Besides, you could get away with murder in Miss Engel's class. Homework didn't even always have to be done. You could claim bad dreams or fights with siblings as excuses. Amazing. They treated her with the bemused, slightly ironic respect that you would adopt toward some plant at a botanical garden that bloomed only once every fifty years. She had a musky scent the boys said came from not washing between her legs. Still, they protected her even as they dismissed her. She wasn't quite real, but they suspected somehow she had something important to tell them.

Unlike most of the other adults Danielle knew. Walking toward the shop's window, seeing the lettering that announced CAMPBELL TRAVEL, Danielle found herself polishing her dislike for her mother to a dull burnish. Then she saw them. They were inside the shop, talking and seated at the table toward the back. Mr. Ellman was trying to get Hilda to listen. He was straightening his tie, yammering on. But she was adjusting a stocking and clearly uninterested in what he was saying. What stilled Danielle was how Hilda kept plucking at her leg. Sticking her ankle out to see if the seam was straight. Mr. Ellman wasn't even distracted by the expanse of pretty calf, which made Danielle realize he had seen it too often to be mesmerized. Which meant they knew each other's body more frankly than Danielle liked to think. Which meant he had probably touched her there and other places. Hilda unbent herself, satisfied at last. Mr. Ellman kept on yakking, though he did reach over to flip down the collar of Hilda's sober dress.

Danielle was beyond the first stage of very cold. Her toes were acquiring the blocky numbness that meant when they came back to life they would surge and tingle with pain. But she couldn't move. The shock of just how fragmented her mother's life was made her stand there. Hilda spoke about whole chunks of her day with Mr. Ellman which she did not share with her daughter. If that wasn't enough, Danielle had witnessed the confirmation of intimacy, the push and groan between adults for which the boys had words as harsh as tools and which she privately found thrilling. And it clearly explained why her mother was a whore and what the cot out back was for. Mr. Ellman might not be paying, but some compromise had been reached.

Mostly, though, just seeing her mother and Mr. Ellman so careless with each other, completing each other so casually, made Danielle feel hollow. She couldn't bear the thought of their readjusted smiles, the glances traded to see if she knew what they were doing. So she went back down to Queen and spent her allowance on cocoa in a tea shop and did homework on the passive voice, even though Miss Engel hadn't assigned them anything. She found she liked the sensation of sitting alone in the steamy shop, the fat cashier paging through *The Globe and Mail,* sucking on a pencil when she worked the puzzle. A thin, tense salesgirl touched up her lipstick and ordered black coffee. A man with a red scarf and brown mustache who was reading a novel stopped drinking his tea altogether, so taken was he with what he saw in the yellowing book. It made Danielle feel better, seeing these adults manage their own apartness in ways that didn't look completely crazy or suggest defeat in the world. Not like Miss Engel's admission of failure over conservative thirteen-year-olds and winter, the dullness of Canada and poor heating. Danielle felt happy suddenly. She understood the passive voice and how it helped people evade responsibilities. She carried this glow back with her to the shop, where Mr. Ellman and Hilda had neatened their clothes and faces in preparation for her arrival. She was proud of her solo, so it barely hurt they hadn't noticed she was late or that her mother still poured her cocoa even though she said quite clearly, "No thanks, I've already had some."

After dinner, she arranged her books on the table and asked Hilda, who was leafing through the paper to find the auction schedule, "Mum, do you fuck Mr. Ellman?"

She'd never seen her mother go so still before, and in the moments before Hilda spoke, Danielle became aware of the absurdly steady ticking of the clock and the rattle of panes in the wind. Everything acquired a kind of scuffed clarity: the worn linoleum, the chips in the blue paint on the kitchen chairs. The furniture seemed alarmingly to swell, thanks, apparently, to Danielle's choice of phrase. Whore. Fuck. She hadn't quite known how quickly words like that could shift things about. Then she remembered how suddenly she'd turned to violence when Eileen Carstairs provoked her.

Hilda put the paper down and Danielle saw a smile amazingly begin to gather on her mother's mouth. "I suppose you could say I do," she said, "though I'd appreciate nicer language, Danielle."

"He's not my father, is he?" she asked, knowing that he wasn't, but knowing, too, that she wanted now to find out who was.

"God, no," said Hilda. "No, not Edward. No, with Edward, it's it's . . ." and her eyes drifted to the clock, trying, Danielle saw, to be clear. But she couldn't. What went on with Mr. Ellman was something swirling and adult, and Danielle couldn't follow it and Hilda did not try to translate. "No, love, Edward is not the man." Hilda sighed and looked back at her daughter. "I wondered when you'd finally ask," she said. "I've nearly said something so many times, but it was hard to know when you'd be ready." She lit a cigarette, without her usual briskness.

"Now seems fine," said Danielle, wondering if this was true and if she really did want the full story. She'd grown used to not knowing, as it had always been hard to get Hilda to talk about the past, which seemed like something sealed over, tough new tar on broken pavement. Now and then, if her mother had drunk wine, she could be cajoled into relating one or two memories about her brothers or the farm. "Ancient history," she called it. "Old as the Parthenon. No need to dwell on it. Lots of bad weather and people in debt. We had to leave, lovey. It's sad talk," she once said. And Jem and Stuart? Out there on the Coast, city men now, who sent cards at Christmas but otherwise had stationed themselves well beyond their sister's life.

"Am I why Jem and Stuart don't visit?" she asked.

"No, it's not you. It's me, not marrying your father. Stuart's gone Christian. Jem doesn't care, but his wife's a bit fastidious."

"So why didn't—" Danielle started to ask when Hilda said, a bit more loudly than she seemed to intend, "Because I didn't want to."

Danielle sat back. The situation was more complicated than she'd imagined. He had died, she thought late at night when she allowed that corner of her mind to open. Or been sent on some secret work for the Canadian government, a fantasy she developed in some detail, though Miss Engel implied that the Canadian government was too boring for such adventure. He was a doctor for lepers in India. He lived a hermit's life in the Rockies, ate acorns and trout. He had some special aloneness that could not be diluted by the daily demands of food, linens, girls and women. But it was both more intricate and cheaper than she'd pictured. No wonder Hilda had said so little.

Her mother got up and went to the cabinet that held a few pieces of Armand's old glassware. "Have a sherry with me, love." Hilda poured out two large drinks, and they sat there for a moment, watching the brown gold of the liquor in the faceted crystal, a softness within an edgy solid.

She'd been very young, was how Hilda put it. It had been an odd time, her parents just dead, the farm and her family gone, and no prospects. Oddly free. Then she'd met up with a man she'd known from home, the family doctor, a libertine.

"A libertine?" Danielle said.

"A man who likes to please himself first and doesn't care if it hurts others." Hilda sipped more sherry. "You look like him a bit, but more like my dad," Hilda added. "I don't see him in you, Danny. And from the start, he never knew. I wanted you all to myself." She sighed and folded her hands across her stomach, eyeing the sherry as if she wasn't quite sure if she wanted another drink or not.

"What's his name?" Danielle asked, and Hilda told her. He lived in Alberta, had never married, and was still practicing medicine as far as she knew. Then her mother put the bottle away and carefully washed the good glasses. It seemed it was the end of the discussion.

"Was he a good doctor?" Danielle asked, her fingers curled on a cabinet knob. He had been, in his way, Hilda said. A good man for stitches. "Maybe that's why I like science," Danielle said carefully, still feeling the burn of the liquor in her throat.

Hilda laughed, and it was nearly normal. "Maybe so," she said then, listening, "That's a wind tonight." As they'd talked, smooth blankets of snow had gathered on the windowsills. They stared at the low slopes of white that had been cars, and Danielle realized that it did not surprise her how quickly blizzards erased the familiar outlines of streets. She went to sleep trying to imagine her father's face. But whenever she thought she had it fixed in her mind's eye, Hilda's features would spread like a film of water across the picture she'd arranged. There wasn't space left for another parent; her mother held that territory, with the same deep certainty of a lake. Danielle had thought that knowing who her father was would carve new places in her. Maybe even make her feel that something, one thing, was settled. But all it had done was confirm that Hilda was the only one who mattered. She couldn't use fists to fight something so large. She'd need other weapons. Danielle bunched her pillow in her arms and listened to the blizzard coat the night. She knew that she would need to leave Hilda one day. She would have to cross oceans. Fly through storms.

After Danielle found out that Hilda and Mr. Ellman had relations, as prissy girls at school called it, she watched them for signals of intimacy. But they simply weren't there. "Hilda, have you seen the folder on the charter deal to Rome?" Did she know what day the holiday blockout started this December? Crisp, mild questions that did not speak of disordered sheets, opened mouths and legs, violent motions. No heat simmered between them. No smiles. Just a lot of tolerant, collegial activity. It amazed Danielle. It meant that you could slice life like a roast chicken: put a leg on one plate, a wing on another, and pretend, flashing your knife, that they hadn't come from the same bird, that no tendon or muscle had actually held the entire thing, improbable as it was, together. That was when she stopped thinking about the cot behind the screen in the agency and how often they used it. She merely used their strategy, that delicate, deliberate separation of the various elements of experience.

Through high school, it became something of a mission for Danielle to disentangle the pieces of her life from Hilda's, and she found various ways to enact her plans. First, she made ample room for boys, with whom she found herself far more at ease than girls. Boys did not ask long, probing questions about what one's family was like and if she'd ever contemplated suicide. They didn't want to listen to moony folksingers through a haze of pot smoke and probe at blemished skin in front of mirrors. Boys were brutally clear about their intentions. They appreciated silence and Danielle appreciated a certain angularity to their thinking. They went after what they found interesting, without hesitation or apology.

But Hilda proved able to accommodate that particular tactic. Danielle would have to do something grander to get blown beyond her mother's protective circle. When it became clear how Danielle might be spending her time on weekends, Hilda said, "Women in our family might get knocked up by a good storm if we aren't careful," and took Danielle to the gynecologist. After that, Hilda's primary fear was that Danielle would get snagged in romance. "A bill of goods, Dan, marriage and men and babies. A big bill of goods. Take your time."

Danielle told her, "Don't worry, Mum, it's just Bobby Hanlon." Bobby Hanlon was fantastically good-looking and as dumb as a wrench.

"It is true," Hilda said, "that you are too smart to marry Bobby Hanlon. But be careful. You get hit when you least expect it."

It occurred to Danielle to marry Bobby Hanlon just to have an easier time leaving her mother, but Hilda again found a way to push Danielle off without diluting any of her influence. Near the end of Grade 13, Mr. Ellman announced to Hilda that a friend of a friend in Paris needed a junior sales assistant at Druot, the auction house. Danielle could have a job, a maid's room, and a small salary if she wanted after graduation. Hilda, excitement darkening her cheeks, asked, "Your French good enough, Dan?" and Danielle retorted, "Aren't the highest marks in the class enough to prove that?"

"You know what I mean, Danny. Is it good enough for Paris? Oh, it doesn't matter. We'll just get you pretty clothes."

As they packed her trunk that September, Danielle said, "It's your idea, isn't it, Mum?"

Folding socks into balls, Hilda said, "It's a good one, isn't it? Why not travel when you have the chance?" Her voice had false bounce, the same kind it acquired when she was pressing a slightly too expensive package on a client.

Danielle sat down, a lavender sachet of Hilda's in her hand. Danielle imagined opening a scarred bureau in her *chambre de bonne* in Paris and having a great wave of Hilda greet her. She did not know if that would make her ill or sad or both. "Why don't you go places, then?"

Hilda stopped fiddling with the socks. Danielle saw how gray had spidered through her mother's hair. Her fingers were thickening at the joints. Then she grabbed a sweater and tucked back its woolly arms. "All I've done is travel," Hilda said. Later, Danielle would see that Hilda equated travel with survival. That she'd endured some difficult circumstances and wound up with work, a daughter, enough money, a satisfactory life. All that journeys meant to her were adaptations to difficulty. She understood, however, that change of scene could mean something less fraught to other people. She wanted, Danielle later realized, to teach herself to live without me. "If it's nice, I'll come and visit," Hilda said, which they both knew wasn't true.

 PARIS, 1973–75

Danielle had not packed the sachet, but once she was in France she wished she had. She missed her mother, although she acknowledged it had been a good idea to come. Hilda's ideas were maddeningly correct, even though, of course, Danielle's French had not been swift enough. But the men she met at work helped, as did the fact that to eat she had to go to the market and accept or reject the beans and tomatoes the blue-jacketed greengrocers selected for her. That certainly made your French crisp, and it made her think as well of Hilda, whose old habits of thrift surged through her. She was often lonely, but it was a sensation as familiar as the lake's wind and did not surprise her. She appreciated the coded French approach to manners and liked living in a place where if you spoke properly and wore the right clothes, people left you alone. In her long, frequent letters, Danielle addressed her mother as Hilda. Hilda noticed and wrote back that it was funny but she didn't mind.

It was working, this distance from her mother and Canada. Danielle was feeling loose here in this cool, tight place. She made friends with girls at work who taught her how to tie scarves and where to put perfume. French women were tougher than Canadians, as practical as men about love, and she found women for the first time to be good companions. She was told she had "allure," and the managers liked her for that and because she came to work on time and did what she was told. She even liked, though she had dreaded it at first, being near old things for sale. She let their patina of experience draw her, the particularities of their histories, not frightened at last that she would become as blank and distant as her mother at those Canadian auctions. She went to the Louvre on the Sundays when it was free, and through the bulky curves of viewers stationed at the most famous paintings, she started to study the way paint could mirror skin. Then, in

November, she met Osman Harris, a boy who was half Turkish and half English, a boy who had a job working with lovely rugs, and after that, all she wanted was to study him.

"I'm a bastard," she told him soon after they met. They were at a café, a bit nervous because it was near Notre Dame and the prices were sure to include the glimpse of the gargoyles they had from their table. Then, because her admission made her nervous, she took a sip of coffee too abruptly and it went down the wrong tube.

He poured her water from a small pitcher, and once she stopped gasping, he said, "No, you're not, you know. You're actually quite nice." They smiled at each other, then he said gently, "Got a bit of lipstick on your tooth," and that had settled it for her. Even in the thin sun of late fall, his black hair caught at least ten colors that she was able to count.

When it was warmer that spring, he took Danielle to his favorite churches. He had eight months more experience in Paris than she, an advantage of familiarity that allowed him to have favorite cafés, squares, and bakeries. For churches he liked St.-Germain-des-Prés and St.-Etienne-du-Mont near the Panthéon. When they came in from the tourist-choked streets, the sudden cool felt like a mild smack. They would sit in the back pews and watch women in trenchcoats cinched at the waist come in and bend stiffly at Sainte Geneviève's altar. The candles they lit were like long, smooth fingers, the flames like wavering nails. The air smelled of incense and damp. Danielle was amazed to find she liked it. Hilda had been bluntly opposed to the mystical and to trappings of priestly vestments and sober buildings. But Osman seemed at ease.

"My grandfather on my dad's side was a minister, C of E, nothing so showy as this," he said when she asked why. But it was more than just his history, though the idea of his Turkishness so boldly entwined with something so sternly English excited her. Maybe it was why he liked churches—he liked the way they could be caves. He used them, too, as groves in which he whispered stories to her. It was hypnotic. He had so many. Hilda had sat on history as if it were a trunk whose contents might spill chaotically on the ground if the latch was lifted. Osman was generous with certain parts of his past. His mother Lale's life in Istanbul, where she'd had a cousin who memorized Rumi, another who would speak only in Russian. He was less forthcoming about his father, Simon, but he particularly liked talking about Emma, Simon's mother. In the murk of St.-Etienne, he told Danielle about when Emma and her brother had first come back to England from India, where she and her family had lived until she was ten.

She spoke Tamil better than English, Osman said. It was a talisman, the language. But it was dangerous and it was certainly the language that unleashed the worst beating she received as a child. The day they settled in London, their father had forbidden them to speak it; it was warping their accents, he said.

They disobeyed him one evening a week. On their governess's night off, when Emma and her younger brother, Andrew, were left alone, they took advantage of it to talk about India, how awful London was, the cook's nasty trifle. Always in the rapid pulse of Tamil. It was better than a lullaby, Tamil. They'd been so absorbed they didn't hear their parents' return, the footsteps in the passageway. Suddenly their father was just there. The nursery door was open and he swept into the room. "What are you speaking?" he demanded.

The children stayed silent.

"Answer me," he said. Emma remembered the blurred outline of his top hat, beating at his side like a misshapen bat, a big Indian one.

"Indian," Andrew whispered.

Osman said that Emma never knew what seized her then. Perhaps it was the ringing fear in Andrew's voice. Perhaps it was seeing Andrew, normally calm, so undone, that made her speak. Perhaps it was knowing that her father would kill Andrew if he could. The weak son who had pulled them back to England with his frail health—he would wring him to death like a chicken if he could. Emma, too, had despised her brother for not being strong enough to manage India. But when her father was about, her loyalties were purely with her brother. "No, we weren't," she said, sitting up in bed. "It was English."

Their father turned to her. "English, Emma?" he asked, almost politely, but advancing. He came across the nursery and grabbed his daughter. He took her to the window, and she felt the velvet slide like cool fingers across her cheek as he wrenched the curtains wide. Then the creak of tight hinges hung in the air as he shifted Emma in his arms. For a moment, Osman said, she let herself believe that this was all he would do, just open the window and cradle her there, just a slight scare, before he sent her back to bed. But the grip of his arms gave him the leverage he needed to hang her out headfirst into the night. With deliberate patience, he let his daughter's nightgowned body slide through his arms, until he held her by the ankles and the hem of her shift. He was careful not to let her scrape against the sandstone, but he let her sway, chestnut hair waving like a sail over the courtyard. The bones in her feet had crackled. His hands were iron rings, pressing sharply on the narrow bands of tendon. Her cheeks and eyelids felt like packed, separate pillows of blood. Then, just as suddenly as he tilted her down, he pulled her back and deposited her on the floor in a white heap. As the air drained back into her body, her heart squeezed and opened in thick beats, as if it were encountering clumps in her blood. He hadn't meant to hurt her. If he had, he would have. She told Osman he'd been a brutal man. She had seen him with servants and heard their cries and seen their wounds and scars. But that was over now, and he was trying to shake India out of her, as if it were a ball of rice caught in her throat.

"Awful, isn't it?" Osman said when he was done.

"You've made it up," Danielle said. "All those details."

No, he told her, he hadn't. Emma remembered everything. All of it. She would sit with him after tea when Simon, his father, walked around the garden with the dogs and she would feed him these stories. Like sugar cubes dipped in coffee. Even when they were grim, he loved them. He was the only one she told.

"Why did she do it?" Danielle asked. Someone was tuning an organ. Low notes hooted through the church.

"Teaching me, I suppose," he said, "about what to look out for." In himself or in the world, he didn't say. The organist played a dark scale. Danielle didn't press for more.

But the stories and their odd, dim glow pulled her toward

him. He had edges and shadows most Canadians she'd met had scrupulously banished from their characters. And if her countrymen had dark pockets in their pasts, as Hilda did, they were tucked away, sewn shut. Meeting Osman also allowed Danielle to dismiss the notion that what she'd been engaged in with Canadian boys was anything more than advanced groping. What she had with Osman was sex, and she knew it because it made her burn with a white gleam. Partly it was Paris, where everything had a ripeness and a flow alien to the more rigid notions of love in Ontario. But mostly, it was this boy who rolled carpets and came often to Druot to watch the sales. Osman wore a lovely leather jacket and had a way of steering her through a crowd with a fingertip at the small of her back that made her feel as if her spine were carrying a live green line of current.

She began to crave him, and to understand what Hilda had warned her against. The slow tug toward someone you weren't quite sure it was prudent to need. She stumbled onto this grim desire for him through a strange weaving of elements: the quality of light and a certain edgy atmosphere induced from too much sex in too small a room. Late in May, he was trying to convince her to make love one more time. She was sore. She was tired. She liked making him wait and watching how the shadows from the curtain gave his shoulders, shapely with the lifting and unrolling of carpets, long tiger stripes. Earlier, they'd been playing backgammon, and he had begun to pout because she won so steadily. "I've got lucky dice," she said teasingly. "I can hex them." He made her roll out of a glass then and was pleased that the trick seemed to work: he began to win. They had made slow love again and slept for a bit. When they woke and Osman pressed her once more, Danielle said, "I'll give you three chances to roll twelve, and if you do, I'll make love to you."

He liked this. She'd known he would. He'd mentioned bets he'd placed in England, the horses he'd won from. He liked the idea of chance and of trying to beat it. She recognized this survivalist strategy from Hilda—dart into the world, try to grab what you can. You never know when suddenly that won't be possible anymore. He propped himself on his elbow and said, "And if I don't?"

"Then I get first pick on your new shipment." He was starting to find carpets he liked and was bargaining now with his boss, Jean Paul, for the chance to buy his own. For each carpet he bought, he received a discount that he paid for with extra hours. They hadn't talked yet about how they might stay in Paris, and Danielle realized that with this request, this tying of her interests to his, she might be counting on him more than she'd thought.

"Not a fair bargain," he said. "Carpets last longer than Danielles," and his finger coasted along her hip. "Even lovely ones." He did not say which was worth more, and she considered that tactful. It had been a rash request.

"What if I gave you six tries?"

He started to kiss her breast. "No, it's still not fair. If I roll a seven and a twelve in twelve tries, then we make love."

"And then?" she asked, cupping the dice and pushing him gently away.

"And that's all. If I don't, then you get the pick." She knew which one she wanted. A golden Bukhara he'd shown her the day before, beautifully knotted. It was old; he had underestimated its value, she thought, because the abrash was uneven. It had been odd to see how much she had learned from Hilda and those auctions with their smell of coffee and dust that she had used to dread.

He pulled the dice from her hands and shook. First a three. Then a six. He was on his ninth try and no seven or twelve had appeared. A pure mystery of chance. Sevens were of course the easiest to throw. At ten, he rolled a double six.

Danielle waited. The odds were good. On the eleventh, one die tipped to reveal a four and the other stood propped against the water glass. Had it settled to the floor, it would have been a three. They knew that. It hung there, and they saw it teeter but not shift. "I think, my love, that counts," and he began to press himself against her.

"But it's not fair, Osman, it didn't fall. Stop," she said, in the voice that had always worked with guilty Canadian boys. "I don't want to." He was taking advantage. She wanted the Bukhara more than she'd known, a flicker of hunger she recognized from Hilda running through her. That was the real reason she slapped him. She wanted the rug, and he was not playing by the rules. He even had another opportunity to roll, but swept the conditions of the game aside. The feel of her quick and open palm on his golden cheek sparked the memory of the peculiar pleasure of beating up on those boys as a girl, the warm crispness of the sound, the pleasure in seeing the red mark rise on a face. Take that. And that.

What shocked her was that he slapped back, and much harder, as lazily as a big cat swatting a cub. But with claws out.

She saw that it surprised him, the effortless smacking back. She had never been so solidly defeated. The shock stilled her, and he took advantage of her silence to take her fiercely, riding only his own body's sensations. She did not mention the Bukhara. He left afterward, and she lay there, wrapped in the damp sheets, watching the edge of a gull's wing catch the last of the light as it cried and circled outside her window. He had her now. It had just started between them, she realized. It would be much harder than she had imagined.

It was the beginning of the dream time in her life, when she was aware that she was dreaming but unable to stop it. Hilda wrote, sensing it. "Dan, how's work? You never talk about it anymore. Who's this mysterious Osman? Where's he from? Dan, write and tell me how you are." But she couldn't. It was as if a dream were the only way she was going to let herself in to the other side of life, the place she'd imagined when she first realized she would have to leave Hilda. It was as if she'd never learned her mother's rough practicalities. Never lived in a country of frankly bad weather with rules that demanded you follow them to avoid freezing. She grew careless, ate less and badly. She was not advancing at her job. Her French was growing formal and old-fashioned because she spent a great deal of time in cafés reading Balzac and Maupassant. She and Osman took books out of the American and British libraries and read those, too. But what she liked to do best was watch water: in fountains, down gutters, in rainspouts, the river.

One night she dreamed she was climbing into a rowboat. She felt the water rock against the wooden sides, listened to the slap of the waves, the implication of tides and fish she'd never heard of. She, who had never learned to swim, pulled offshore through the glass-green breakers, settled into the motion of rowing out to sea, oarlocks squeaking, hands chafing, shoulders aching with the unfamiliar movement. Even so, it had felt natural, but natural as a dream does, with a pulse from some source of life nearby but unseen, propelling you forward into landscapes you cannot predict, whose customs and contours you do not understand.

By the end of July, Osman was spending a great deal of time on the phone and traveling out to customs at Roissy and was less attentive. His technique for acquiring solitude she later realized was this: one of his friends would be on hand to escort her for an evening or two; he would be away a few days, and then return. One night, sitting in the purple twilight of the place des Vosges with his friend Cédric and drinking a kir, she understood that it would always be like that with him. She would never quite be able to tell where he was. He would come and go, and it would not be because he didn't love her. She swallowed the last of the sweet wine. Pigeons curved plumply in the sky, their watery shadows a pale stain on the square's golden buildings. The glass scraped against the metal top of the café table. "Cédric, he's not with another girl, is he?" There was some urgency to the question. Her period this month was troublingly late.

The young man was so startled, offended even, by this North American bluntness that he lit a cigarette, offered her one, and said, "No, of course not. He's just not here right now. He is very attached to you."

"Of course," she said, and accepted the Gitane, though she didn't often smoke.

"Would you like another kir?" he asked.

"That would be lovely," said Danielle, who later invited him back to her room, because it was preferable to being alone and imagining Osman somewhere, enjoying time without her. Cédric knew why he had been asked, and they did not make love but lay fully clothed next to each other as the summer evening deepened through a spectrum of blues. They smoked, and he spoke of being in love with an older woman who did not love him. "Poor man," said Danielle, stroking his sleek, dark hair. "That's the way things are, aren't they?" he said, and kissed her gently.

He lifted himself slightly to light another cigarette, his face all orange angles in the momentary fire of the lighter, and Danielle wondered how the French could make such a poisonous activity as smoking look so essential. "You look pretty in this light, Danielle," Cédric said, and pressed her kindly back to the pillows. In the morning, he was gone and her throat hurt from the night's rough tobacco. She lay in bed, feeling light and clean and old, watching the sun make the curtains' cheap weave apparent. In three months, she and Osman were married, a four-month baby anchored in her belly. She had no idea if this risk had been one worth taking or not.

"A baby?" he'd said, and immediately touched her breasts. But nothing in their shape had yet changed except that they were growing slightly denser. "A baby?" he'd asked again. He looked exhausted. They were in her small room. It was Sunday morning and they'd just finished Saturday's bread, jam, and coffee. A small wasp hummed about the jam jar's lid. "I'll make more coffee," Danielle said, as if they were going to start a vigil that required the alertness the hot drink brought. She was conscious, as she crossed to the gas ring, of the slight soreness of her nipples as she tipped the old grounds into the trash. He sat naked on her bed, looking out the window. Doors opened and closed as neighbors along the corridor came and went. Church bells clanged. A pigeon flapped past. It was the same kind of silence, silence like a large bowl, that had fallen between her and Hilda when she asked about her father. The kind whose breaking matters. The kind where you become aware that words both are flimsy and mean everything. When the coffee was ready, Danielle dressed, and they sipped it without speaking. "Let's go to the museum," she said, because her head was starting to ring with fear and she needed to say something that sounded vaguely normal.

Osman still said nothing. He put his coffee cup down and said, "Did I tell you how my father used to beat me? The scar you always want to know about? The one on my lip? He gave it to me when I was seven. And the one on my shin? From pushing me into a table when I was eleven." He sat there, still not looking at her. She'd known they were there, those stories. The ones that didn't smell of tropical fruit or feature hookahs and turbans. London stories, grimy and fractured.

She knew, too, what he was saying. That he didn't know what piece of him might hurt her or a baby. That he was safer alone. She remembered how he'd hit her, the ease with which the blow had flowed from him. "I used to beat boys up," Danielle said.

"You did?" he said, and looked at her for the first time. She nodded and came to sit next to him. He smelled of sleep, coffee, his work: sweat and wool. He would always smell like that, she knew.

"They teased me about not having a dad, so my mother told me to hit them. I liked it. That was the odd part. I really enjoyed it. I even missed it when they left me alone."

They sat there for a few more minutes, quietly measuring each other's capacity for danger. The wasp investigated the tan flakes of bread crust, then buzzed its way back out the window. "Anything else?" she asked him. "What else should I know? Do you cheat on me?"

"No," he said, "not that. I'm bad with money. I don't care about it. I can't give you lots of pretty things, and that will make you angry. And I like, I like—" he said, and sat upright, pulling the sheets around his lower body. They fell in folds of white and shadow, and through them she could see the lovely heft of his legs. She did not want to live without those legs. "I like not knowing what's going to happen all the time." He looked at her directly and touched her hair. "That's not good for babies."

She thought about it. Her stomach twisted a bit, with the baby or with this conversation she couldn't tell. "Os," she said, "no one ever knows what's going to happen."

They had gone to the Louvre then and stood for a long time without talking in front of the Ingres in the large red hall. The odalisque's long back, her calm, her pretty headdress, spoke of some essential order, even as she embodied the most sensual, spontaneous elements of life. Studying the figure, Danielle felt she could tolerate being a woman, even with all the complications of fertility. One just had to make space for it. But later, strolling in the Tuileries, she became overwhelmed at the equipment children required. All those prams, small shoes, miniature cycles, and *barbe du papa.*

Danielle said, "Osman, I need to sit down," and he found her a seat on a bench, then went to fetch a cone of chestnuts. When she saw him coming back across the park, tall and straight, so lovely, so unlike the careful Frenchmen fussily reading their papers and tending their pipes, she felt a terrible burst of love, of the kind that's closest to anger, love in spite of itself. When he sat down again, she asked, "Will you marry me, you bastard?" and he had said, "Of course I will, idiot," and then, as he leaned to kiss her, he spilled the nuts from their white sack. They bounced in dark-red jumps across the sandy ground, jets of steam leaking from their plump bodies.

They had gone to the mairie in Osman's arrondissement and been given sheaves of paper to fill out. Completing the forms woke Danielle up abruptly: one couldn't dream and answer a *fonctionnaire*'s questions at the same time. He bought the wine for the party they had in the kitchen at the hostel in the twentieth, where he had a room. It was a day of thick gold light, deep September. She wore a new scarf that friends at Druot had given her. The residents drank the good wine with pleasure, and Danielle let herself be rocked by the sea of languages they spoke, not bothering to see which parts she understood or not. The hum of quiet celebration. Osman came over to her and kissed her lightly, gave her a plate of cheese and bread and pickles. Married, she thought, I've married that man who is standing in this bleak kitchen. The man who is pouring wine for his Senegalese friends and making sure the sad Greek woman has food. Who rolls up and sells carpets for a living. Whose mother is Turkish. Who's never met Hilda or been to Canada. Who's been beaten. Who tells me stories. How strange, she kept thinking. How lovely.

It wasn't until she told Hilda, however, that she began to doubt herself more thoroughly. "I've married the most beautiful man. We're having a baby." The words echoed back at her with perfect clarity, because Hilda was as silent as midnight on the other end of the phone. It was possible then for Danielle to hear the edge of insincerity in her voice, and her fear in the diminished echo. She was wearing her prettiest suit, a moss-green tweed. In a month, that would no longer be possible. The seams would pull against her belly, already swelling to a partial globe. She'd even polished her shoes, as if Hilda could see her. She was wandering home from work on a roundabout route when she saw the empty booth; she'd been promising herself to call all day. Her room had no phone and the line at the PTT was too long at lunch, so she'd broken a hundred-franc note and had a fistful of change ready for the transatlantic call. Her view was of the rue de Buci, whose market pulsed with fussy shoppers. The pyramids of tomatoes looked ripe enough to burst even this late in the season, and still those thin French fingers weren't happy. Rain began to spatter the glass panels. Clouds as round and heavy as black pearls filled half the sky. The other half was flawlessly blue.

"Mum?" Danielle asked. She watched a woman yank along a poodle who wanted to pause and sniff a vegetable stall.

"When's the baby due, Danny?" Hilda finally asked.

"Early March," Danielle said, and for the first time wanted to cry. It did not seem possible that her body had done this to her. It was telling her it was ready, but it hadn't bothered to ask.

"I'll be there. I'll reserve a place in that hotel that serves tea in the morning, not coffee. Helen Marlow told me it wasn't too dreadful."

It made Danielle rather sad how much and how quickly Hilda could still calm her. Wasn't that the point of leaving? Not needing her anymore?

"I'm signing off now, Dan, no point in wasting your sous. What's done is done."

"Thanks, Mum," she said, and stood there even after she'd hung up, watching the rain blur the bright market, caught by some feeling she couldn't quite name, until a man banged angrily at the door of the booth. She walked home in the rain, not minding that her pumps got soaked. I'll never be French, she thought. I don't really respect shoes. She listened again to her mother's voice on the phone. What she'd heard there, she realized, was the flat recognition of defeat. Hilda had lost her bet that Danielle would somehow be different. This was a pattern that had been meant to end. But it hadn't, Danielle thought, as she made her way past bakeries and buildings stiff with wrought iron. The air smelled of smoke and hot bread, rising and expanding. Oh, she thought again, when she grew aware of what to call the feeling that had stilled her: I am both sad and happy, in equal measure, filled with them equally. The Germans probably have a word for it, one of those long nouns that look like a great linked train. But in the languages Danielle knew, happy and sad were bottled separately, not quite mixable. But they are, she thought. I am doing it. And then she was home.

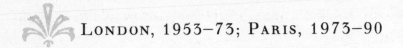

When Osman first saw Danielle, he was struck by the way light carried itself on her body, the way even the stingy French sun seemed to love her skin, perch gently on her shoulders as if it were a feathery cloak of energy. All his life, he'd needed light like that.

His first memory was of lying in his nursery and seeing a flood of sun stain an ivory wall. The light was alive, a pale, wavering bird of it. He lay in his crib and watched it, the high clouds blotting its shape to something else. A camel, a blowing tent, a shirt hung to dry. Then he remembered how his mother's hands pulled the shade down. How she shut it off.

His next memory was of his father, and it was clearer. Simon stood in the hallway in the narrow brick house in Chelsea. The rooms were lean and long, and his father filled the living room with his shouting. In fact, the only wide, generous thing in that house was the sound of his father's anger. "Why did I ever marry you? What did you expect? I'm a bloody antiques dealer, Lale. Just piles of old chairs no one else wants. Old chairs, Lale." Simon had damaged his right hand when he was a boy and he had to cradle it to his body if he didn't want it to drag. His mother sat like a piece of a raven, not big enough for an entire bird, just a wing or a couple of tail feathers, dusty and crumpled. But then his father was the one to tuck him in that night, and what frightened Osman most was that the anger seemed completely banked, his father suddenly as safe and ashy as coals raked over for the night. He had it that well hidden, which meant it could leap out anytime.

Usually, Osman could dodge him. Simon when drunk was like a clumsy bear. He snuffled, his arms flailed, and if he connected with something, it usually hurt him more than what he'd hit. He would smash into the sideboard and howl, clutching himself, eyes screwed tight in pain. He had to clamp his bad hand under the good one, but because its nerves were damaged, it proved the better weapon. Osman knew he had to avoid contact with that right hand. The bruises were always worse. When Simon was bad, Lale and Osman's younger sister, Yasmin, locked themselves in the bedroom. But Osman stayed outside until cold or dark or neighbors looking drove him inside, usually all three. No one offered to help, the idea being, it seemed to Osman, that they were lucky this happened only once a month and not every day. Simon Harris had steady work, didn't he? And he kept his wife and kids in clothes? Partly, too, it was the misfortune he'd brought down on himself by marrying that Turkish girl. Hadn't they been students at university together, very young when they'd gotten hitched? Did he think things could go smoothly after such a rash choice? Couldn't be easy being married to that moody little hen. No wonder he had to drink. So Osman would sneak in, chilled but alert, and draw him. If he could get his father to chase him, yell, and swear that he regretted the day he was conceived, then the chances were good that his father would collapse on the sofa and sleep. But sometimes it took longer. Sometimes it never happened. There were days Simon wouldn't stop until he had the boy in his hold and would alternately cuff his ears and sob. The next morning Osman would wake in the living room, his head ringing, hair still damp from his father's sorrow.

When Simon was quiet or gone, his mother taught him and his sister Turkish in the dark. "Don't tell your father," she told them. "Just for us." He loved the idea of keeping a secret from Simon, of engaging in something furtive and vaguely wrong. Lale breathed the language to him in a soft river, and it rolled into his sleep, entwining with English like a vine. *Güle güle.* Go with laughter. What he said to her as she closed the door. Turkish was a language for confessions and whispers. Nights when his father was at his shop, his mother would stroke his hair and teach him rhymes and tell him stories about Nasreddin Hodja, the man who rode his donkey backward. Nights when Simon raged and drank, she would mutter prayers and say this was not what she was born for. She had been a student, and an Istanbullu. She had wanted to teach; her father, for whom Osman had been named, would have, in his own strange way, been proud to have a daughter as a scholar. Sometimes she told Osman whole stories, not just fragments of her disappointment. One night, when Simon had clipped the boy in the face and made his nose bleed, Lale brought Osman chips of ice wrapped in a tea towel to stanch the flow. Then she leaned into the hill of his knees.

When Lale was ten, she saw Bey Habibi for the first time. He wore the yellow turban of the believer who had made the Haj, but looked about as animate as a fossil pried from a cliff: an ancient shape curled into itself, frozen in a historical era whose true significance remained vague. He came to them, in his rather dirty white robes, through a side entrance of

147

their house in Galata. Not the grand front door. Not the back entrance for servants, but the side entrance, for everyday friends and family, the one that gave onto her mother's sitting room with its divans and rugs. It was slightly more private, and suited Bey Habibi's mission, which, as Lale learned, was to teach her brothers Arabic on the sly.

It struck her as very odd, she told Osman. Her father, an exporter of glass, had delicate sensibilities about the West. He spoke German and English because of his education and his work, but since the first war, he had wanted his family more clearly linked to the Allies. With the help of tutors, he taught his six children—three girls and three boys—both French and English. The first language was spoken at the midday meal, the second at supper. French became melded with the taste of soup and the way light hit silver, the way that roses unfurled in heat. But Lale's dinnertime English rang with the brittle edges of crystal, a state occasion of a language.

Turkish was for early mornings and for bedtime, the cusp tongue. The words of dreams and the barely felt veil of waking in your bed and not knowing what side of sleep you were on. For whispering to sisters in the summer twilight. For hissing curses at brothers allowed to talk with Westerners, who laughed like breaking glass.

And that was not the only luxury the sons were granted. The boys rode, east of the city, on a farm that bred nimble, arch-necked ponies. They came home smelling of damp leather and hay, and Lale would wait in the hall to catch it on them. She was even more jealous of their ability to attend actual school. And now there was the secret Arabic. Below her father's veneration of Mustafa Kemal, she found out that he loved the slips and curls of the old, illegal language. He went so soft and whispery when he greeted Bey Habibi.

Lale had seen her father with the visitor, drinking tea the customary way, sitting on cushions in the study. Bey Habibi looked like something in a Sumerian frieze she'd seen in the museum, and her father looked exceedingly uncomfortable, his knees in his handsome suit at peculiar angles to each other. "Why is that old man here?" she asked her mother, who told her, "To talk with your father, nosy girl," then broke a thread with her teeth, having sewn a tear in a pillowcase. But later Lale slipped away from the women and found out that Bey Habibi was in one of the rooms at the back of the house, speaking a language she guessed was Arabic. After Bey Habibi left, her father would be in a state of nervous contentment. It was clear it pleased him enormously, the knowledge that in his long, cool house that smelled of sea, with its many small rooms and courtyards, Arabic was running through the hands and mouths of his sons. It pleased him the way water trickling in fountains did: a subtle shifting of sound and texture in a familiar landscape. A note of rightness that could undo him, for which he might well pay. Since 1923, it had been illegal to write or speak the language, Lale told her son. The call to prayer even came in Turkish. Persian, too, was shaken from the country, as if it were no more than dust caught in a carpet. This was a time of change; educated Turks were supposed to turn unblinkingly toward Europe. Her father was risking a great deal to satisfy this nostalgia.

The next time the tutor came, she followed him again down the corridors and sat there on the cold tiles, listening. She wanted what they had, those boys. The language sounded hot and vigorous, even passing Bey Habibi's old lips. It was a kind of fuel. It could make you grow tall. It was ancient, and its holiness was meant to temper men, to teach them where they stood in relation to Allah. Speaking it, you learned your place in the universe, your size.

Whenever she could, she sneaked off to follow the teacher through the house and to plant her ear on the splintery panels, listening to the scrape and pull of the language in her brothers' mouths. It bored them, she could tell, to do the recitations, as did Bey Habibi's scholarly fussiness. She knew she could have learned it, she told Osman. The words would have bubbled from her like fresh tea. But then, of course, one day her father caught her. That, too, was part of fate when one was a girl. Not to get away with much and to suffer the wrath of men. She heard him coming, the slap of his leather-soled shoes, the harder bite of his heels. Then his smell of jasmine, with which he dotted his handkerchiefs. She didn't even try to hide. He didn't speak, merely grabbed her by the collar and dragged her back down the hall to his shuttered study.

She submitted to the beating, knowing that to remain limp across the cassock was to lessen the pain of his riding crop on her thighs. He wasn't as brutal as he could have been, but he was attentive. The slaps sounded wet on her skin and she could hear the effort of his breathing. He didn't speak, but she knew both that she wasn't to eavesdrop anymore and that she wasn't to speak of this old language being learned in their modern house. She was not to expose the tricky, contradictory threads that wove her father into who he was. He would not explain himself to her.

Osman lay still, feeling his mother's thin hands on the top of his knees. "At least you are a boy," she said. She took the tea towel from him, which, in the dim light, looked as if it had been used to blot ink. He didn't love her less after this, but he loved her differently, more distantly. It would be dangerous to side with someone on such close terms with home-made cruelty. After this story, Osman began to pretend he was asleep when his door creaked open and a slice of light stole across his blanket. He would sense the weight of her gaze, judging his stillness.

Around this time, they began spending more time with his mother's cousin, Nislahan. She had a flat in a shabby building near Hampstead Heath, but you couldn't smell or hear London anywhere once they started to talk and cook. When Lale's father died, there hadn't been money to send Lale back for the funeral, so they had held a gathering at Nis-lahan's. Simon had stood by a window of the small living room, his flawed hand tucked like a wing against his chest. He refused to sit or drink the bitter coffee while Nislahan's tall sons huddled near the television, swearing in English and Turkish when Manchester United came close to scoring. He stood there as Lale and Nislahan wept and pulled trays of *börek* from the oven, wept and poured raki for the men. The flat smelled of smoke, honey, coffee, and musk, the smell nearly of a church, Osman thought, but darker. The boy felt strangely at home, even listening to Nislahan's husband complain about his work on the railways, the long hours, the ungrateful customers. The boys, too, when they weren't eating or watching the screen, moaned with operatic precision about London, which hated Turks and foreignness, which never let you belong. He understood, as his clothes absorbed their tobacco and his tongue picked out flecks of coffee grounds, that this lack of English kindness meant they were allowed to express their discontent. They wore disadvantage like a scarf. It gave them a decorative, reckless edge.

One of the ways they exercised their anger was to hate Simon. It was an affront, being so English, so easily accepting of royalty and rain. His father ignored them as well, sipping weak tea with his left hand, watching the storm smack glass, and waiting to be restored to his cramped and tidy British life. They teased him for the stiffness of his face, his obsession with the old. At Nislahan's, people were expected to be mobile, funny, possessed of large appetites. History, if you knew anything about the Ottomans and their predecessors, was a trap, and here, perched on Europe's edge, they could occasionally believe they'd escaped the worst of it. But Simon, steeped in antiques, served as an irritating reminder of the pasts they'd put aside. Osman had almost felt sorry for his father stooping there so awkwardly by the window, so clearly not a part of the Turkishness that made his mother, even saddened, for once look plump and whole.

But then Simon had caught Osman laughing at one of his cousin's ruder jokes. He had seen that his son understood the quick spurt of Turkish and called the boy over. "You understand it? Have you studied it?" Osman saw his mother watching, her eyebrows high, coffee cup stalled on its way to her mouth.

"Just from listening," Osman said, looking at Lale. "Just from hearing Mum and Aunt Nislahan. Just a little bit." Neither he nor his mother knew what he would suffer for this disloyalty to England or this tolerance for the foreign.

But it turned out his father wanted to make use of the boy's skill. Osman saw his mother's cup settle back to its saucer. Her face softened. Knowing this language would make Simon's occasional transactions with Turkish carpet dealers that much simpler. So Osman had to pretend twice: first that he had never quite learned the language and then, in front of the dealers, that he did not understand. He was introduced to them those days in the shop off Portobello Road, as he casually cleaned furniture, as Ozzie. Ozzie Harris. If the price they offered was good, he'd raise the feather duster. If the deal seemed to be sliding in a strange direction, he would dust furiously. Simon never bothered to ask what various words meant. Nor did he show as much interest in the foreign rugs as he did in English antiques. The rugs were for points of color in a room. Something on which a desk or table would be placed. Where Turkish things seemed to belong, Osman thought. He felt guilty about colluding with his father against the dealers, who were usually quite poor and wore cheap leather jackets in which they hid lots of pens, calculators, and cigarettes. But he did not like how they smelled or how they spoke so derisively of his father and the other shopkeepers. They used words he didn't know, of course, knots of curses, he suspected, but the general sense was clear. It was easier once the dealers left. Simon would clap Osman on the back and steer him, hand gripping his son's shoulder, toward the pub, where he treated him to a pint. "Your part of the proceeds," he'd say, and order himself another. Osman would look at the blunt English faces, listen to the ruddy cheer of the room, the thwack of darts meeting cork. Those were the times Simon seemed not to mind his hand, even to notice it.

Simon never spoke of the damaged limb. He never mentioned his childhood at all. The only person to tell Osman about his father's side of the family was his grandmother Emma, whom they visited infrequently. Emma and Simon did not quite get on. They were tight and quiet with each other. Teaspoons nicked saucers with edgy frequency. Still, Simon paid her dutiful, seasonal visits, to which Osman secretly looked forward. Emma noticed him; it was a pleasant sensation. He and his father went to Kent one year just before Easter to deliver their annual basket of lilies. After tea, Simon went walking along the edges of the crater. That much Osman knew, that his father had survived a bomb dropped during the Battle of Britain, a bomb that destroyed the wing of the house that had held the library. The crater had softened to a berm fringed in Queen Anne's lace each summer, barely noticeable anymore unless its story helped you see it. Osman stood at the kitchen window watching Simon walk the rim, one of Emma's Jack Russells following. They watched Simon pick his bad hand up as if it were a hammer and stuff it in his jacket.

"Has he ever told you what happened?" Emma asked. Osman shook his head no.

"Do you want to know?"

He wasn't sure. Shouldn't his father have told him? And what sort of compact was he entering with Emma by agreeing to hear her version? In his world, allegiances, open or otherwise, could get him into serious trouble. But he did want to know. The hand was fascinating, even when you got to see it every day. Curled, darkish red, its palm split and stiffened with a ropy scar. "Yes," he said, a craving for story winning out over worries about loyalty.

It was just this time of year, Emma told him, when she had heard a buzz in the sky one morning. It was a plane, and through the old glass of the windows, full of bubbles, swirls, and imperfections, she saw the black, whirring spot growing larger, beginning its assault.

She and her husband, Arthur the clergyman, gathered their two daughters, but no one could find Osman's father. The whirring grew louder. She turned to run through the kitchen and then the dining room, shouting for her son. She didn't see the boy until, stooping to glance in panic, she found him gripping the table leg, his head tucked between his knees. She grabbed her son, who would not release his hold. All her energy focused on prying Simon's hands from the cherry gateleg, but the child had sunk his entire body into the one solid thing around him. The whining was getting louder. She ripped him from the table, which came crashing down around them as they rose. Simon's arms wrapped around her neck as hard as they'd held the wood. Emma found she could barely breathe. Running, she heard the first whistle of a dropping bomb. Just as it hit the rear of the house, she tore through the door, her son a dense weight on her chest, warm and heavy as church silver heated by candles. The earth shook, and in the stench of smoke and the sudden heat of fire, Emma became aware that the plane was buzzing past them, going on, its work mysteriously finished. The girls and Arthur stood in the middle of the garden. Through the haze, she saw that the library was gone. She watched the pages float, books blown to paper birds.

Later, a man from the village came to say that they shouldn't touch anything in the crater, go near it even. You never knew when the last surviving wall might collapse. So Arthur's desk, a huge rolltop affair he'd inherited from his father, stayed on its side where it was, exposed to rain, drawers shot wide. The desk looked like an unmade bed, an unwanted guest. Once, while in the garden, Emma saw a pigeon settle on a blown accordion file and take the grosgrain tie in its beak and pluck, testing the pleated cardboard's suitability for a perch. Weeds grew. Files softened. Brass dulled.

We adjusted to the destroyed house, she told Osman, seemed even to move with confidence around its wound, the way people were said to adapt to the loss of a limb. But Emma knew it was not as simple as that and had new compassion for soldiers coming back from Germany and France, stumps blunted in white gauze. Something integral was gone, and you were never the same.

The girls stayed away from the garden, but Simon kept wanting to explore it, Emma said. One morning in late August, when it was very hot, he approached the lip of the crater, a fistful of dandelions dropping from his hand. It was hot, Osman, I wasn't thinking. And so, she said, she decided to let him look, just once. The wreckage was quite a lot more interesting up close. A great moldiness had gathered around the books, which bloomed with mushrooms. Black mold spidered vellum. Birds had made nests in the walls and frames of paintings hung at strange angles, their gilt catching the light in a cheerful way. Seedlings were sprouting in wet newspapers.

Then Simon fell, Emma said, and a piece of shrapnel spiked the center of his palm. No one at first thought the wound was particularly dangerous. Arthur had been of course furious and she hadn't blamed him. She took Simon to the best doctors. She babied her son, even. But it hadn't healed. Nerves had been sliced. He grew silent and moody. He wanted only to read books and go to museums, she said. He was like that all through school, because the injury made it difficult to play sports. He started mucking about with old tables and chairs people had stowed in attics and sheds. Then he went to university in London, but he spent most of his time looking at furniture. Then he met your mother, and for a time, he was fine. She was so pretty when she was a girl. Had Osman known that? We thought he would get better.

Simon was still poking about the crater. The terrier had caught an exciting scent; its docked tail beat feverishly. Osman looked at his grandmother, at the way the story still sat with her. He felt old. He'd expected to feel something else, learning about his father. More aware or stronger. But instead he just felt tired. Adults and their scars. It weighed so much. Emma turned to the teacups and began to rinse them. He helped her and noticed how careful they both were to blot the fragile china dry, then settle it gently back to its proper spot in the cupboard.

For a time after this, Osman toyed with asking his father more about his childhood. But in an odd way, his father's silence on the subject was something of a relief. Lale had more than enough history to spare. The most personal topics Simon brought up were the stories of the furniture he sold. Safe, dry knowledge that did not make you feel guilty. Simon spoke about his best antiques as if they were dignitaries or diplomats with whom they were privileged to be spending the afternoon. Osman learned which shapes of legs and chair backs went with which names. Even how to make a piece not quite so old look gently venerable with sandpaper, acid, varnish, and paint. "Isn't it cheating?" he asked his father once, and Simon had said, "Not when dealing with the general public," who, according to Simon, seemed destined to be cheated. Who were the general public? People on the Tube? His mates at school? Who fell into that category, and once you were in it, could you ever get out? It had something to do with what his father called being common, that at least was clear. The general public didn't appreciate beautiful tables and sideboards, so studying them became even more important to the boy. He might distinguish himself that way.

When they weren't tending to the furniture, Simon would leaf through great picture books of British estates and show his son the elegant divans and sideboards, the writing desks crafted more from gold, it seemed, than wood. It was the only time he remembered his father being happy. Sitting at his desk that overflowed with invoices, scissors, and swatches of fabric, and beaming at some remarkable example of marquetry that shone from a room inside a gloomy Scottish castle. That was what Simon liked: how such a forbidding building could hold such hot moments of beauty. Osman would sit next to him and listen, scarcely breathing, proud that his father knew so much. Pleased that Simon would use the same words with him as he did with clients and other shopkeepers. The language of the trade, musty with significance. It was the only time when he felt purely English.

He looked too much like his mother to be mistaken for a British child. He was often called a Paki and used the long legs he'd inherited from his father to dart away from fights with boys the color of suet. He used to think that if his mother just lost her accent, his father wouldn't be so angry and he wouldn't have to run so fast. Then he thought that if he and Yasmin and Lale just moved to Istanbul, they would feel more at home. But when he was fifteen, his mother took them there during summer holidays. She had saved house-keeping money and a small legacy from her father. Simon minded his shop and made it clear he would not have wanted to go in any case. That, Osman noticed, didn't bother his mother, who was looking, he suspected, for reasons to stay in Turkey. But the city was hot and crowded, worse than London and with twice the smell. Muezzins howled like cats and woke him before dawn. All he wanted was to climb steep old streets and take ferries back and forth across the Bosphorus. But they were caught in a tight net of family. His grandmother was as bent as a blackened hook. Being held by her was a little like being scratched by a claw. The relatives he met all cried a great deal as well and seized his face between their bony hands. "My son, my son," his grandmother kept saying. They did not pay nearly as much attention to Yasmin. Cousins, aunts, uncles—such a profusion of family, abundant as grapes—kissed him gently and often on both cheeks. They admired his Turkish, which had seemed to freeze. They called him a beautiful boy. They moved from feast to feast, one great bowl of fruit and platter of *meze* to the next. Osman kept watching his mother to see if she looked less dusty or tired than at home, and he could not decide if she was happy or not. He was embarrassed to admit that he was glad to return to England. The first night back, he had kicked a can all around the block just to have a chance to feel his feet scuff the pavement's familiar cracks, to see lights in all the right windows, to smell the boiling cabbage. Horrid, homey London.

Simon, as if to counteract anything that might have tempted his son in Turkey, began insisting that Osman come and watch the shop with him on Saturdays. Lale worried that it would interfere with his studies, but Osman liked it. He earned a bit of cash. He got a chance to read. When his father went off on buying expeditions, he was able to draw a small circle of privacy around himself. A world of his own creation, territories and edges that he constructed. By the time he was seventeen, he spent every afternoon there in its stale gloom, polishing mirrors with faded silver backs, wiping dust from candelabras. His mates groused that he was never free to go and drink or play snooker. But he liked the sense of mastery he was gaining with the objects that his father sold. And besides, if he hadn't been working, he would never have met Gwen.

She was tall and wore drapy, pale clothes and reminded him, not unpleasantly, of a stork. She had long white arms, eyes that seemed partly to slant. She was looking, she said, for a gift. Could he help her find a small chair for a child? They had one that he'd recently touched up. It couldn't have been more than five years old, but it looked, with its craquelure and the rough spots he'd sanded in, at least forty. She looked at it and said, "This is lovely!" He told her, not quite believing he was actually saying this, "You know, it's not genuinely old."

She had said then, "Of course it's not. Doesn't make it less lovely, does it. Perhaps, though, that means you could give me a bit of a bargain on the price." That was when he looked at her more closely.

Gwen liked racing. Horses were so well made, she said, and they liked speed. It wasn't just jockeys pushing them, they liked the motion themselves. She was thirty and unmarried. She taught violin. Sometimes she would play for him after they'd been down to watch the races at Epsom. Short, vigorous fragments of mazurkas and tarantellas. He could tell that she wasn't quite expert, but she enjoyed herself, which he supposed was the most important thing. "You're too young to be sad, Osman. Nothing's happened to you yet," she told him once, and he wanted to say both that she was wrong and that it would, she would see. As if sadness were a sign of maturity. But then she would kiss him slowly and all he could think about was her white skin and the tiny folds gathering inside her elbow and how that flaw, with its hint at the gravity yet to settle fully, was what he liked best about her. After they made love, she fell soundly asleep, breathing quite heavily through her nose, and he would watch her, keeping track of the way the veins flickered in her eyelids. You could tell, she said, when people were dreaming by watching that. Her lids beat all the time, but she said she never remembered what she'd seen while sleeping.

She broke it off that summer. She had a job playing chamber music on the ocean, some string quartet. "All mournful matrons and sniffy old men. Don't want to hear anything but Mozart and Bach. Dull as mouthwash. People bring dogs that start scratching in the middle. No fun for you, Osman." "You're a love," she told him when he dropped her at the station, laden with her blocky instrument case and battered luggage. She could barely reach over the stack of it all to give him a chaste peck on the cheek, as if he were a nephew.

He went to the races after she had gone, watching tails and manes streak past, and then the oddly stationary clouds of dust the animals kicked up in their wake, absorbing, without being quite aware that he was, the names of the horses, the odds the touts posted. So he started to bet, more than Gwen would ever have allowed. He made deals with himself. That if she came back, he wouldn't mind losing five bob on some nag named Shining Tulip. But mostly he did well. Mostly, he started to win. He studied the racing sheets, began to understand why good blood often won out, why antecedents mattered, but never made his bet till he'd actually seen the animals. He needed to watch how they might rile one another, which one looked hungriest. He was quiet as he handed over his money. He made no fuss if he won or if he lost. The old men who hung over the rails began to notice. When they asked him his name, he told them Ozzie. August came and went. Gwen did not come to the shop. He went to her lodgings and found she had moved, her name hastily scratched out and someone else's scrawled on top of it.

The only person he told about the horses and about Gwen was his grandmother. Simon refused to visit her at all now, so Osman went by himself. Once, as they sat in the glow of the late afternoon, watching the sun decorate the mitred edges of the steeple, she asked him, "What's next for you, Osman?" It surprised him. She was usually more interested in the past than in the vague and dangerous future. Besides, he wasn't used to being asked questions like that. Lale was too preoccupied with making sure Simon didn't destroy them with his temper or drinking. They barely even whispered in Turkish anymore. Yasmin had won a scholarship to a girls' boarding school and sounded relieved in her letters to be so far from home. So there was no one with whom to mull over such private thoughts now Gwen was gone. With his friends, he smoked and watched girls pass on the streets, but time with them felt like having sour water creep around his ankles. No one had work. Some of his schoolmates had started dyeing their hair in strange colors. It made them look like slightly malevolent tropical birds. But then you saw their faces and all you saw was London.

"Don't know, Grandma." She looked like an old leaf. Veined and dried to beige, curled into itself. There'd been more there, he knew. She'd had something, some heat or strength. It made him think she might understand about Gwen. "I had a girl, but it didn't work out." It amazed him that he could compress his girlfriend—her tarantellas, her pink gums, her bedsitter that smelled of incense—into such a small sentence.

"It usually doesn't," Emma said, and pulled her sweater tighter. The light was thinning out to blue. The sun glowed like an orange pearl.

"I've been playing the horses at Epsom. I've been winning," he added. "Let's go in, it's getting colder." He gathered the tea things and noticed as he followed her how she had gone round in the back. As if she were hoarding a large question mark on her shoulder.

"Hah," said Emma, holding the door for him. "Good for you. Save the money. Make sure you don't give it to your father.

Travel a bit," she said. "See other places. Take that money and go abroad." She toweled her hands dry and said, "It's a pity not to see things while you can. I was so glad to have seen a bit of the world before coming here." Before, he thought, she married and had children. Before she belonged to anyone. She looked then as if she might lean close to touch him, but he pulled back, not wanting to embarrass either one of them.

When she died the next summer, having tilted over from a heart attack into her roses, Osman had come back from the service dry-eyed and sat in his room to drink the first pint of whiskey he'd ever bought. He drank until he cried, and then he slept. He woke up and looked at himself in the mirror and saw in the heavy light how much Simon occupied his face. Saw where his father lived in his cheekbones, eyebrows. Saw how his mouth looked as if it belonged to Simon and had only been loaned to Osman. He scrubbed himself then, until his skin shone red. Years later, comparing photographs, he realized how much Simon had looked like Emma and how she, too, lived daily on his face.

In March of the next year, twenty, skinny, and in a thin jacket, Osman left for Paris. With his winnings from Epsom, fifty pounds his grandmother had willed him, and a handsome gilt frame he'd bought at an auction himself, he climbed on the train to Dover. His mother was there to say goodbye; his father had drunk himself into a fury. Lale pressed a few more jumpers on him, as if Paris were as cold and distant as the steppes. As if it were bound to be more threatening than London and required the protection of wool. His French was thin, curled into odd sounds by his English accent, which the Turkish in turn had pulled in funny directions. "You can't go to Paris," his father roared. "You barely speak English. Do you think the French know Turkish?" His language skills weren't excellent, he had to admit, speaking at home clearly being dangerous.

Lale had found him later that night and said to him in Turkish that he should leave quickly. His father would forget faster that way. He sat up in bed and saw again how she had shrunk to such a scrap of a raven. He wanted to ask her if she would be all right. He wanted to ask her if she would survive his going. But she threw a block against it. He could tell when Lale wasn't reachable. She pulled her fear into a dark fist that he was not to disturb. She stood there, though, just watching him. Perhaps she was thinking that they were made of something that didn't bluster like the English. Something older and fiercer. Something that a drunk's anger couldn't harm. They were too subtle for such a blunt quality. "Go," she told him again.

So he had. And he had hated Paris at first, hated the way the French were so easily ruffled by bad weather, bad meals. Mincing whingers, he thought at the start. Then the gold and gray of its buildings and sky began to work on him. He sold the frame to a dealer on the rue Vielle-du-Temple and got a fair price. He liked the lively smells and life at the youth hostel where he had a room: all the strange accents and odd spices that scented the large, dimly lit kitchen. Usually, the common language was a broken French, and he would often sit with a beer and a bowl of soup and talk with tired students from Senegal who corrected his grammar with great gentleness. He met women who were less gentle but had other skills. He wrote his mother that all was well; he didn't know how to tell her he was not planning on coming back. Her answers were quick and falsely bright. Things were well with them, too. His father was often away. He wondered what she would have said if she had written him in Turkish, what would have slipped in that her formal English would not admit.

Mostly, however, he was too exhausted to think about his parents. He'd found work, as a helper in a warehouse that shipped and imported carpets, and he spent his days lifting, folding, and stacking rugs into thick piles. The building was down on the quais and during his lunch break he would eat his sandwich and watch barges on the smoky river, repeating words or phrases he'd learned from the Senegalese. France. It seemed more like a condition than a country. Something you never quite got over. The men who ran the place were weary from constant travel, and they looked on their buying trips to China, India, and Iran as long suspensions from decent wine and pretty women. They were anxious not to have to interact overly with foreigners. Jean Paul, the man who hired Osman, had looked at him and said that it was obvious he wasn't French, so what was he? *Anglais*, Osman said. Not completely, the Frenchman said. Turkish, too, Osman admitted, and the man: "Do you speak it?" and that had sealed it. It was the second time being a hybrid had actually helped. He was speaking more Turkish now here in France than he ever had at home. Great bursts and twists of it to the shiny, impatient men who wanted to bribe him to get their rugs sent first and faster. Men whose energy and greed reminded him of his cousins, men whom he both recognized and feared. He would not let them take him out for raki and *meze;* he didn't know what else they might want of him. The point of being here at all was to find out what he wanted for himself. Instead, he would spend nights hunched over supper and let Victor the Senegalese patiently untwist his awkward French. At one point, he realized that he could speak no language with complete authority. That if he opened his mouth, anything in one of three tongues might spill out. That was when he started to look harder at the rugs he was helping to fold and ship. That was when he grew much quieter and language stopped mattering much at all. But then he met Danielle.

She glowed, and in Paris that was a feat. In a city of gray buildings, water, and humors, she was a tall moving skein of life. He'd seen her coming and going from the auction house, giving the sash of her mac a quick tug at her waist and cheerfully stepping into the mist. He followed her. Later, it was little wonder to him that his children turned into voyeurs of a sort. It was in his blood, this lurking at the edges, collecting information, assembling it until one was sure of one's position.

But she surprised him. The third day of sitting at the back of the tea salon where she went to read the paper before going home, she waved at him. "I nearly called the police," she said, "but then a friend of mine said, 'Oh no, that's only Osman Harris, the rug man from Jean Paul's. He knows a lot about carpets. Looks like he's got a bit of a thing for you. He's quite harmless, just follows girls about, trying to find out where they're from.'"

She'd sat there in the crowded shop, chairs scraping

linoleum, a vague smell of stale pastry coming from the front, and he thought his heart would shatter she looked so beautiful in her raincoat and her tousled hair holding even in the dull shop a tawny light. He had to be careful with what he said. It would carve the shape of things to come. "I come from a long line of spies," he said. "It's genetic." Here he became unexpectedly tongue-tied. Why had he said that? He came from a line of fearful people, who watched to keep from getting smashed for the wrong sort of skin, accent, tone of voice.

"Spies?" she said. "Double agents? Dark cloaks and code names?" She laughed, a sound like a well-oiled door swinging wide, quiet but inviting. "Oh, come have tea," she said. So he had and they had sat in that salon, whose name he could no longer remember, though he could find it if he wanted to. Of course he could.

He felt as if he were inhabiting himself just below the skin but that the rest of his body had been hollowed out, scooped away, leaving only his heart quivering in the empty barrel of his body. He felt she must see it, clanging there like a drum. But her eyes weren't fixed on his chest in wonderment. Rather, she seemed, after her initial bout of bravado, to be wondering what she ought to do. She twisted her napkin into a long, curled shell and said abruptly, "My name's Danielle Campbell."

He had said "How do you do?" and they had sat there, silence growing bumpier and bumpier between them until for no reason she started to laugh. Later she told him she knew from that first moment when he'd spoken of spies in his beautiful voice that they were going to be lovers. But how were they supposed to manage the first awful minutes together? There was so much tedious information to wade through, the favorite colors, the vegetables most hated.

So she had laughed and so had he, and then, within the next two minutes, he had grasped her hand and they had grown silent, finished their tea with their free hands, and gone back to her room, hands still clasped in the garlicky crush of the street.

He wanted her, there was no question. But something else tugged at him as well. The quiet of churches. Walks through towns on the edge of Paris, down streets, past houses and people he didn't know and into local churches. Thinking about what was next and what he might want. The steady cultivation of a place for himself away from his parents. Away from London. From his mother's angry relatives. From all that damaged history. Cobbled streets soothed him. The pungency of incense did, too. A calm inside of which he could calculate risk. But then Danielle was pregnant and he stopped wondering what he might become. There it was; his future found him. It was oddly comforting, this sudden sense he had of lacking choice. A sense that fate had tracked him in the form of this tall, pretty Canadian. When Danielle told him, he had thought of his mother and Nislahan, of their long, braided conversations, the screen of cigarette smoke that surrounded them, as they polished family misfortune to a seamless finish. The way things were. The way they had always been. How foolish he had been to think he would be able to shed a whole half of his past, a world that hedged everything with Maasallah. Wonder of God. He did not

169

know whether he believed in God, but he felt that some large wall had suddenly dropped in front of him, blocking forward motion. His life had arrived. He would have to accept that.

He did not tell his parents right away, partly because his mother was the source of news and change right now. He and Danielle had been married two months and were living in her tiny room when he received the letter from Istanbul. He did not open it for several days. Its slim whiteness with a square stain of bright stamps sat on his bedside table. Danielle saw it but did not ask whom it came from. When it had been there a week, she said one evening while they were out shopping, "Do you have news from your mother?" He liked that she could talk like this, so indirectly. She gave him room. He opened it the next morning after she had gone to Druot. His mother was in Istanbul, living with cousins. She was working, for the first time in many years, and as a tour guide. She enjoyed getting a chance to lecture the English for once, and be paid for it. It was peaceful to be home at last, to care for her mother, to see her aunts and uncles. A necklace of relatives, she wrote. About Simon she said only that it was when he stopped drinking, after Osman left, that she realized she needed to return to Turkey. And not even because he had made her so unhappy. She had two beautiful children, after all. But she woke one day and knew she should never have left her real home, Istanbul. Yasmin was coming soon to visit. He was welcome, too. She would always love to see him.

Osman told her briefly he was married and expecting a baby. His wife was Canadian. He paused when it came to describing Danielle. "She is beautiful," he wrote, "tall and strong." It was all he was able to say. He wrote as well to Simon, saying much the same thing. There was room at the bottom of the page to invite him to Paris or to say that he and Danielle would come to see him once the baby was old enough to travel. It was quite a large space, two inches of pale paper. He did not fill it.

At Christmas, he sent another card to his father, who was now alone. Yasmin had decided to stay with her mother in Istanbul. Lale's letters were more and more cheerful. Her English was gradually growing odder, its punctuation less careful. It made Osman try to imagine his father in the tall, dark Chelsea flat. "Ask your father to come," Danielle said. She liked the Parisian delicacy toward women in her condition, and it made her generous. But his father had answered stiffly and rather belatedly that he was too preoccupied with business to manage a trip. So he and Danielle had Christmas alone, attending services at the American Cathedral, singing carols. The day itself was as bright and sharp as holly. They made love, and after, Danielle fell deeply asleep. Osman pulled the sheet down and looked at her swollen breasts, which she'd taken to calling the shelf, and watched the blue veins lacing the fine-grained skin.

He also began to sleep a great deal, a sympathetic response to the dreaminess of late and heavy pregnancy. He was almost glad that Hilda couldn't come until May, thanks to a murmur in her heart that the doctors were trying to manage. He'd spoken with her several times on the phone they finally had installed, and she made him feel uncomfortably awake and aware of reality's sharper edges. Without her, he and

Danielle were able to ease into the baby's first, murky weeks when sleep and waking blended into each other inside a fog of milk, tears, sheets, and baths.

He was unbelievably tender with the baby, a boy they named Sasha. It had been Osman's idea. "Not like anything on either side," he said. "Sort of dashing and Russian. He can run from wolves with a name like that." Danielle had smiled and said, "Something new, you mean, a little fierce," and agreed that it fit the tiny child, who looked like neither of them, with his dark-red hair and slanted blue-gray eyes, and who howled operatically for the first months of his life. When Danielle was ready to cry in frustration, to swear at her husband and the men responsible for these creatures, he would take the infant and sing Turkish lullabies that returned to him from childhood. Where Sasha had been rigid with frustration in his mother's arms, a hard sausage of a baby, once his father held him he slackened into peace.

"You would have been the better mother, Osman," Danielle said sometimes, not bitterly. She was dying to go back to work at Druot. She missed the easy camaraderie, the thrill of the sales. They needed the money. Business had slowed at Jean Paul's. "Go back," he said. "I will stay with the baby." Each morning, she pumped milk and they laughed at the absurd machine even as she cried, "Ow, ow, ow, my God, this is painful."

Then she'd dress in clothes she was carefully preserving from milk and rents and lint and go happily off to work. She was better at that part of life. She found ways to make the concierge take packages that he would never have thought of. She paid the bills and did the wash. He loved watching her hang laundry, clothespins spiking from her lovely mouth. That spring, he allowed himself to become dreamy again, to walk slowly through the city with the baby, whom he fed and coddled as he sat reading in one park or another. But he had to be careful when he told her how he'd spent his day. She could grow cranky and pinched if he wanted to talk about a new book he'd discovered or even if he'd spent money on roses. He would kiss her, biting her lips, showing how gorgeous the flowers were in the crystal vase he had bought her as a wedding gift, and she would cry a bit. He would speak to her in Turkish then, which she found oddly soothing, though sometimes he would add in English, "You're going to make the baby sad before it has to be, Danielle."

That time in his life broke when Hilda arrived, grim-lipped, in late May. She brought with her a spell of dark, hard rain that seemed to hit her mac and steam, she was so full of heat and anger. The flat was too small. Danielle should not be working. The baby was spindly. Hilda frightened Osman into getting a second job at another shipper's warehouse. Despite her nonexistent French, she went out and bought a larger crib. Then, one Saturday morning while she and Osman went to fetch fresh bread, she said to him, "If you don't shape up, Osman Harris, and give my daughter a decent life, I will have your skin and take away my daughter and your baby." She lit a cigarette that she was not supposed to have and offered him one, too.

He accepted, though he didn't often smoke, too rattled to refuse. Hilda was something he'd never seen in a parent before. All he'd known through Lale and Simon was rage, sorrow, and dampened quiet. Their new incarnations, his father

173

as teetotaler, his mother as tour guide, were unknown and unfathomable to him. But Hilda's competence and credible threats were not qualities he'd expected to encounter. "Danny says you're good with rugs. There's money there if you're careful. I will loan you enough for the first year. Before I leave, you are going to rent a new flat and an empty space for a shop, and you and I are going to start stocking it." And so they did. They found a one-bedroom on the rue Amelot and a tiny shopfront on a street off the rue des Francs-Bourgeois. Hilda waved her wads of money about, and the landlords and real-estate people scrambled to help, despite her complete lack of style and her imperviousness to the French language. After they'd signed the lease, all she'd said was "That's something at least, not having to spend all that money on the métro." Hilda found it dirty, after Toronto's. Bums in tunnels did not impress her. She actually appeared to enjoy France, if only because it gave her a chance to exercise an energetic critique upon its obsessions with clothing, cheese, and scent. The money these women spend on an avocado! she'd cry. Outrageous. But he brought her handsome *gâteaux* from good patisseries and he saw how much she liked them, savoring their delicate crusts. Even more, he saw how thick the tie was between mother and daughter, the coded way they spoke, the sudden resurgence of Canadian vowels in his wife's mouth. They looked complete next to one another, Hilda and Danielle. They touched each other so easily.

Osman promised Hilda he would not let her or Danielle or the baby down. He promised he would do what it took to keep them well. Hilda looked at him and said, "I at least believe that you believe that." He had to laugh. He liked her even though she scared him. She said, "Go and buy your wife a pretty something. Every mother needs to know she's still a lady."

He missed her when she left in July. So did Danielle and Sasha, who seemed to cry uninterruptedly for three days. "Do you want to go back?" he asked Danielle, and he was terrified because she did not answer right away. Later that week, she woke him in the middle of the night. "No," she said, pressing her milkiness close to him. "I want to be here. Otherwise, she owns me." He kissed her and soothed her to sleep, rubbing the small of her back where pain gathered. Slowly, they began to feel they would manage. I will make you happy, he told her, letting her hair drift through his fingers. I will make you proud. He wondered then about Simon, if he had said the same to Lale. He wondered if his parents had had the same fine intentions. He lay there, unable to sleep, holding old memories of his mother's face pale with fright, his father's clotted with anger.

They were helpful, those faces. They kept him working. They kept him from buying carpets he could not sell. Roses they did not need. Too many toys for the baby. It was a cramped life. They saw few friends. They did not play backgammon or visit churches. "We're grown-ups," Danielle said, patting the baby on his narrow back, when her husband mentioned they had not had a party in ages. "We don't have time."

That September, three days after Danielle discovered she was pregnant again, Druot fired half its staff. There'd be unemployment. They could stretch it out. But Osman was going to have to sell carpets at a brisker pace. The problem was that he grew more and more attached to the rugs he bought and sold. That was not how it was supposed to be. You were supposed to assess, to be dispassionate. Danielle was better at it than he. She could take in at a glance what the market would bear and knew just when to mark up or down. What was more, she loved the fight. But she was sick with this new baby. She felt as weak and unhappy as she had felt alive with Sasha. Nothing was wrong with the child, they were told. It was just the way some babies took hold. She was instructed to rest and needed no encouragement. By January, the city was dark and shining. Though it snowed and froze quite often, women refused to give up their heels. Small dogs went skittering down the steeper streets. Fog with an industrial tang to it settled over the Seine. Osman slid back and forth to warehouses, buying rugs he thought were ugly, the ones in popular, chemical colors. But no one wanted them and he had to auction them for half what he'd paid. Danielle grew puffier, more frightened. "It will be all right," he told her as he held Sasha, crying from a spill on the sidewalk. "It will be all right."

"That's not true, Osman," she said. "I wish it were, but it's not."

They would not ask for help, though they thought about going to Toronto to run Hilda's business. She was planning to retire and move to Florida, weary as she was of Canadian winters. Somewhere there was heat, light, and everything moved at a pace built for the tired. She could send them money, Osman said, but Danielle refused to ask. Nor would she think of turning to Simon, who had sold his shop and lived off a tiny pension in a Council flat. Lale and Yasmin

176

had nothing to spare. "We just have to tighten our belts," she said, and began counting out bills to pay the rent.

One evening in early June, he came back from work and Danielle said, "Os, I'm feeling a bit off. I'd like it if you could take me to the clinic."

She had toxemia. She nearly died, along with the baby, a tiny girl they named Sophie. A week later, when she was finally home, safe but tired, he called a man he'd met once while working for Jean Paul. He would not handle anything himself, he explained. He would not be near any of it. It would be too dangerous for his family. But there would be space available for shipping in his next load of carpets from Turkey. He would arrange it with the men there. They could unload what they needed in Paris, in the slip of the warehouse where he received his merchandise. He would prefer not to know more. He would like to assume that it was nothing that would harm people. Perhaps just more rugs than they said. Leather goods or electronics someone had forgotten to put on the bill of lading. The man on the end paused and said, "Of course." They arranged a price, Osman for once bargaining as hard as he could, refusing to yield. They would do this only sporadically. Osman would not be told in advance, but it was perhaps from now on safer not to sign for anything. To let the clerk be responsible and then leave the shipment alone for a day or two. An account would be set up.

He called Danielle to tell her he would be late that night. There was a business meeting he needed to attend. She did not believe him, he could tell. But all she said was "See you later. Bring back some milk. We're low."

He did not want to let her go on the phone. "Where are

you sitting?" he asked, though he already knew. There was only one phone and the extension was short.

"In the red chair," she said. "With Sasha on my lap."

"What are you wearing?" he asked.

"My bathrobe and slippers, and Sasha has on his blue pants and the yellow sweater Hilda made him," she answered slowly. "Are you all right?"

"Kiss Sasha and the baby for me." He then went out and got very drunk for the first time since his grandmother's death. He went to sleep in a hotel near the Gare de l'Est because he did not want Danielle to think he'd turned into his father. At dawn, he woke and walked back home, smelling bread he would not let himself buy. Men like him didn't deserve its hot, simple goodness.

Sophie was a perfect baby. She gave no sign of having caused much less been troubled by her mother's difficult pregnancy. And it seemed that with her birth the skies cleared: the summer was scoured free of rain and chill. Sasha was upset at his sister's eruption into his life, but Danielle was healthy. Rugs started selling again. The money from the other arrangement arrived on time and Osman wondered if he should make another phone call to stop it altogether. When Sophie was four months old and their debts had been paid, he called the man again. But it proved not to be possible. Osman's place was quiet. It was easy to get in and out. They would double what he was receiving. But he didn't want to do it anymore. The man had said, "It might be complicated for you, I think, if the police were to show up at the flat." And so it went on. The irony was that the longer the situation continued, the more successful he became through his own business. Commerce surged, even though he still was not good with money and let Danielle handle the books. He grew wildly lucky with the rugs he was able to buy, the clients he attracted. His shop became known for his taste, his discernment. His photo appeared in magazines. But the man would not let him stop, and he could not insist. They would speak of his pretty wife, his boy and girl. He would hang up each time, ashamed and frightened.

So began the part of his life when he did feel himself to be a spy. To notice who came into his shop and when. To assess to what extent a stranger could be trusted or not. To investigate who might threaten all that he had carefully built and tended. "You're turning into a lizard," Danielle said. "Getting inscrutable." But she did not pry, glad in a private way she could visit her mother, whose heart was slowly clamping down in the thick heat of the Florida coast. Glad not to have to eat flageolets and drink thin wine the way they had when Sophie was small. Glad they were able to buy a new flat a few blocks away and, a year later, the shop where Osman sold the rugs. Even gladder, though she never said so, that he had proved himself a man who appeared able to resist his temptations. "You don't get dreamy anymore, Os," she told him once when they were walking with the children in the Tuileries, and he was startled. Hadn't she and Hilda wanted that to happen? It struck him as well that he had quite forgotten how to be aimless. There were prams and schools to think of, clients to contact. Danielle's illness and the beauty of his children had raised in him a terrific fear. If he were less than vigilant, he might lose them.

He used the shameful money only for them and his mother. He bought the children handsome bicycles and taught them how to clean and oil the well-made machines. They took modest vacations in Saint-Jean-de-Luz. Quiet luxuries, ones that wouldn't attract suspicion or envy. They'd been in France long enough to mind being showy. The gifts he provided would tell Danielle and the children that he loved them, tended to them, anticipated their worries. A sturdy house of attention.

They believed in it. They all believed in it. Even when Hilda died in her sleep in 1984 and they'd both been numb with sadness for a year. Even when the children got sick or taxes were raised. When Paris felt cramped and cranky. When disputes arose with suppliers or clients. He did not waver. Women tried to tempt him and he was tempted, but did not act on it, not knowing who was trying to expose him. Money quietly filled his account. The slight ripples of extra activity at his warehouse went unnoticed.

As time passed, and Danielle remained happy and the children grew straight and lovely, Osman allowed himself only two indulgences: books and beautiful carpets too large to sell. Books in French and English, books on furniture, history, religion, and cities. Great worlds he'd like to travel, because he did not dare leave France, leave his family unattended. The carpets he let himself buy were great stories in their own right as well: where they came from, where their designs had first been born, who might have woven and then owned them. When the children would come after school to visit the shop, he would watch them hop from one medallion of color to the other, weaving private games of luck and disaster as they danced from one patch of color to the next. Sophie took the red sections, Sasha the blue. Those afternoons, dust rising in fine plumes from under their feet, their high voices calling in a bumpy mixture of English and French, the stacks of carpets muffling the horns and taxis on the busy street, he would feel, for a fraction of a moment, safe.

He thought he'd anticipated all possible danger. He assumed it would arrive from outside in some dark and pointed form. A policeman, a gun. An oily lawyer, even a rogue car, a hungry thief. Against those, he had locks, attention, probity. He sharpened his mind to danger, a habit he remembered from being Simon's child. He did not expect it to arrive in the form that it did: a bruise on Danielle's thigh that would not heal. And another that appeared without bidding on her arm, a blemish the shape and color of a bundle of dark grapes. Then came a cough, and a consultation.

The doctor was a young, still Frenchman who blushed when he delivered the news at the start of September 1990. The first thing Osman said was "It's a mistake. You've mixed up the results." But it was Danielle who said, "No, I'm quite sure Dr. LeBlanc is correct," in English, holding her husband's arm with gentle pressure. "I feel it, dear," she said, looking at him. "I knew something was wrong." It would be best to check it now, the doctor said, to do more tests. To see how far the illness had progressed.

She sent him away right there. "I don't want you to see me all poked with needles," she said. "Go talk to the children." He couldn't leave her. He didn't think he would continue to stand if he walked away from her. She was wearing her dark gray suit that swam so beautifully over her body. Where had the slight fold of skin around her eyes come from? He swore he had never seen it before. "Go," she told him, and he finally had.

He began the long walk back across the river, watching and hating every person who strolled past clasping a long wand of bread, tucking a blanket around a child. Anyone who looked carelessly alive. It so exhausted him, the precision and size of this hatred, he had to stop for a coffee. He was going to have to tell the children something. They would be home from school soon. What language would he use? They flitted back and forth between languages, depending on situation and need. English for tears and supplications, raging fights with one another. French for school, parties, Sundays, frigid politeness, and a desire not to be asked what they were thinking about. Having two languages made them believe there was a word for everything. He bought a pack of cigarettes, lit one, but could not move, remembering for the first time in years the moments when women had left him. He remembered Gwen, his first girl, pecking him on the cheek at the train station. He remembered getting drunk when Emma died. He remembered the first letter his mother had written from Istanbul. He remembered when Danielle was ill with Sophie. He remembered the shock of Hilda's quiet death. But those times had not prepared him for the extent of this grief. Those sadnesses hadn't carved a home for themselves in his stomach and spread in star-shaped tentacles through his mind and body. He could not believe that people had felt this way and the world had lasted. He sat there in the growing dark, resisting the picture of Danielle's body on fire with dark cells. He sat there trying not to see how those bruises stained her arms and legs, whose curves and lengths were as essential to him as bread or air. He did not understand how it was he was still breathing.

PART FOUR

LIGHT TRAVELS

PARIS, 1975—90

In the Paris apartment, the ceiling sloped and the bedroom window held a cramped view of slate roof, antennas like crow's legs, a smudge in the background that meant the river. When it rained in Paris, the streets got sleek as fish, gleaming like trout and bass that lay shingled on beds of ice on market days, as abruptly dead as the rabbits hanging by tawny ankles. Sophie hated when the wind made them swing. In Paris, women had thin calves sheathed in glossy stockings and wore glasses as if they were jewelry. Bodies in winter smelled as ripe as pelts. It was home.

Paris was a city that looked best in blue, Danielle had told Sasha when he was about five, twilights, winter dawns, long weeks in the fall. This made his mother happy, because it was her favorite color. Any kind. Those were words Sasha knew from the earliest times. Cobalt. Navy. *Bleu marine. Bleu foncé.*

Bleu clair. Danielle would give them to him, like beads or berries, and wait as he searched them out in carpets and in picture books. Those early words and colors came in both French and English and they melted together in Sasha's mind. It wasn't until he first went to school that he was absolutely sure they were separate languages; they'd swum together so easily until then. The strict protocol of the French playground and classroom taught him not just that the languages were different, but that they codified separate reactions to everything from weather and meat to dogs and soap. Each one had its borders, places the other couldn't penetrate. He realized one afternoon when his mother came to pick him up from the *école primaire* that no one would ever mistake Danielle for a Frenchwoman. Her hips were too loose when she walked and her arms swung. Wind disturbed her hair and she did not mind. Sasha loved that, how the light caught his mother's hair from behind and made it glow in a spiky golden shadow.

One of the first facts he knew about her was that she loved maps. If she was careless of her appearance, she was focused and steady when it came to scale and latitudes. She would spread out the huge Plan de Paris sometimes and show them where they lived, where the school was, the fastest way to walk to the Buttes-Chaumont. They used the kitchen table for the task, tracing the streets that ran through the city like little blue canals, the paper crackling when they leaned on it with elbows. Sometimes she would bring out the Canadian map and show them Ontario and Saskatchewan. She would talk about the lakes she and Hilda had visited. The bear she had seen. Fat and clumsy, snuffling in a blackberry bush. She had no photographs of herself as a child, and she took pictures of Sasha and Sophie with irritating frequency. Artifacts, she said seriously, so you'll remember. The maps made her thoughtful and still. They could sit there for hours. Canada, flattened, lay there like a great trapezoid, whereas Paris unfolded like a web. When she talked about Canada, the stories came out straighter, full of Hilda being sensible and Toronto's straight streets, though there were gaps. She never mentioned a father. She didn't talk of grandparents. But when she talked about Paris, about meeting their father, the stories started to twine together, each one overlapping into another, turning knotty.

Dinners often went like this. "Osman, please pass the—" Danielle would say, pointing, and Osman would hand her the bread and say, "Too much and you'll get—" and she would say, "I don't want to hear it. It's not as if you're—"

"Oh, don't even start with that," he'd counter, not peeved, "when I'm out earning pennies to keep body and—" and Sasha would say, "When was the last time anyone—"

"Finished a sentence in this family?" asked Danielle, munching the heel, which they always saved for her. "New baker at Clouet's, I think. Baguette tastes like sponge." Sasha felt safe then. Maps, bread, the fragments of talk. Safe.

If Danielle managed the day's practicalities, Osman presided over darker necessities, like real stories. Every night until Sasha was ten and Sophie was eight, he would come to their room and reveal to them threads of where they came from. If Danielle's family seemed vaguely defined, Osman had more than enough relatives to spare. They would select a cousin, an aunt, a grandmother, and he would unfurl a story. About London and the way it smelled in winter. His grandparents and their dogs and roses. What his school was like. What his mother cooked. Some of the tales he knew himself, some were inherited. One of their favorites was about their great-grandmother Emma in India. Danielle had showed them in the atlas what the country looked like, a green triangle with a curved and buckled edge to represent the Himalayas. But they couldn't see it until Osman told them the story of Emma's haircut, and then there it was, a whole country, floating in their minds. That was what Osman did: give the invisible shapes, smells, textures.

Emma and her brother, Andrew, had an ayah whom they both loved very much. An ayah, Osman explained, was a nurse. They saw her more than they did their mother and she had full responsibility for their care. She liked to take them to an Indian barber on the sly. "His shop," Osman told the children, "was an apron of dust below the third largest banyan on the main road to Manipuram." No sign announced it, no wall defined it, but that space belonged to Ravi and his long steel scissors, his glittery talcum powder, and the parrot that refused to speak in anything but Telugu.

"What's that?" Sophie asked.

"A language, ass," said Sasha.

"Enough," said Osman. Ravi had inherited the large, angry bird from a customer as payment, and barber and bird hated each other with great dedication. Ravi did everything with elaborate care. He was always trying to persuade clients to try a new lotion, and often rearranged his bottles and scissors to create a more alluring display, getting angry with customers when they didn't praise his efforts. It did not matter that most of Ravi's clients had been coming to him for many years. Often the dust from the road was so thick it was easy to miss the flash of scissors and the sullen green flare of the parrot shifting on its perch. Yet Ravi nursed a fear that potential customers strolled toward Manipuram in search of a barber, unaware that under the third banyan they could, for the price of a few annas, receive an excellent trim.

"What's an anna?" whispered Sophie.

"Indian money," said Osman quickly, glaring Sasha to silence. He continued: Ravi did not like to acknowledge that his customers came primarily because his shop was where people went to trade gossip. Partly this happened because he asked abrupt and personal questions that so surprised them with their cheek that they answered frankly before thinking. Partly it was because his clientele came from all stations and so the news had more than the usual levels and layers to it. Information could be gleaned from houseboys who served tea planters in the foothills and pale Parsis through whose long fingers the area's moneylending flowed.

After explaining caste and Parsis, he described Ayah the way Emma had: she had a scraggly braid through which a blue thread was woven, a glassy song of bangles gave each step or gesture its own fanfare, the spokes of her arms were ashy with dryness. She was always the only grown woman there.

Had she been in love with the barber? Did she simply like to court danger from time to time? Perhaps she liked Ravi's air of well-being and seriousness; perhaps it was his curving mustache, of which he was inordinately proud. It served as another feature on his face, with as much ability to express mood as his mobile mouth and sensitive eyebrows. It seemed to take on the job of his eyes, which were a muddy brown that revealed nothing but a mild and constant despair.

As the son of a local sage, Ravi had some right to his didactic ways and would lecture the children in a hypnotic blend of Tamil and English on the proper names for the various avatars of Krishna and all the titles of Good King George, to whom he was strangely attached. As he cut hair, he would sing bits of the *Ramayana* to his own peculiar tune. They could hear him before they saw him.

Ayah instructed Ravi to hang a sheet between two sprouts of the banyan, so they would not be seen by a passing official or a memsahib on her way to visit a lieutenant with dysentery. As puffs of heat made the sheet dance, Ravi lined up his pomades in their vials of cloudy glass. Dark oily red in one, something thick as tamarind paste in another, tilting a bit on the uneven ground. Before he tended them, Ravi sharpened his scissors on a black whetstone, well saturated with palm oil. The sound was a thick irritating scrape as he lectured his customers on the importance of chewing three cardamom pods a day to ease digestion in the hot months. Once inside the dusty semicircle of Ravi's territory, one had to participate in the drama of his preparations.

Ayah always guided Emma toward Ravi first. The barber wet her hair with a sandalwood comb swiped clean in a basin of water. The teeth of the hand-carved tool were sharp, uneven, but he lent a pleasing briskness to his work and Emma had told Osman she did not mind the occasional snag. Afterward, she knew her hair would carry a note of the wood's warm spice. Then she would feel the buttered slackness of his fingers as they and the cool leg of the scissors brushed her neck. As he measured and trimmed, he would alternately sing and lecture, and though Emma could not see him, she smelled him in a cloud around her.

Ravi never spoke to Ayah directly; she was lower-caste than he and it wouldn't have done. But when the three of them came, his voice would acquire fresh edges and he would chatter to the children about the price of mangoes at the market and the strange ways of that poor thin major, as if Emma and Andrew were as interested as he in this spreading of news. Ayah would listen with her sari drawn over her mouth, behind Ravi, and poke neem-tree leaves at the parrot, which ignored her. But the other clients, who'd ceded their places the moment the English children arrived, pulled in closer.

Of special interest was watching Andrew's pale hair fall to the ground. Emma, smelling now of coconut oil and sandalwood, watched from the safety of Ayah's lap as the fringes of blond hair fell to the ground. "Why would that be important?" Osman asked. "Think about it. To see a man who would grow to be a sahib have his head touched by an Indian, to have hair that many Indians held as holy scatter in the dirt below a banyan tree."

The children were silent. That was part of the ritual. To let Osman give them the moral, which they never understood. "It was a wonderful and dangerous joke," their father finally said. Never at the expense of the children, but at the expense of their countrymen, and even more at the expense of their terrible father, who was known for his cruelty with the troops under his command. To watch this bad man's son be shorn was to participate in a carefully staged gesture of pure and total disrespect. And yet, Osman said, Emma always emphasized the tenderness with which Ravi touched them, despite his loud voice and the jumpy motion of his mustache. He blessed them in Tamil at the end of their haircuts, carefully scraped up the blond and brown feathers, and tossed them into the coals that kept his tea water bubbling all day. They would sip milk in chipped glasses and wait until the bitter stink of burning hair had faded, surrounded by the squatting, patient men who had been pushed aside when they arrived.

"Protest," Sasha said sleepily. Sophie, too, thought she understood. No words, no spit. But anger that spilled along different lines.

The stories, Sophie knew, were supposed to be some kind of inoculation. Protective pieces of knowledge about the way families worked. Some of the world's hazards. It was dangerous, her father implied. Go out armed. Go out aware. But where Sasha felt safe when Danielle unpleated maps, Sophie felt secure at her father's shop, which smelled like dust and wool. Not moldy dust or grimy wool, but the vaguely magical dust of other places where the carpets had once lived. Osman said he could tell from the smell where the carpets were from before he even saw them. There was Persian dust. Turkish dust. Indian dust. Danielle said that as far as she was concerned, dirt was international, and internationally unpleasant. Osman would smile and say her nose had gotten stuffed from too many Canadian winters. "Hah," said Danielle, but she wasn't fussy anymore. Still, she didn't like the task of cleaning the shop. Gradually, it became Sophie and Osman's, their outing. "So what do we do first today, Sophie?" her father asked in French.

"Clean the windows," she said. It was her favorite chore, Saturday afternoon's work. Nonetheless, he always asked and she always answered. It was better than the rote responses of church, which Sophie also liked, but secretly. Her parents would not have approved that she attended. They liked churches as specimens of stone and glass in interesting proportions, and as places that preserved quiet and held music. But not for their real and holy work. Osman went silent and a bit stiff at the mention of God, and Danielle said, "Stuff and nonsense," sounding like their grandmother Hilda. So Sophie sneaked off on occasional Wednesday afternoons with her delicate, cough-ridden friend Marie Claire, who had the distinction of sporting a scimitar-shaped scar on her chest from open-heart surgery. Marie Claire needed God to keep her fragile little body upright, that was clear. The way Marie Claire talked about him, God was like a large finger that reached down from heaven and poked at the base of your spine to make you stand straight. He believed in obvious rectitude, it seemed. Sophie, who was healthy and tall for her age and had never considered that she needed anything at all except occasional protection from Sasha, was impressed at this open admission of dependence. Marie Claire, mournful and patient, explained that of course Sophie was damned, because she had the misfortune to be born neither French nor Catholic. She wasn't clear on which condition was more likely to make Sophie burn. This made Sophie laugh, but then she realized she liked the steadiness of church, its cool, evocative dimness. It could lull you, she saw, which might be useful. But if Wednesdays were for tentative explorations of the mysteries, Saturdays were devoted to Osman and the rugs.

The pail was in the lavatory, with the wiper inside it. It was too heavy for her to carry when it was full, so her father lugged it, hot and sharply scented with ammonia and vinegar. The large square window held discreet lettering in the corner, like a tidy smile with a flicker of gold in it. *Tapis Orientaux, O. Harris, propriétaire.* Late in the afternoon, the streets were quite empty, and the only sound apart from the rumbling taxis was the braid of water that rushed along the gutters. Sophie brought out the stepladder and the stack of saved *Le Monde*s. The wiper squeaked against the glass and sent down soapy rivulets. Sophie, on the ladder, mopped these wet strings dry with bunched-up pieces of newspaper. They moved slowly across the window, working in vertical strips, Osman squeaking, Sophie catching the moisture and rubbing it away. In their wake they left the bright clarity of glass. When they were done, they stood back from the window, and instead of the blurred gray that had been her reflection as she wiped away the dirt with old news, Sophie would see her father next to her, bouncing back at her in partial truth, because there was still the dust to scrape from the inside.

Osman could have paid for someone to clean the windows, but he didn't. The same way they could have had a new car. Instead, they drove a battered and inconspicuous Renault named François le Fort that both Osman and Danielle babied as if it were their third child. *"Le pauvre François,"* Osman would sigh as the car jerked slowly up hills. By the time he was twelve, Sasha was embarrassed that they did not own something grander than this small blue car with the dented fender. Osman kept it polished and Danielle swept out the sand, mud, and leaves. Still, it was crowded, rusting at its edges, its age advertised for all to see in its old-fashioned shape. Why couldn't they have one of those rounded beauties Citroën was making now? Because, his father said, we live simply. They were not supposed to reveal too much to others. Friends were kept politely distant, and the French, with their elaborate devotion to privacy, did not insist. Part of it, Sasha suspected, was linked to Osman's work. But when he asked his father what he did, Osman always said, "I'm a shop-keeper. I sell rugs. Nothing fancy about it."

So they kept the Renault, and kept it tidy, even as rust fanned over its body. But the day it had labored up the pass outside Saint-Jean-de-Luz, near the end of their vacation, his father's mania for discretion for once had not mattered. Sophie was quiet as she looked out at the steep road, leaning her lead on the bony pillow of her elbow. Her hair was in tight braids. Danielle had a map partly accordioned on her lap. She wore a cotton dress and her shoulders were speckled with nutmeg freckles. She, too, was quiet and looking out at the blue pines and the narrow cleft toward which they were heading. Osman was in shirtsleeves, his holiday jacket neatly stashed in the back. He was smiling slightly, and rested his arm on the door where the window had been rolled down. Wind rushed in and swept back Sasha's bangs. The air smelled of juniper and salt. The sun was slanting and orange. They were heading to the pass for a picnic supper and a view of the ocean as the night settled. "Look, Sasha," Danielle said suddenly, "it's a falcon." She pointed to the circling black slightness in the bright sky, and Osman pulled over to the shoulder. "Oh yes, let's stop," Danielle said. They tumbled out from the cramped seats, and as they craned their heads to the sky, they saw that the bird had dipped lower. They could even see the dense chest feathers and the mottling flecks of brown against the white. They could see the curve of the talons, their perfect sharpness. Though they were not at risk of being hit, the car was at an odd angle off the road, not quite safe from traffic. For once, they were making a nuisance of themselves. Sasha noticed that the other motorists rushing past looked annoyed at having to steer around them. Some even honked at the family with the cocked elbows, staring at the sky, not caring for that moment about the hazard they might cause. But the sound wasn't loud enough to mask the bird's cry, a sharp descending line that it sang as they watched. Then the thermal it had ridden gathered strength and lifted the bird elliptically back to the air. When it was only a mild black cross in the sky, which was turning boldly red, they nosed their way back onto the road. They said nothing. Osman rolled the window up. Sophie smiled at some private thought and played with the end of her braid. Danielle folded the map. They were perfectly happy. It settled like the lightest of burdens in the small blue car. They breathed it in. They let it tug them gently.

But soon after they got back to Paris, Danielle had gone to the doctor and it seemed impossible that any of them had ever known such a peaceful moment or could have been so careless. Her illness was with them the length of the school year. Those months, Sophie measured time not by tests and holidays but by whether or not Danielle was at home or in the hospital, feverish or cool. Their father first told them in the kitchen, gripping the back of a chair. Danielle was ill; something in her blood. She was staying overnight to have more tests. He said she would be fine too many times and lit too many cigarettes. Neither Sophie nor Sasha believed him. "Does it have a name?" Sasha asked.

"Not yet," Osman said, which made it worse. If it were called something, there would be ways to attack it. It would have a known pattern. It would curve this way, then that, and the doctors could follow, with medicines designed to outwit it. Marie Claire's father was a doctor, and he had names made of intricate syllables for things as simple as a scrape. Sophie told Marie Claire her mother was sick and Marie Claire said it was the will of God and Sophie smacked her. Marie Claire and Sophie both cried then and went to church to pray for God to help Sophie with her temper. But her temper would not be stowed away like one of Danielle's maps. It was large and scarlet. She could feel God watching, scolding her. She told him she did not care.

Danielle's sickness made Osman collapse inward. He tended his worry in a dark ball at the center of his stomach, but those bad months made Sasha sharp and stealthy. He spent time in libraries reading about blood, as if mastering its chemistry might have some impact on the disease that had settled into his mother's body. He was at ease with facts he was too young to need. All the learning made him look smaller than he was, furtive. The sickness only made Sophie angry: she would wake in the mornings with her teeth clenched. She was tempted to throw bottles out the window at the healthy, stupid head of the concierge snooping through neighbors' mail. She dreamed of knives and scissors, broken glass, even during her mother's good spells.

Late in April, Danielle was home, resting in her bathrobe, and she asked Sophie to come and sit with her. Her mother looked as if light were no longer interested in coming near her. Her skin couldn't hold it anymore. The last time Sophie had touched her, in the hospital just before she came home, her fingers had the slight roughness of fine sandpaper. That was when Danielle explained, for the second time, about periods and cramps, telling Sophie that these events would happen soon and she ought not to be frightened. That she should tell Osman when they occurred and he would help her. Sophie had nodded, mortified that her mother didn't remember saying just the same thing last year, but also amazed that Danielle's body had once been able to process blood so simply. Now, looking at her mother, she thought it would chafe her lips to kiss Danielle. Seeing her mother in the chair, her red robe only slightly masking the eerie thinness of her legs, Sophie heard herself say, "No."

"It's not catching," said Danielle, who rose like a piece of wire unbending and went slowly to her bedroom. Sophie looked at the empty chair that still held the slight imprint of her mother's weight. She sat in it, feeling its worn velvet arms, smelling the ghost of lavender Danielle had left. She rose then and went into her parents' room. Danielle was lying on the bedspread, awake, eyes trained on the flaking ceiling. Sophie went to her and lay down. She circled her mother's wrist with her fingers. Danielle's bones pressed against her rough skin and made it pearly where the bones came closest to the surface. "I know you hate this," she said, and stroked her daughter's hair. Her own had gone and she wore turbans now. They lay there as the afternoon deepened into night. They hadn't spoken, drifting in and out of sleep, until Sophie woke and sat up, horrified. For a moment, she was certain Danielle's heart had stopped. She pressed her warm, firm fingers at her mother's throat and found the small warble of the pulse. She did not want to lift her hand away, as if that were all that was keeping her mother there.

For a time late that spring, the doctors found drugs that seemed to work. Osman managed to eat more. Sasha played football occasionally. Sophie found she was on better terms with God. At dinner, which Osman cooked, they would remember to interrupt and tease each other sometimes. He would tell them stories about clients in the shop, new rugs he'd bought, dealers who had tried to cheat him. Stories about the push and pull of business, stories that meant he was alive. But then in June, Danielle want back to the hospital, and over four nights, Osman's stories changed.

He came to say good night to them. In the midsummer evening, he stood there. "Would you like to hear a story?" he asked. "I've been thinking about this one." At fourteen and twelve Sasha and Sophie were too old for the bedtime ritual, but they didn't answer, which he seemed to take as a positive response and sat on Sophie's bed. He lit a cigarette and began. Once there was a king, Osman said, whose domain lay in the desert. He loved the rocks and the dry plateaus, but his nomadic blood pushed him to travel in lands where springs were only slightly sacred. He'd seen France, Spain, Italy, and even when these countries were arid, their citizens were familiar enough with moisture to be quite casual about rain and streams. This bounty of wetness made the king thirst for gardens, not the thrifty plots of palms that fringed his oases, but spilling acres of lilies, fountains, moss. It is said his desire took root when, in Spain, he held the slick ribbed feet of a frog and looked into its eye of melted gold. But he had a measure of wisdom, this king, and he was wise enough to know that his fate had made him a man who would rule only over stone. He was even aware that he was king in name only, because no one could claim something so implacably itself as the desert.

But he was hungry for something. Water had awakened his appetites and he returned to his silken tents for the first time in his life unhappy. Having bestowed on his wives and children his gifts of candied nuts, cuckoo clocks, and mirrors, he sat in the billowing light, untempted by ripe apricots and trained doves. He was aware for the first time of a dissatisfaction for which he did not have a name or a cure. It was as if the things of his world failed to assuage him, because he invested power now in what he'd seen on his travels, other worlds' solutions to design, beauty, health. That frog, those palace gardens, those spires of stone, had made him doubt his own kingdom's worth and so his own.

Sasha said, "Where was this?"

His father said, "A desert. A place where there were nomads, camels, oases. Palmeraies." Sophie could tell he liked saying this last word. The coal on his cigarette glowed more deeply. "Stories do not have to be precisely located to be useful, Sasha. They don't have to conform to regular geography."

Sasha shifted in his bed, turning on his stomach and bunching the pillow in his arms. He liked his stories exact. Danielle told them bits of real life, like how the métro had been built. Or how to tell when Madame Dupont, the concierge, was in a good mood or not. Practical pieces of information, reports on how much electricity had gone up last month and fluctuations in the population of Paris over the last ten years. Danielle read newspapers. She had let them know what was going on beyond the chaotic flap of school, Osman's shop, her own work at the auction house, bills and marketing, keeping the flat tidy enough to find the telephone. She was the one who translated events like bombings in train stations; wars in poor, dry places; droughts and storms that burned forests or ripped at coastlines. Danielle had kept track of emergencies for them. It did not matter that their kitchen was always in disarray and that as a family of foreigners, they were always scrambling to meet scrupulous French standards of appearance. If Danielle was abreast of troubles, they were somehow fine. "How do you know all this?" Sophie asked her once. "I'm Canadian," Danielle said, as if that explained it. "She means," Osman said, "that she's from the New World, and that North Americans are more efficient with information than Europeans." "Oh," said Sophie, still lost, but aware that her parents were exchanging, over coffee, one of their secret, married smiles.

But now that Danielle was sick, trouble had leaked in everywhere. Early in her mother's illness, Sophie had lost the sash to her school uniform. Osman's lunches were not warm. She saw that Sasha's query about the exact location of the desert was his way of saying he missed his mother. Osman seemed to understand, however, and told Sasha: "This story unfolds in the Syrian desert, three hundred miles northwest of Baghdad. Major economic activities: rug weaving, sheep herding, the cultivation of dates, figs, palm oil. Religion: Islam, mixed with remnants of animism. Primarily nomadic. Beautiful and feisty women with a preference for silver over gold. The color blue is valued, because indigo is hard to come by." Sasha settled deeper into his bed. "May I go on?" their father asked. "Yes," said Sasha, his voice muffled in the pillow's down.

The king kept having trouble sleeping, Osman told them. He grew thin and pale. Nothing could please him, not the baby camels, not the annual sale of horses over which he usually presided with enormous glee. One night, with his family gathered about him, the king thought of telling them he was going to renounce this princely life. He had clearly acquired some demon of the spirit, and rather than risk infecting them with his malaise, he felt he should abandon all trappings of power and control, admit his weakness, and seek to cleanse it. Become a wanderer of the desert. Depend on spirit and will and the generosity of traders to provide for him. It began to please him, this thought of a dry and simple life.

As he watched the lighter carve curves from Osman's face, Sasha wondered where his father got these stories. He and Sophie were too old for them. Too old to be sharing a room, but there was little space and they'd arranged privacies for themselves. A curtain on brass rings hung between the beds. They changed at different times. They were discreet, without speaking about it. They studied there together, in silence. Sometimes they did not even wish each other good night. But they did not reject the story. They knew it soothed him to talk.

Osman inhaled and tipped the furry ash out the window.

"So the king was in despair. But that night, the most lovely of his wives sang to him and stroked his hair, shot through now with silver. She sang ghazal after ghazal, and for once, the king slept. It was a long sleep, one that the dawn could not budge. He slept through the total heat of the midday and woke just at dusk, when the temperature started to drop and the sky turned violet. Small supper fires crackled orange outside the tent and the smell of mint tea drifted into his sleeping chamber. For the first time in weeks, he felt refreshed. He did not turn to the collection of lovely European objects he had amassed—the gold-rimmed porcelain, the silk-tasseled pillows—and wonder at the use of his desert kingdom.

"He had had a dream, he told his manservant, Salim."

"Why does Salim have a name and the king doesn't?" Sophie asked. "Shouldn't he have a name, too?"

"What would you call him?" Osman asked her.

"Farouk," said Sophie.

"That's Egyptian," said Sasha scathingly. "This is Syria."

"That's the problem," said Osman. "You give him a name and you run into history. You try to match him with someone else's face, territory, or war, and there you are: stuck with a bunch of facts and no story," Osman said, sighing. "May we just call him the king, Sophie?"

She relented, but gave him a private name. Hassan. King Hassan. It sounded sad and noble all at once, which was how she imagined him.

"So what did he dream?" Sasha asked.

He had had a vision, the king told Salim. A giant rug. A rug the world had never seen. Huge. A garden rug. Forest-colored wool. Pearls for the eyes of animals, rubies to line the tongues of dark lilies. But who would weave it? Salim asked, nervously making tea, which he was glad to see the king at last sip. "Bring some olives, please," the king asked, "and I'll tell you the rest."

News of the king's improved state of mind spread quickly—they'd seen Salim fussing at the cook to make the food look more enticing—add a rose to the plate, would you—and his people gathered from all around to await his appearance. The king rolled back the flap of his tent and stepped into the green dawn. All about him stood the nomads, who looked to him as their leader. He had again slept well, was freshly shaved, and called to them in a strong voice.

"In what language?" asked Sasha, not being able to help himself.

"A form of Arabic," said Osman smoothly. "An older variety than is now spoken. May I go on?"

Sasha nodded. "The king asked his people for assistance in a grand project. They would not pay fealty in dates and amber this year, but they were to weave him a carpet in squares of wool in colors as vivid as indigo and pomegranate allowed. They were to make the finest yarn, combed and softened in sheep's milk."

Sasha and Sophie turned over in their beds. Carpets. Osman's obsession. They no longer visited him after school at the shop, and though Sophie still helped clean the windows, neither she nor Sasha quite understood the appeal of all that ragged, faded wool. If Danielle had been there, Sophie thought, she would have said, "Idiocy, Osman. Kings know better than to like rugs. They're too sensible. Good kings prefer gold or timber any day." To which Osman would have said, "Not this king, Danielle. He is a man of taste and distinction." But with Danielle in the hospital, Osman could say what he liked. Still, he must have known they did not want to hear more. He pulled the sheets to their chins and they let him kiss their cheeks. He pulled the curtain between them. They didn't speak, but lay there, listening to one another breathe and, outside, the swish of taxis through the night, the call of friends on the street after a party. *"Bonne nuit, bonne nuit,"* a young woman kept saying, her voice tickled to silliness. Too much wine, Sasha thought. But to Sophie, she sounded merely as if she was in a pretty dress and enjoying summer, knowing how nice she looked in silk and lamplight.

Osman returned the next night, this time with no cigarettes. They had come back late from seeing Danielle and the *tabacs* had been closed. His hands were nervous and Sophie gave him a pillow to clasp to his chest. Danielle had looked pinched in the face, though she assured them she was feeling fine. She kept plucking at the needles in the crook of her elbow, trying, it seemed to Sophie, to hide them from her family. As if that would mask the silver trellis from which the plastic sacks swung. "I'll be out soon," she said, her hand a small knot under the white sheet. "These doctors are a bunch of nellies." That had made them feel better; it was Danielle in her firm Canadian mode, being superior to French anxiety, but then Osman had not said what the slight doctor wanted to talk to him about before they left. Tonight they all needed to hear what the king was doing, even if it did involve carpets. Anything not to think about Danielle and the way she'd stroked their hair and asked if their father had done anything about learning to make decent eggs. Were they helping? Was the house a disaster? Yes, they said to both. Wasn't it always when she wasn't there?

"Where did we leave off?" asked Osman.

"The king told his nomads they were going to make rugs," Sophie prompted.

"Yes," said Osman. "The women began to heat water in great cauldrons near the palms for the roots, leaves, and stems they were going to use to tint the dyes. And while the potions were stewing they were singing—"

"In Arabic," Sasha added.

"In Arabic," Osman continued, "and as the stuff brewed, the boys and girls rounded up the sheep to be shorn. The sheep were fantastically dumb, but they quite sensibly liked to avoid being sheared. It hurt their skin and frightened them and reminded them that humans are not gentle creatures. But once the animals were cornered, they went still. The children had rough black scissors and snipped off gray mats of the wool. The sheep with their yellow eyes stood impassively as the camp filled with floating tufts. Then, when they were shorn to their skins and you could see the muscles of the skinny backs through their pelts, they were let go. They sprang back up the cliffs like stiff, white crickets. During the day, everyone spun the wool as they followed the herds from pasture to pasture, twisting the wool onto wooden spindles, turning it to coarse hanks of thread.

"When they'd gathered the spun wool into sheaves, the dyes were ready. It was men who plunged the wool into the dark water." It looked, Osman said, like a woman's hair. The way a woman douses her hair at a stream. He stopped for a moment, and they all were turning pieces of the same image over in their minds. Sasha remembered how last summer Danielle had stood to her waist and whooped in the ocean at Saint-Jean-de-Luz, dunking her head in and out of the water, over which hung a low quilt of fog. Osman remembered that, later that night, he had kissed the salt from where it had gathered in white frost on her jaw and teased her about still not being able to swim. Sophie remembered the way her mother moved more happily after being in the ocean, her joints eased of something angular that they held the rest of the year. But then she had gone to bed, abruptly tired. The first sign she was sick.

"Go on," Sasha said, a little more roughly than he meant to.

"So the wool is dyed," Osman said slowly. It turns different colors. Red from cochineal insects, for which they had traded with Lebanese dealers from the coast. Indigo from Africa. Rose from the rinds and seeds of pomegranates. Yellow from mustard. Green from minerals mixed with alder leaves. Brown from the shells of cashews and pistachios. The wool steeped and absorbed the color, and the women stirred and sang, encouraging the dye to bite deeply.

Then they left the wool to dry in the sun. This was a critical step, said Osman, because all the elements had to be invoked to make good wool and so a good rug. Fire to heat the water in which the wool was steeped. Wood from the earth to heat the fire, and now air and light to complete the process. Sophie wondered if they all craved light in their family. All Osman's stories took place in warm, dry places. The predominant color of Paris was blue-gray, smoky with damp. Osman's stories were like an alternative source of power. She would never have admitted it to Sasha, but they still warmed her.

The men's hands were dyed to the elbow with whatever color they'd plucked the wool from, Osman continued. Yellow arms. Red arms, and blue. A whole array of color that eventually washed off, but the children would gather dabs of color on their cheeks from their fathers and uncles as they darted among the great clots of drying wool. The men did not mind their antics. First, they were tolerant of children. Second, they were happy to do their king's bidding. He was strict but fair in helping them resolve troubles with dowries or horses and in measuring the worth of a goat—and the ones with nimble-fingered wives looked forward to the display of their women's skill. They were glad, too, he had shown his strength again. They did not like being leaderless. Small fights had been breaking out like sharp, bright fires across his territory. This new task distracted them from rivalries, and they put their knives back into the sheaths. Their wives were grateful for the respite, and though weaving was a far more onerous task than handing over baskets of dates and polished chunks of amber, they applied themselves to the chore at hand.

Osman stopped then. Sophie said, "Go on, Papa." Sasha said nothing, and lay propped on his elbow, waiting, too.

But Osman said, a bit wonderingly, "I can't. I don't know what happens next." He kissed them then and sat there, his back against Sophie's bed. In the morning, he was gone. He had left to get cigarettes, his note said, and to go to the bakery. But he was still away as they readied themselves for school. They ate the heel of the stale baguette for breakfast, its crust softened in water, then toasted, a trick Danielle had taught them to rescue bread past its prime.

The next night, Osman was smoking again. He moved as if his muscles ached, Sophie saw, but his voice eased gently into the story. "The men settled in to lay out sketches and found themselves surprised."

"What did they write with?" Sasha asked.

"Their knives in dirt, and then when they were pleased with what they had, they took sticks of charcoal and sketched the designs on parchment they had traded for. Is that satisfactory?"

Sasha said he could see that, and Osman went on. Yet when even the clumsiest of the men went to draw a pattern, they found their hands pulled in directions they had not expected, crafting beaks of long-necked birds and tails of curious spotted cats, the dark arms of trees they'd never seen. But what surprised their fingers most were the fish that were born into their designs: bright with muscle, blue-skinned. Some spouted jets of water, others were human to their waists. There were shepherds who ran from the area around the fire where they scraped their pictures, fearing charges of heresy, but their wives, less nervous around miracles, told them that their fingers were being directed by Allah, not some *djinn*, and that they should buckle down. They showed the patterns to their wives, who said, "Looks complicated."

"Sounds like Mum," Sasha said. It was something that Danielle might have said. She loved the simple over the complex, the clear as opposed to the veiled. None of them could talk about that right then, so Osman continued: "But as they tried to coax the wool across the warp and to make the first of the knots, they found they couldn't. It was as if their hands were being directed beyond their control. Some got nervous, as their husbands had, but they couldn't bear the thought of revealing weakness in front of a man, and so they let the wool fly across the looms they set up underneath animal skins stretched taut on wooden poles. They worked for twelve hours at a time, even in lamplight, wasting sheep tallow, because the patterns that emerged were so beautiful. Even their fingers were spared, growing none of the usual blisters and calluses that weaving gave them. The combs they used to tighten the pile moved smoothly through the rugs in progress, and they sang as they worked, above the rasp of the metal on wool. There had been just enough yarn. The dyes had bitten with deep richness. When they snipped the pile short with the same black scissors the children used to shear the sheep, the wool was lustrous and soft, as if silk had miraculously been woven in as well."

The next step was to wash the rugs, Osman told them. They let them settle in the irrigation ditches, and women and children stamped on them as the water rushed through the heavy wool. Slowly, the dye that would have rubbed off on fingers and heels flowed away. Then they hauled the carpets to the banks, where they dried like big rectangular flowers on the chalky banks, the sun baking their colors fast.

Then came the call from the king: within three days, he wanted the rugs they had woven to be presented at this tent. The shepherds and their families became excited. Everything had gone so well. Fish and flowers leaped from their carpets. Each shepherd was sure his panel would be the most beautiful and would serve as the medallion, would be the one chosen as the setting for the most precious rubies and pearls. On a winter morning, the men set forth from their camps, breath like translucent puffs of wool marking their passage, looking forward to the boasts about who had completed the finest piece of the king's rug, each man sure that his family alone had felt the spirit of the Lord upon him as they made their contribution.

But then a hush fell. A pair of cousins from different camps noticed first: one had knotted the tail end of a strange fish while the other had shaped its head, although neither of the young men had a word in their language for the creature's name. Each panel had emerged as a piece of a whole. The shepherds looked at where the edges of their carpets stopped and called out "Half-cat, green vines" or "Blue fish and prow of boat," and waited until the weaver of the cat's front paws, grapes, and stern came forward. And so they sorted themselves into a great, laden whole, arms sweating, faces taut from both the weight of the rug and the surprise.

The king laughed and admired their elegant work and, after they had laid the panels down and adjusted their robes, sent them out to a feast of foods spiced with rosewater and cumin. While they gorged on stuffed meats and watched the sky—it was a strange color for winter, too pearled, as if the good weather might be breaking and a storm was on the rise—boys wielding slender needles sewed the great garden of wool together, using loop after loop of golden thread. Then after they had rested, they set about embroidering the eyes and scales of the fish with sapphires and seed pearls drilled with the tiniest of holes by burins the king had bought from jewelers from Amsterdam. The enormous carpet began then to sparkle.

When the last goat knuckle had been spat out, the last clear glass of tea drunk down, the king called to them from the entrance of the tent. "Come and see what you have made." What the shepherds saw was a riotous green rectangle, an expanse of woolen field, branching trees, pillows of roses, birds sipping nectar, wild cats and antelopes darting past lush bushes, and everywhere a flower or root had not curled, the leaping creatures of the sea they knew had once flowed over the routes of the caravans. A sea so rich with fish that sometimes still they pulled a hook from the spongy bed of a camel's hoof. Together, because it was clear the rug was blessed and because it was time, the men and their king prayed, grateful for the chance to be so oddly touched by God.

"Is that the end?" Sophie asked, because Osman had paused.

"No," said Sasha. "It can't be. There hasn't been a conflict yet. Every story needs a climax, then a dénouement." He was imitating Monsieur Griffon, his literature teacher, who had a southern accent about which his students were merciless. "Something else has to happen."

They had visited Danielle again that afternoon. She was grayer in the face than she had been before. She didn't call anyone a nelly. She had just held Sasha and Sophie and not cared if they'd seen the tubes in her arm. Afterward, Osman took them out for supper, an unheard-of luxury. It was a simple bistro and they'd eaten omelets. The waiter had overcharged them and Sasha was the only one to notice. Osman had just left a tumble of bills and coins on top of the check. They could see a bit of the Seine from where they sat. They had homework to do that no one mentioned, which made

Sophie nervous. The other diners were older men and women, couples, not families.

"When is Mum coming home?" Sophie finally asked as Osman scooped the extra change into his pocket.

"It's not clear," Osman said. She remembered he'd said exactly that, because he said much the same thing now. "It's not clear what has to happen. We'll finish tomorrow night." He forgot to pull the curtain between them, and Sophie thought Sasha would tug it closed, but Sasha seemed to ignore it. She watched her brother until his profile dissolved in the dark and all she could see was the slight hump his body made in the sheets.

The next night, Osman came to their room and said that he knew the ending and that it was a sad one. Did they still want to hear it? Danielle had looked better today, that was why he dared approach them with the story. The doctors were talking about having her out by the end of the week. A specter of something normal seemed to be creeping toward them. It meant they might go to Saint-Jean-de-Luz as they always did. It made them a little reckless, Sasha saw. Danielle had outfoxed the nervous-nelly French. It meant they could endure hearing stories that didn't finish well. It meant situations could relax into happy surprise when you least expected them to. Even so, it was still not clear what was wrong with her. All they could say was *"C'est un problème du sang."* Blood trouble. A tricky sort of cancer, perhaps. Why couldn't they just clean her out of the old stuff and pump in new, Sophie had asked early on, but Sasha had scornfully said that it was all more complicated than that. So explain it, Sophie had said, but he hadn't been able to and wound up kicking the kitchen table and stalking to their room.

Sasha finally asked the question. Sophie was thankful and angry in equal measure. She both wanted and did not want to know at the same time. "So she's not going to die?" The air was gauzy with smoke. Osman sank to Sophie's bed. He found her foot through the covers and held it at the arch. He was the only person who could touch her feet without making her scream with ticklishness. *"Chatouille,"* he said, squeezing her ankle, as if he were thinking the same thing. Claiming one small gift. *Chatouille,* the French word for both pussy willow and tickle. It sounded like what it meant, for each one. "It doesn't look like it," Osman said. "Not the sort of thing that happens to Canadians."

"Tell the story, Papa," Sophie said then, loving the feel of his hand on her foot, not wanting him to let go.

They had left the tribesmen in their devotions, Sasha reminded his father.

"I know where we are," Osman said. They were praying so mightily that they did not feel the trembling of the sand below their knees and arms. Or perhaps they did and thought they were shaking with fear at the strangeness of the ways of the Lord or fatigue at having been his puppet. Perhaps they were addled with feasting and felt the sensation as a weakness in their heads when faced with such a luxury of green. They were used to it only in vivid, irrigated strips at the edges of the occasional river or near ditches. Green, the color of Islam, the holy color, and they'd been so deprived of it. It might have disoriented them. In any case, none of the men, except perhaps the king, had an idea that the strange cast in the sky and the metal taste to the wind were signs of the army of a neighboring ruler coming to claim this part of the desert as his own. A man admired for the deftness of his sword. He was the one to deal the last blow to the rope that staked the tent, which flew into the air like a pale, enormous bat, leaving the garden of wool exposed.

"Not fair," Sophie cried. "Why, just when it was done, does it have to get taken away from him?"

"He hadn't learned the proper lesson," Sasha said, and his father cocked his head and asked, "What was he supposed to learn?"

"Only God is whole, and the rug pretended to be, so Allah sent the enemy king to destroy the other." What everyone says about Oriental carpets. The flaw woven in so as to proclaim only Allah's perfection in the universe. Yet human error assured those flaws, and they were the very places Osman loved most. Where the knot pulled loose, where the weaver ran out of one color of yarn and substituted another. Or even better, where her fancy took over and the design blossomed strangely forward through the rug.

"Clichés," Osman said, "won't help you get to the bottom of this king. What do you think, Sophie?"

"I think he knew what was going to happen. He wanted to give his people something beautiful before he died."

"How do you know he dies?" Sasha said hotly.

"She's right, Sasha," Osman said, and continued. The troops came thick and fast. Even on his black mare, slashing at the enemy soldiers, he knew that he would lose the fight. In the carpet's center, his head on a lily pad, the king died.

Around him, shepherds bled onto arched necks of lions and spread tails of peacocks, blood soaking the fountains and the roots of the trees. Where the dead or injured did not lie, the carpet was shredded by the sharpened hooves of the invader's horses, animals bred for war and damage. When the battle was over, the women came to gather their men and to keen in sounds they had never made before, as if they'd learned them from the foreign birds their fingers had woven. As if the songs they'd sung that made the valley ring only days before were now being played backward through their voices, which made the music strange and melancholy. All night, the women carried the men back, and spent the next three days burying them. Then they took their children and their sheep and headed north to better pastures, taking with them their looms and wool, but promising themselves only to make small domestic rugs and saddlebags from now on. They would reduce their dreams and joy to manageable sizes.

Only one fragment of the carpet survived, rolled into a rough tube and hastily tucked into the robes of the youngest shepherd, a small bent man whom no one bothered to harm or to protect. He used it as his prayer rug, as did his eldest son, who passed it down through generations until, thanks to many pairs of reverent knees, the rug lost its fish, grapes, and spatter of blood, returning to the resilient browns of the desert. One night a housewife in Tripoli was cleaning out a closet, saw a bundle of what looked like dirty raffia, and promptly tossed it in the trash for a tired old servant to burn the next day. The rug, it was said, flamed gold, and the servant, not knowing why he did so, fell to his knees in prayer.

Then their father kissed them and lit a cigarette in the

still summer night. He sat there on the floor, legs crossed, tobacco smoke twisting.

"What's the moral?" Sasha asked, sitting up. They hadn't expected such an abrupt ending. The sheets rustled. Sophie was quiet in the next bed, but had flung the covers off.

The cigarette's coal pulsed brighter as Osman inhaled and twitched the sheets back over his daughter's body. It was just blue enough to see the tendrils streaming from his nose. "I don't know," their father said.

Osman was wrong about Danielle. She did die, at the end of the month, just as school let out. None of them were with her at the time. It was as if all their hope were in her way; she couldn't leave with all that worry and fear blocking her path. So she slipped out in the middle of the night, just as the nurses changed shifts. Like a coward, Sophie thought furiously. Just creeping away. The last thing she had said to her mother was that she had earned an 11/20 on a history homework. "That's all right, lovey," Danielle had said. "Try harder next time." If she'd known she was going to die, why hadn't there been something more? Something firm and burnished? Why had it been so ordinary?

Sasha didn't say what she had said to him last. Sasha didn't say anything at all. He just lay on his bed and let the summer heat gather around him as he stared out the small window.

Their father rolled carpets in his shop and wept. If you glimpsed him from the window, all you saw was the wedge of a man's strong back, the black wing of his hair, the deft tugs that curled the rug to a cylinder edged in fringe. It was only when you walked into the shop and faced him that you saw his cheeks were snaked with tears. Marie Claire's mother invited Sophie over and watched her carefully as she served the girls bread and chocolate on tiny china plates. They were too old for snacks in the afternoon, but Sophie found the treat soothing. She and Marie Claire went to church twice a week that summer. Osman found out and said nothing, just held her jaw in his hand. On the sagging velvet prie-dieu, Sophie prayed that her father would stop weeping. But God wasn't listening to girls of mixed blood and no distinct religion that year.

Osman told them that as soon as he sold his business and the apartment they were moving to New York. Why New York? Sasha asked, stabbing at a slice of ham. They were pretending to eat dinner. Their faces looked wrinkled, the way faces get when you sleep in the middle of the day, but none of them were sleeping much. The flat smelled of bouquets that friends had sent. The flowers were turning slightly rotten in the heat. Why did people send them, Sophie wondered. They lasted such a short time before they also died. It was ten days after they had scattered Danielle's ashes in the Seine, off the quai aux Fleurs. They'd sprinkled out the silty handfuls late one night in July, as it was probably illegal. Sophie had not been able to stop weeping there by the old stone walls, as tourists in pink and yellow shorts stared at her. Sasha had stood to one side until finally, hands balled to fists, he cried, "Shut up, just shut up, she would have hated that."

"Hush, Sasha," Osman said, but his son's outburst did allow them to move slowly back home. Since then, Osman could have told them they were to ride camels instead of the métro. Eat only mustard and pickles. They didn't care. There was no known pattern left. Paris hung about them in a straggling veil of sightseers and dried-out plane-tree leaves. With its shuttered restaurants and dusty parks, the city was barely recognizable. This was the time of year they were always away on vacation.

"Because it's a fresh start. Because business is good right now in the States and I have colleagues there. Eat your ham, Sasha." Because, Sasha thought, none of us have ever been to New York. Because his father had no memories waiting there. It struck him then that it was as good a place to go as any. There was no one left here or anyplace else. No Hilda, no Danielle. Their father's parents glimpsed only through Osman's stories and letters. A cluster of aunts and cousins to whom they had no attachment. A thin crust of French friends, who were decorously thoughtful and discreet. Osman could have moved them to Moscow or Paraguay. They were in the desert. They did not expect that to change anytime soon.

When the weather began to cool in the fall, Osman started to make stews, potatoes, food deeply rooted in British fog and notions of what put flesh on your bones. Sophie and Sasha liked it. It had a solidity that gave them an anchor, a shape. At least at the end of the day, the kitchen smelled alive. And it didn't smell like Danielle's cooking, had none of her wine, garlic, and lemon, and that, too, was helpful. Osman's French came out those days in stiff creaks, as if pieces had rusted away. He always spoke English now with Sophie. "Make the dressing, Sophie," he would say, knowing without looking up that she was done drying the curly fans of lettuce. From the moment she got home, he kept her gently busy with small errands—fetching bread if they'd run out, setting the table, and then, after supper, doing lessons. It was lightly tiring, all this activity, and it helped her sleep better. Only much later did she think he'd done this intentionally.

By October, Osman had moved out of his bedroom and onto the sofa in the living room. Sasha took to creeping in each morning before school to watch his father. The light that fall had a smoked edge to it. It was free of color. It made him feel that he was watching everything through a fire's haze. The room acquired a bit of Osman's scent of tobacco and old wool. But apart from his body on the sofa, the room remained unchanged. Sasha, eating bread and jam, would stand like a heron, one foot's instep planted on his knee, oddly balanced. He did not know at first why he would go and watch his father. Then Sasha realized how his heart unclamped when he saw the slight shifts Osman's body made below his blanket that meant he was still breathing.

That December, as they packed up the flat, Sasha and Sophie played this game for the last time. They would be in New York by the turn of the year. Their father had found them an apartment, as they had to learn to call it, and enrolled them in schools as well. Everything was shifting in this new, unpredictable land of motherlessness, and later Sophie thought that's why she and Sasha, too grown-up at fifteen and thirteen for such idiocies, had returned one last time to their old competition. Osman had told them they were to roll up the large Shiraz in the hallway, but after they'd cleared away the desk and the trash basket, without a word, they found themselves stationed on either end of the carpet. Sasha owned the rug's blue patches, Sophie the red. Sophie's knees shook with the effort of stillness. The object was to get to the other end without having your feet touch a lozenge of the wrong color. But as she inched toward the center, she tilted and her hand grazed a piece of Sasha's territory. "Out!" he shouted, and pounced. The burn of the wool on her cheek, the fine grit wearing into her skin, the knowledge that the fingers which gave the carpet its soft twine of animals and trees had been deft and expert, made it even worse to lose her balance and tumble into Sasha's world. He had her pinned. He'd grown so much these last months and his weight was hurting her. But it had been so long since he had touched her that even so she let him lie there for a time. Then they got up and rolled the carpet, as if nothing else had happened that afternoon.

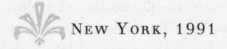 NEW YORK, 1991

In New York, the view from the apartment on East Eighty-fourth Street was larger, more angled, louder. Everything about New York was bigger, seemed spiked. The voices, the cars. Then, in February, it snowed and muffled all the strangeness under thick layers of white. It was easier this way. There were fewer details to absorb when frost obscured shop windows and people were muffled in long coats and scarves. Wearing new boots, Sophie began to learn her way about the neighborhood, to find a favorite path between home and school, which was slightly farther east, on the river. "How long are we going to live here?" she asked her father soon after they had moved. "Do we own this place?" she pressed, gesturing at their five square rooms. How attached was she supposed to get? How many impressions should she acquire? But Osman shook his head. He didn't know, he said. They were renting, and he had a year-long lease on his carpet shop downtown. They would see how it went. But did she like it all right? Was she happy enough? And to keep her father from worry, Sophie told him yes, that she was fine. But she did not say that she missed the rich stink of the French, their perfume, their cheese.

She cultivated those memories privately, sharing nothing that might trigger Osman's hooded look. Even without reference to the past, he was growing more and more quiet. When he did talk to her and Sasha these days, it was mostly in ways she suspected would surprise other parents. "It is a strange rule of fiction," he told them one day in March, as the snow was beginning to melt, "that the person who speaks the least is always perceived as the most intelligent." The information he imparted ranged from biological curiosities of snails to the habits of nomads in the Turkish highlands. He was full of these small flourishes, which emerged like tidy scarves from the sleeve of a sad magician. They often arrived during supper, a meal he prepared with enormous care and precisely measured spices. His cooking changed here in the New World, taking advantage of the steady stream of produce from California and South America. Raspberries in early spring. Unheard of in Paris. She and her brother sat there after their father had made one of his pronouncements and chewed the delicious chicken slowly. Living with Osman was making them behave like sentries at the threshold of their own lives.

It was impossible to say whether or not their father liked New York. He offered few opinions. He'd found a shop on Fifth Avenue in the Twenties, on the eighth floor of a building that housed other rug sellers. He had hired a young Tibetan man to help him. But he seemed to spend much of his time on long walks in the park and rooting through museums and bookshops. Their conversations with him grew more general, clipped of the familiar. He told none of the old stories, mentioned none of the names of the characters that had filled his tales. As if they were neighbors exchanging greetings in an elevator, not living in the same house, circulating the same molecules of air, bumping into the same pieces of furniture they had lived with for years in France.

The one sign that the children were more than merely his acquaintances was the presents he would occasionally leave on the mail table. He attached their names to the item intended for them—a reproduction of a dour Braque for Sasha, a field guide to mushrooms for Sophie. They took these gifts seriously, examining them like runes for symbol and import. But Osman never spoke about his offerings and certainly didn't invite discussion or even thanks. The gifts further padded the apartment's silence. What was there to say about used books on pythons or Machu Picchu, gone soft and grubby with someone else's fingers and scribblings?

So they had all become quieter in the volubility of America, where they now spoke only English. Meals with Osman were now like meals in the monasteries they'd sometimes visited in France, salt passed, dishes cleared in a rhythm they all three seemed to understand without needing to speak. A liturgical steadiness found its way into how Sophie lighted candles and their father asked her and Sasha about their days. They answered dutifully, in full sentences, submerging the parts that might disturb the evening's surface. They talked of classes, weather, books assigned for reading. Sometimes he played music in the background. Sometimes he read them a story from the newspaper, but never told them anything made up or dredged from some corner of his family lore. His voice, though thinner, was still beautiful, and when he spoke, they all forgot to eat. They were growing thinner in this sturdy country.

Kirghiz, Khotan, Gebbeh, Shiraz, Sophie found herself whispering as she walked to school that spring, a cloak of names to keep her from harm in the place she was sent to learn the strict geometries of popularity and beauty in this new city. A girls' school this time, instead of the cheerful mix of everybody in Paris. Osman thought she would like it better, only being with young women. But the students here were even sharper and tougher than the girls at home, and Sophie missed Marie Claire's soft faith and attachment to hair ribbons. It was not home to her, this place. The names of these green cities in the desert warmed her, the names of towns and people who wove the rugs that had blanketed their floors in Paris and their father's shop. She walked carefully because of carpets, a small, crimped gait, never allowing herself to step in the triangles that decorated the Gebbeh, the hawks in the Shiraz.

Mumtaz, Qum, Samarkand, Kashgar. At school, there was protection only in the library, where she waited before classes began. The corkboard floor reminded her of the ceremonious quiet of her father's shop. No shoes there, a beaker for coffee, and the piles of carpets absorbing and distorting sound effectively as fog. The stockinged feet of the women customers moved shyly. Their smiles were slightly strained. They didn't understand at first that with her handsome father, it was more than finding the right shade of tan to match a sofa; you acquired a piece of history you had to learn to tend as carefully as you would a garden or a child. Or the way at least he used to tend his children. Maybe, at their ages, they weren't supposed to need as much attention. Maybe he'd used up all his energy getting them safely across the ocean, and now that they were here, he was just catching his breath and waiting to see what should happen next.

Sophie slipped off her own shoes and into her favorite chair of cracked leather. Outside, it started to rain, and the trees that lined the street looked cold inside their iron fences. She had five minutes before French. She took out her notebook and wrote: "This morning I had a dream of horses and dogs running past me, chasing Sasha to the edge of a cliff. He stood there laughing. There is no more milk in the house. Papa listened last night to opera. Fourteen cigarettes in the ashtray."

She edged the page from the spiral binding and folded it into a tiny triangle, a paper sail. Darting to the door and off to class, she tucked the note in the Hebrew-English dictionary. She had seeded books in social studies, poetry, history. Now and then she saw one flutter to the floor as a student pulled a book from the shelf. What surprised Sophie was how often the stashed note drifted against a table leg, unnoticed. She retrieved it when she could and slid it back into its place.

Since they'd moved here, Osman had taken them once a month to someplace they could watch light on water. It was better than good wine, he said, or home-cured tobacco. Sophie got the sense that in looking at the wavering reflections of buildings, trees, and sky, she and Sasha were being asked to consider the essential fact of their mother's death. They walked to Central Park and watched waves on the reservoir try and fail to look fierce. Once they traveled west to watch the oily expanse of the Hudson River creeping away from the jagged piers, insisting on its brown and creamy self. In March, when the weather was awful, they watched the stiff water of seascapes in a museum and listened to the juicy squeal of rubber boots on marble.

They rarely mentioned Danielle's name, but these public excursions as a family made them all conscious of the space she would have filled next to Osman. Sometimes Sophie could see them as other people must, a family with a hole, moving haltingly, because a piece was missing. During these afternoons, Sophie supplied in her head the details and observations that Danielle might have, pointing to the unfamiliar parking meters or to the puzzlement on that particular dog's face. Last week, on the way to the fountains in front of the Metropolitan, she had spoken her thoughts aloud, and Osman, to their horror, had begun to cry noiselessly in the April light. She hadn't realized how much she sounded like her mother.

Instead of seeking light, her father was acting as if he'd been deprived of moisture his whole life, as if he hadn't grown up in England, whose whole history was ringed in climate. In New York, they were closer to the sea than they had ever been, on an island, even, whose tip, their father told them, was made of dense, packed trash. How much bigger had it grown, Sasha wanted to know, exactly. And their father told him: from 9,750 acres to 11,240. Without looking at a book. Sometimes Sophie was amazed that Sasha and her father's skin remained intact, that the lines of their lacerating tests of knowledge hadn't whipped their arms and chests with long, thin scars. Neither of them relented. That was a new facet to life here as well: Sasha obscurely angry all the time, usually at Osman. Sophie thought how Danielle would have hated their sparring. Facts were to help you understand things, not hurt people. She would have found a way to make Sasha be less indignant, over an open atlas and a cup of cider.

During these walks on whose edges their mother floated, trips that grew as mute as their dinners, memories returned to Sophie like burned bits of paper escaped from a fire. Bath time in Paris when Sophie couldn't have been more than six. The porcelain sink, the clawed tub. The hand-held shower and the thin blue mat, their mother's shirtsleeves rolled up past her dimpled elbows. "Wasteful," their father would say as she sprayed the shampoo from Sophie's head. Sometimes Danielle would turn the silver needles of water onto their father, who would dart, laughing, out of range. The water coiled their mother's hair to wild dark vines.

She remembered when she was seven and Sasha nine and Danielle took them to the Luxembourg Gardens, saying, "I've got a treat for you." She stood there in that manicured place, along the *allée* of cropped plane trees, and pulled a red Frisbee from her shopping sack. How the French mothers had scowled, how their beautifully dressed children had gaped at the foreigners' hoots and shouts, their frantic darts and swoops. The dust they kicked up. Then Sasha tripped over a section of overlapping wire arches that protected an expanse of grass clipped to the consistency of a green pelt. The French, Danielle would snort, treat their lawns better than their wives. And they treat those sorry excuses for dogs better than their mothers. "Danielle," Osman would sigh, "tolerance." When Sasha fell, park attendants and two policemen came running, not to help him, naturally, but to snatch up her brother at the nape like a ferret. Danielle was there in an instant and told them to drop her son, in quick, harsh French that clearly startled the gendarmes. She had looked like a lady until she opened her mouth. She held Sasha in a tight crescent to her breast and hip and yelled. Sophie had been so mortified, so proud.

But the most complicated part of what Sophie did that spring and summer was this: she pretended Danielle had not died and was merely traveling. It was a habit she knew she shouldn't engage in, like gliding into Sasha's room to see what he had in his bureau. It was wrong, it was stealthy. It cost her, made her feverish. Still, those few moments when she could float in that strange place of believing her dream had a kind of pillowed calm that made her burn less dreadfully. What was difficult, however, was that she wasn't able to stop with just imagining. She would let herself pretend that Danielle wrote her letters, which she then found herself composing. She wove in words from the books Osman gave her. Danielle, she decided, would have liked the South Seas. Sophie wrote about how storms made the halyards clank against the sailboat masts so loudly it sounded like prisoners rattling chains. Birds' nests woven tightly as cloth found on a climb to an active volcano. Melons hollowed out for soups of orange fruits. Descriptions of wharves and currents.

She even let her imagination move to this point: she could see the letters jumbled in jute bags, next to triangular heaps of green bananas. They might smell of diesel. The stamps would be like square bits of butterfly wings, from countries Sophie looked up in her school's encyclopedias. Vanuatu. Tuvalu. Specks of black in the atlas, and if they were big enough, a microbe's worth of green. Often the star that designated the capital was larger than the island itself, the name of the city sprawling into the ocean.

Sometimes Sophie cut out pictures from the atlas and encyclopedias and pasted them in her notebook. The vandalism didn't trouble her. No one at her school seemed much interested in anything but clothes, vengeance on less popular girls, and the reedy boys they saw at dances. No one in this place of glinting surfaces would miss small and foreign Vanuatu.

Nothing in this new place felt quite real, so the sense of consequence was lessened here. In Paris, she wouldn't have dared. The memory of Madame Frontenac's ruler that came with an infraction of the rules was still vivid. In Paris, school and uniforms were sacred. But here, where no one believed in corporal punishment, Sophie doubted that slicing up encyclopedias would earn her more than a trip to a person the girls called the Frog, a lady with a wide, tremulous mouth to whom you were sent to talk if you didn't eat or hand in homework for a few days. Still, she was careful in her crime, working when the librarian left for a moment or at the very end of the afternoon, when the tired woman propped her head on her hand and fought sleep.

Sophie had noticed people liked to watch her, and she didn't enjoy it. They wanted her to confirm the stories they had heard, to tell them the exact shape of her strangeness. There was no mother's name next to their father's on the parent list. Then there was the father's accent, the darkness of his skin and her own. She's Gypsy, she heard someone whisper. No, just French, someone else corrected. The mother's dead. The mother's crazy. The brother's beautiful. They are Jews. "How rich are you anyway?" one girl asked, and Sophie had replied honestly, "I have no idea." Speaking of money in France was about as acceptable as wearing torn stockings. When she asked Osman that night, trying to get a sense of how wealth was measured in this blunt country, he said, "I will say two things, Sophie. One, we have plenty for a comfortable life. Two, you should never ask that question again."

Enough. They had enough to live in a safe neighborhood. Enough for raspberries out of season. Enough to send her and Sasha to their private schools. She wanted to tell the girls who gossiped that she knew almost as little about her family as they did. But feeling it was safer to have people believe these flickers of talk, Sophie did not say anything to disrupt her classmates' vague impressions. She had no desire to be known by these foreigners.

Instead, she took it upon herself to put everything she knew about herself and her family in her notebook. Favorite snapshots she had filched from the photo albums Danielle had loved assembling. Transcriptions of Osman's old stories. Then the notebook's scope grew to include possible futures for all of them, especially Danielle. Pictures clipped from magazines of people and places Danielle might have liked. Song lyrics she would have enjoyed learning from her daughter. All this was glued into the pages, along with the glossy strips of paper illustrating life in the tropics.

Sophie used one of Sasha's X-Acto knives to perform her surgery. Violating Sasha's sanctuary frightened Sophie much more than slicing up American books. So far he hadn't noticed or, if he had, had said nothing. Whether this reserve was good or bad, Sophie didn't know. Absorbed in her work of piecing together the fragments, she didn't quite mind, which she knew would make her careless. Then she'd suffer her brother's anger, an emotion scoured clean of heat, and all the worse for that: it was as cool as science, as mercilessly timed as Switzerland. A refusal to acknowledge her presence, to the extent that he would bump into her in the hallway as if she were no more than the corner of a bookcase, the arm of a chair. Something, however, told her that Sasha could play that terrible trick, the only thing that reliably made her lose her head, and that she would survive it. She thought about this as she added photos of Tahiti and words she had stumbled on in dictionaries. She was sure she was creating something essential. Her father looked at her curiously one night and said, using French for the first time in ages, "You're growing up, Sophie." She replied, in English, "So what?" and was sent to her room, burning with the shame and pleasure of rudeness.

A fathom was a measurement of depth, six feet. Old-fashioned, no longer in use. Chiefly British. A verb and a measurement, a dual definition that Sophie found thrilling. A length coiled inside the murk of not understanding: "I simply couldn't fathom what she meant," said the dictionary in its example, and Sophie accepted, without knowing why, that of course women could not be fathomed. She grasped that there was something the world, and men in particular, failed to decipher in the cloudy ways of women, their veils of perfume and scarves, their coy skirtings of directness. As a six-year-old in France, having just begun to master the language, she told the mother of a friend, *"Je veux rentrer chez moi."* The woman had said, *"Non, non, petite, je voudrai."* Girls' desires, she learned early on, were to be expressed conditionally. Girls' desires were conditional. They depended. Someone might notice your wants. Someone might not.

Dear Sophie: The weather has turned stormy here. It is the rainy season, but it is less rain than curtains or sheets of water that travel over the ocean. They drench the port, the boats, the children, and just as suddenly pass. Within minutes, shirts and palms and docks steam in the hot sun. The food people eat is all white, bananas, taro root, except for tins of imported vegetables and meat. Everyone drinks milky instant coffee all day long. I am going to the Marshall Islands next.

There was no attempt to sound cheerful or forbearing, just reports of birds seen, islanders met, geological notes, but no mention of traveling companions or difficulties. Sophie wondered if Sasha's stance was more useful. Avoid thinking about her, talking about her, excise her altogether, because there was nothing you could do. He told her she should start a life list, but she had: Sophie kept track of betrayals. Birds were too tame and mild by far. They had nowhere near the allure and danger of the people you loved.

Sasha crouched, not quite feeling the rain finger its way down his neck. His binoculars were growing filmy, his breath made wavering columns of fog. It was April, and chilly in the mornings. He was still getting used to the sharper climate, but he was pleased. He had found the vireos. He knew they were here; he'd heard the distinctive call, like someone crying "Three-eight, three-eight." At least four chicks filled the twigged cup. It amazed him, the complete focus of the parents, the babies' unabashed greed.

He pulled his notebook from a plastic sack and jotted, "Nest near 76th and Central Park West. In bush next to cherry tree." Binoculars around his neck, the birds blurred to an indistinct lump. A jogger thudded past. A dog stopped, nose twitching, at a garbage can. A church bell started to clang. It was time for school and Sasha stood, rain fumbling down his collar. In moments, he had left the green tangle of Central Park and was running on the sidewalk, jostling other dark-jacketed young men to get inside before the red doors locked. It had surprised him, he thought as he climbed the stairs suffused with a terrible blend of sneakers and bleach, to find so many birds in New York. Since March, he had taken to walking across the park to his boys' school on the West Side.

That open space was the best thing about the city, the only part he thought an improvement on Paris. It gave him the chance to develop an obsession, a funnel into which he could pour himself and keep the rest of his life at the level of a distraction. This school with its hymns and insistence on ties. The blank modern apartment where the light got trapped and their old furniture looked so ill at ease. Sophie and Osman growing thin and pale and silent. Turning sixteen without Danielle to make a large and messy cake. Instead, he trained his mind on the problem of taxis and herons sharing a home. It was wild everywhere, it came to him as he pressed toward the second floor, even when it looked as if it wasn't. Soon he would start looking for the coyotes he heard were living in the Bronx.

In his room at home, Sasha kept his field notes in immaculate order. It bothered him that he had sensitive long fingers whose nailbeds turned purple in the cold. He didn't like being so irritated by temperature. He planned on being a biologist, to spend long, muddy hours in bogs and valleys, but his body was not suited for the work. Every night after supper he went to his room to reread his entries. On May 5, the robins lost a chick. He had steeled himself and sketched the small creature, its head and beak translucent pink, its eyes too large for the small skull just tufting with pinfeathers.

The vireos were thriving, nearly ready to fly. On May 10, he'd caught a glimpse of the white flirt of a mockingbird's tail. He told no one but Sophie about watching the birds, and even to her he did not describe what he did in detail. He just did it. Outside, the city clicked and whistled. Taxi doors slammed, tires whined on macadam. It was getting warmer and the breeze stirred the curtains his father had insisted on. Too spartan otherwise. Sasha didn't protest. He found it easier to give in on small matters. It allowed more time to look up birds.

Boys here, just like boys in Paris, were magnetically lured to music, cigarettes, girls, their bodies' own shaggy development. But the girls here were even crisper and more brittle than the girls in Paris, and Sasha found it easier to spend the money he earned working in his father's shop each weekend on wildlife guides. He tried to parcel it all quite neatly. School in one box, where without fuss or much effort he excelled. Life at that level was simple. Do the problems, attend the classes, stay out of harm's way. He didn't engage in tricks as the boys in his physics class did. During a lab on pendulums, some students purposely dropped the silver ball so that they could sneak a look at the slender legs emerging below the strict white coat and pursed lips of the stiff but lovely Miss Hofstader. The design of this accident was far more precise and challenging in terms of physics than the experiment itself, and the results were exceptionally satisfying. No underwear, claimed Jeff Beattie, who'd muscled his way to the ball first, nearly knocking Miss Hofstader off her feet and earning him a trip to the dean's office. A dark warm slash of flesh and hair and some strangely spicy smell. That's not what he said, but their collective imagining sent them off supposedly early to lunch but actually to the most distant bathroom they could find for a quick, fantastical rendezvous with Miss Hofstader. Sasha, even, too, but later, at his own discretion, and even though he knew that Miss Hofstader didn't like men: he had followed her and seen her go into a bar frequented only by women. He didn't write this down anywhere, fearful in an inchoate and unnamable way that his work would be discovered and her secret revealed.

Sasha wrote half in French and half in English, using whatever word came first. He kept entries in his life lists and his diaries scrupulously clean of personal reference. He avoided, if possible, a *je* or an *I*, trying to be a mere lens, an instrument that reflected the light and reality around him. It wasn't that he didn't like himself. It was more that the *I* was an inconvenience, an obstacle to the knowing of the world that was his project, just as his body and its sensitivity to cold was an irritation, an impediment. Sometimes Sasha wanted only to be a mind, a vast, translucent sheet of receptivity. But whenever he had these fantasies, he would spend night after night waking, wrapped in sweaty sheets, his head flashing with glimpses of women's legs and globes of pink-tipped breasts, nipples straining against cotton nighties. Worse, sometimes his dreams were laced with the naked heads of baby birds and human hands he thought belonged to his mother. What was even more disturbing was that between the vireos' anxious programmed stuffing of bugs down the gullets of their squeaking chicks and his vision floated the memory of these breasts: languorous and heavy, lightly batiked with veins.

It was then he would get up at dawn and roam the park for days in a row, tracking like a dog the faint signs of the birds.

As school wound down, Sophie began to notice that Osman's stares were deepening. His eyes would get caught on the armchair Danielle had liked to sit in or the handle of the pan she had used to make omelets. But Sophie didn't try to help her father anymore. With the rising temperatures, it became clearer to her why exactly she was reluctant to spend too much time around him. It was more than his silence or his cryptic gifts or the pressure of his sadness. It was the penance, she realized, that he had to endure for his inability to keep their mother alive. She for one was not going to risk contamination with love that didn't work.

But she also kept herself away from him because of the strange territory her body was now entering. At fourteen, she had suddenly gotten rounder, years, it seemed, after other girls. To her horror, the other day he had gently brought up bras, to which the only possible response had been to flame dark red and storm from the room. Usually, she could control herself better. But that was awful. He had noticed her shape, he had been watching it.

After school the next day she forced herself to head to Bloomingdale's. She had never been inside the black-and-gold store, but she had seen the mannequins of women's torsos in the windows and their shiny silver skin on which filmy bits of underwear seemed to float. There was no one her age swirling through those doors, and she nearly turned back when someone elbowed her forward and she found herself inside. She had money to spend; she could be a customer here, she reminded herself. That it was her father's money, saved from groceries, seemed not to matter. Besides, she thought, as she walked up the mirrored makeup section, it was so crowded, no one would notice her.

On the fourth floor, in the lingerie section, she circled the displays, fingering gauze, lace, and silk, letting the different sensations register. So much of it was scratchy, would raise a rash on soft skin. A saleswoman came up behind her and asked nonchalantly if she needed help. "No, thank you," Sophie said quickly. "Just let me know, hon," the woman said. She was stout and had half-moon glasses tethered to a beaded chain. Sophie kept wandering, looking for some simple arrangement of cotton and straps. At least the woman hadn't questioned her right to be here. She must have looked as if she belonged. Sophie stopped in front of what seemed to be a less alarming display and looked at the sizes. American notions of largeness and smallness still eluded her. She grabbed a range of the bras, some in cotton, some in something shinier. The saleswoman had stepped somewhere else for a moment, and Sophie slipped into a booth and locked the door without having to submit to the shame of having her selections counted and gauged. Then she untangled the bras and hung the flock of them on the door hook and stood looking at herself in the three panels of the mirror.

She knew girls in her class came here in giggling clusters to buy lingerie, and she would have liked to have invited someone along to help. But she didn't talk about homework, much less bodies, with the New York girls. Friends were unreliable. She watched the volatile struggles for ascendancy in her class with fear that one day they would capture her, too. You could stay someplace only so long until things happened that involved you.

After stripping down to just her trousers, Sophie unhooked a bra labeled 36C. The cups were cavernous. She put her arms through the contraption and reached behind her back to hook the eyes into place. In the mirror, she saw how the silk sagged forlornly. She could not maneuver the complicated device that would shorten the straps. One side jerked up, but the other still drooped, so one breast was uncomfortably pressed to her chest, while the other crouched in the pouch of fabric. Slightly panicked, she tore the whole thing off. A piece of lace came loose and feathered to the floor.

She pulled the next one off its hanger. At least there were no hooks; it was made of champagne-colored nylon and you had to slide it over your head and then somehow persuade your breasts to settle in properly. But she must have put her arm in the wrong place. One cup managed to slide over a breast, but the other one was left hanging loose, the glossy fabric crinkling uncomfortably against her ribs.

Sophie had cried five times since Danielle died. Once in June, when Osman told them that their mother was dead and her terror got wrapped in tears. Once in July, when they'd watched Danielle's ashes swirl into the river. Once in December, just before packing up the neat silk nests of her mother's scarves that lay in a bureau drawer. Once when Osman had, that April, when he heard her voice sounding so much like Danielle's. This was the fifth time. She sat on the ground and folded her shirt to her face.

A soft knock made the door rattle slightly. "Are you okay in there?" Sophie could not stop crying. It was as if her grief had sprouted a root, thick with sap and full of energy, that anchored her to the low beige carpet. A key slid into the lock and the door opened a crack; Sophie saw it was the sales-woman who had stopped her earlier to offer assistance. She stood there, not saying anything. From the floor, all Sophie saw were the veins under her hose, like heavy strands of wool come loose from a skein. "What's your name, honey?" she asked, easing herself onto the stool in the corner. She shut the door behind her. It was a voice with some sand to it, but not overly rough. Sophie looked up, still hiccuping, and told her.

"I'm Esther Lefkowitz," she said, and pulled her glasses to her nose. "That bra you've got on is the worst possible design. No one gets it right. There's always a boob hanging out somewhere. Laundry left out to dry."

That was reassuring, as was Esther's casual way with breasts. She had said "boob" so frankly. "Let's see what you've got here," she said, and helped Sophie stand up. "Lift your arms over your head," Esther ordered. In a moment, the bra was a toast-colored ball on the floor. Esther paid it no mind. It was a bad bra. It did not deserve to lie smoothly on a hanger. "Put your shirt on, Sophie, and then pass me the other ones you got."

None of them met Esther's criteria, apparently. She sighed heavily through her nose. She looked at Sophie, the bras clamped with one arm beneath the bulk of her own bosom, and said, "Here's the system, Sophie. A is for the little guys. B is for something with, you know"—she made a small flutter with her ringed hands—"a little heft. C is for the heavy artillery, and D, that's for the grapefruits. Got it?" Sophie nodded. "So I'm going to get you something simple. White cotton. Colors are for when there's somebody to show. And there's nobody to show right now, am I right?"

In ten minutes, she had explained the digits to Sophie— "32 is for skinny numbers like yourself. When you get a little meat on you, it'll go to 34, and so on. Do not be a rude girl and ask me my size. Past a certain point it is better not to know"— and Sophie stood at the counter wearing a bra as plain and white as a bandage and holding another exactly like it folded inside a brown paper bag. "Thank you, Miss Lefkowitz," she said. You could barely tell she had been crying.

"It was my pleasure," Esther said mildly, flapping a hand at her as she headed back to the changing room to help another customer. "When you grow out of those, just come back and we'll find new ones." Esther seemed to take it in stride that Sophie's body would keep changing.

Sophie walked up Lexington Avenue as dusk started to cool the city down from the bake of an early-summer afternoon. Men and women surged out of the subway and onto the sidewalk, all angles, elbows, anxious fatigue. The air smelled of exhaust, softened asphalt, and a slight breath of the river. The nicest thing about Esther was that she hadn't asked where Sophie's mother was or why she was not with her. Sophie hugged her brown bag closer. The cotton on her skin felt soft. The straps bit a little into her shoulders, but it was a pleasant tightness. New York was doing its best imitation of Paris at this time of day, and it made Sophie catch her breath. She watched the line of blue that edged the buildings. The way the shop windows gave off smoky gold light. The sky closer to liquid or paint than sky. She took her time getting back to the apartment. She looked at the twilight, she passed right through it.

Coyotes like to hunt at dawn. They'd been seen near Van Cortlandt Park, which he'd located on a map that was now folded in his backpack. Sasha rode the subway north. He had never been in this part of the city. The people on the train with him were sleepy from working all-night shifts but were still surprised to see a young, white, vaguely foreign face going to this section of the Bronx. It was nearly light. They were interested only in going home, eating, getting clean, and crawling into their sheets. He took the train to the last stop and looked at his map to find out where to go next.

The day's heat had yet to settle. There was no one on the sidewalk, and the light was a smudged yellow at the horizon, which he glimpsed in segmented lines as it appeared through the gray blocks of buildings. The park smelled green, even under a layer of gas and trash. Coyotes like to eat mice and rats. They would find them here, he expected. Coyotes are pouncers, not like wolves, who run down prey in packs, taking turns at exhausting the caribou or deer. Coyotes work through stealth. They slide through grass so carefully they make less noise than snakes, one scientist thought. Light travelers. The best way to hunt them is from the air, and even then they are hard to pinpoint, they run so fast and so jaggedly. When caught in traps, they will gnaw a foot off at the ankle.

The idea of a bloody stump caught on iron teeth impressed Sasha. Animals like staying alive. They fight hard to do so. He allowed himself to think a tiny thought that blackened a piece of him even as he did so. She had not fought hard enough. She gave in too quickly. It meant she had not loved them enough; their stories, their dinners, the falcon, none of it had been enough for her. She wanted something else they could not give her. If they had been enough, she would have struggled more.

The park was straggling, untended. He left the path he'd been walking on and entered a more shadowed place where the air was even damper. Beer cans glinted on the ground, hot-dog wrappers, potato-chip bags. The usual American trash. A rat scuttled past. Sasha crouched down on a small black boulder through which threads of lighter stone ran. They might be anywhere. They were. There was probably one watching him right now. He listened to the hum of the city as the light grew stronger and revealed yet more garbage on the scuffed earth. Still, he sat there. Another rat ran past. He took out his map. Five different colors, like patches on a quilt, marked the boroughs. He guessed he was looking at it more to say good-bye than anything else, then got up and walked back to the entrance of the park. He passed an elderly black man doling out bread crumbs to a chattering mixed flock of grackles and pigeons. The man nodded at Sasha, who nodded back. Sasha paused and asked, "Excuse me, but have you seen coyotes here?" He shifted his backpack a bit.

The man looked out at the boy from under the brim of his soft hat and said, "Forget coyote. There's things a lot more dangerous in this park to pay attention to. You get along home." He went back to scattering crumbs.

The whole way back to Manhattan, Sasha kept seeing that

composed face, the delicate motion of the man's wrists as he fed the birds, the small space he'd carved for himself between humans and animals. When he got home, he took his backpack and jacket off and hung them where he always did, on the chair in the front hall. It was only five-thirty and the apartment was still muffled in silence. You could always tell if someone was awake; the air smelled differently, had been stirred.

He knelt on the red-and-blue Shiraz and, not knowing why he did this, pressed himself down on it. He stretched himself on the rug facedown, like a ragged star. It was softer than he remembered. Dustier, too. He heard footsteps and knew from their weight that it must be Sophie. She stopped when she saw him; at least her walk froze. "Sasha?" she asked, tiptoeing closer now.

"What?" he asked in French.

"What's wrong?" she answered in the same language, and then she sat down. He did not answer. He did not speak again either, because it was clear to them both that everything was wrong. He smelled the freshly laundered cleanness of her nightgown and heard her shallow breathing. "Did you see any birds?" she finally asked, nervous, it seemed, at his silent prostration.

"Do you think she just gave up?" he said in English, rolling over finally to look at his sister. Her eyes were still thick with sleep, her hair slipping in partial loops out of its nighttime pigtails. She looked like a small girl, but she also didn't.

"Do you?" Sophie whispered.

"I don't know," Sasha said, and traced the outline of a lion's woolly muzzle. He saw how carefully the person who had made it had outlined the animal's teeth. Even in the three knots of wool devoted to the fangs, you could tell those teeth were sharp enough to tear flesh from bone. Sasha thought he might understand why someone would care about getting details right: it was a way of letting people know you had been there, of being sure of one small thing. Then Sophie lay down. They did not touch each other. He watched a sunbeam start to aim in their direction, staining the floor with light.

Once school let out, Sophie began to spend afternoons at the shop with her father. Despite her ambivalence about him, it was clear he needed watching. Sasha was often gone, apparently looking for whatever wildlife New York had to offer. He would come back from these forays silent, ravenous, and scratched on an arm or his face. He offered no information about where he'd been or what he'd been looking for, and Sophie didn't dare ask him. His hair was growing longer, but he wouldn't cut it. Once, she'd tried to say she'd go with him to the barber, and he stopped long enough to glance up from a huge bowl of cereal and say, through a mouthful, "Get lost."

That was reason enough to spend more time with Osman. But in addition, she soon realized that women had discovered her sad, handsome father. They swarmed to the shop. Business had thrived all year. They wore as much black as Parisians, but they smoked less. Their laughter was just as sharp and tricky, though. They would try to stroke Sophie's hair and say how pretty she was, but she found if she stared hard enough at them, they would keep their distance. Besides, they were after Osman. His daughter's approval was a secondary concern.

Sophie saw how they worked. They came in clumps and flirted collectively, coaxing the stories of the rugs from him. Then they'd place a compliment right in front of him, where he had to step on it. Their praise—of his expert knowledge, his accent, his handsome clothes, his good taste—made him blush. He had never done better business. But Sophie saw, too, that he was getting worse rather than better. After the women left, he would sit at his desk and smoke. He no longer was teaching Sophie about the rugs and watched in silence as she helped Nawang fold the ones the ladies hadn't wanted. Once the Tibetan man had left, it sometimes took Sophie four or five times of calling to Osman before he turned to her and she reminded him they should go home for supper.

He stopped taking them on trips to inspect water, and then he stopped cooking, using as an excuse the hot weather that descended on the city that July. They were discovering that everything in America, including temperature, was more extreme. The first part of that summer, they ate salads and bread, food it took minutes to prepare, or Osman would order out, large volumes of Chinese or Thai that none of them would eat. Most of the dishes ended up in the fridge, slowly aging in their angled white containers. After he went to bed, she would leaf through her mother's old albums and write down anything she remembered about their life in Paris in her notebook. The name of the dog in the café at the corner.

That the trash collectors came on Thursday. That the best sheep's cheese came from the market stall run by the old Basque man.

Like Sasha, Osman started taking long walks at unpredictable hours. Sometimes that August, Sophie would wake up in the middle of the night and know that no one was home. She would lie terrified in her bed until she heard the click of a key in the lock and the quiet creeping of Sasha's or Osman's feet. They never seemed to bump into each other, as if they'd discussed beforehand who got which piece of the night. She could not read or sleep or do anything but lie there, deeply, hopelessly awake. If she concentrated, she felt, they would return home safe.

She even let herself imagine that one of them would come into her room and sit lightly at the edge of her bed and tell her what he'd done as the humid summer wind rattled the blinds. Telling a story with a gentle flourish, a tilt of something to make her laugh. But that had not happened once here in this spiky blue city. It had not happened once.

Sasha knew Osman remembered everything. It was how his own mind worked. He could tell, when his father sat smoking in the living room, that all that floated in front of him were Danielle's scarves, the music she liked, the way she'd sliced onions, impossibly fast, the only times he'd really understood the word "minced." He could tell that they wove around him, those memories, roping him to the chair. Each night, when Sasha looked at him, he saw that Osman was shrinking more deeply into the chair. It was at that point he started going out every night without fail. At a certain moment, the new memories had to push the old ones aside, didn't they? There couldn't be room for everything.

It was something of a relief when school started again. Sasha had to stop roaming so much because of all the work he had to do. The rhythm of classes took over and made all of them feel more solid. Osman even gave Sophie money to get herself some new clothes. He seemed a bit more lively with the return of the fresher air. He was still walking at strange times, and the unsettling gifts began to reappear, but he was going to the shop. He was ordering and selling rugs, after all, and wore a tie to work. In October, a client invited him and the children for a weekend to her house in the Hudson Valley. Sophie agreed to go instantly, glad for a change from the city and eager to keep an eye on the woman who'd asked them. On the phone, she sounded suspiciously breezy.

Sasha, to Sophie's astonishment, wanted to come as well. Her brother was growing more feral, as if apartments and sisters and other trappings of civilization should be skirted at all cost. It wasn't even his hair or how he smelled—something had invaded the way he moved, which was becoming padded and spooked. Perhaps he thought the countryside would offer new birds to catalogue. Perhaps he had a limit to how much solitude he could bear.

Threading their way north in the rental car, Sophie noticed how long it took for the city to thin away. She was navigating, having made sure to occupy the seat next to Osman. They listened to the radio on the way out, a cycle of

Beethoven string quartets. Osman hummed a little. Sophie allowed herself to think they might have a fine time.

And they did. The client turned out to be married, with two young children, whom Sophie happily scurried after most of the weekend. The man, John Madden, was tall and friendly, and got Osman to look at all the old rugs his father had collected as they smoked cigars. The wife, Rosalie, cooked tureens of elegant soup and asked Sophie about Paris, her school, and how she liked New York. As Sophie kept one of the small boys from tipping over a kitchen chair, she found herself talking. She found, as Rosalie sprinkled a bit more basil into minestrone, that she had an enormous amount to say about those topics. That she could have talked to Rosalie, her lively face misted in the steam of her boiling soup, for a very long time.

They didn't see much of Sasha, except at meals. He had brought his binoculars and spent most of his time outside, scouting the woods that surrounded the farmhouse. It turned out that John also liked to watch birds, and Sophie and Osman watched in astonishment as Sasha began to speak. About the Baltimore orioles he'd found nesting in Central Park that spring and the red-tailed hawks he spotted above John and Rosalie's meadows. About all the species he'd noticed and the ones he hoped to see, the countries he hoped to travel to in pursuit of the birds.

When they left on Sunday afternoon, the Maddens wished them goodbye from their front porch. They, too, were packing to go back to the city, but even in their rush and fluster, they paused to wish their guests well. John propped one little boy on his hip, while Rosalie clutched the other to her chest, leaving each a free hand to wave as Osman, Sophie, and Sasha pulled out of the driveway.

They said little as they curved around the back roads that led them to the highway. Sophie watched the trees that fronted the narrow lanes, seeing in the late-afternoon light just how orange many of them glowed. "What kind of trees are they?" she asked, and Osman and Sasha answered in one voice, "Maples." The trees Danielle had always talked about. The ones that made the syrup that she brought back from visits to Hilda. It was sweet and amber, but its essence was mild compared to these trees at their peak, flaring crimson and gold, looking royal. Danielle had told her years ago that the maples that turned these grand colors flourished only in parts of the States, Canada, and northern China, their leaves bursting into reds and yellows because of cool nights and hot days. The prettiest, she said, were supposed to be in North America. Danielle had called the changing foliage one of the treasures of the New World. Sophie thought how lucky those boys were to have a mother who let them march so loudly through the house, a mother who made such good soup.

But then she grew aware of Sasha. He was sitting in the front seat this time, the map unpleated on his legs. He wasn't looking at creased segments of New York State, however, he was staring at his father's profile. "We're all thinking of her, Papa," he said. "We all are." It was the trees. It was the memory of Danielle crowing about the syrup, holding the brown jug above her head and saying they were in for the treat of their lives. How they had scoffed at her thick pancakes, accustomed as they were to thin French crêpes.

Osman kept driving, staring at the twisting ribbon of pavement. "And what good does it do you, Sasha?" he asked in a voice that sounded to Sophie as if it had been scorched, rough and damaged. "What do you want me to do? Turn the car north and drive us to Canada so we can mope around her childhood home? If it would do any good, I'd go." His voice rose and broke further, and he pulled to the side of the road to look at them, his eyes swimming, "Is that what you want? To talk about her? But I can't," he said. "I can't. I can't say anything."

Sophie and Sasha were quiet. Osman put the car back into gear and slowly steered them toward the city. They did not speak the rest of the way back, and only Sophie noticed when the copper and yellow of the country trees gave way to Manhattan's faded brown leaves as the sky darkened and the air chilled.

Soon after that, Osman stopped getting up in the morning. "Are you sick, Papa?" Sophie asked the first morning. He was smoking in bed, a great fountain of it coming from between his lips. He was wearing ragged pajamas. He did not look at her. "Just tired, Sophie. Go to school." She did, and paid especially close attention to her classes that day. It seemed a good idea to keep herself from thinking about her father's long, dense stillness in the bedroom. The windows hadn't been open, the room blanketed in old smoke.

He was still there when she got back. "Did you go to the shop today?" she asked, not daring to come in because she hadn't been invited.

"Nawang opened for me," he said. He looked at her then, for the first time. "I just need a few quiet days," he said. "Don't worry."

She nodded. "Do you want some supper?" she asked, but she already knew he wouldn't eat, that he hadn't been able to eat all day.

When Sasha came back from school and they had poured cereal for themselves, Sophie said, "Papa didn't get up today," and explained that he was just lying there and smoking.

Sasha chewed, swallowed, and said nothing. "And what do you expect me to do about it, Sophie?" he shouted at her suddenly, rising so quickly his bowl tipped on the table. "What am I supposed to do?"

Sophie felt her throat tighten, and to keep herself from crying she watched as the beige O's of the Cheerios bobbed on the white puddle of milk. "I was just telling you, Sasha. I just wanted you to know."

He fetched a sponge and mopped up his supper. "Sorry I yelled," he said, the bowl clattering in the sink. Ten minutes later, she heard the door bang. Sophie spent the evening cleaning the kitchen, scrubbing the stove, tidying the refrigerator. Then she worked two chapters ahead in Spanish. It was such a soft and curly language. It soothed her to work out its tangles, to persuade her tongue to wrap around it. When she went to say good night to Osman, his light was out. She crept in his room. He seemed to be asleep, at least he was breathing as if he were, and so she took the full ashtray and replaced it with a fresh one. Danielle had always done that for him. She had hated when he smoked, but it hadn't kept her from being kind to him.

All week, Osman did not go to work. He dressed only to go buy coffee and cigarettes, then either lay in his bed or sat in his chair and stared at the ceiling or the wall. He wouldn't say much more than that he was a bit tired. That Nawang would do a good job in the shop. That Sophie was not to worry. But he did not reassure her. She went to a church on Madison Avenue and told God, but even though God seemed a bit less exclusive in America than he had in France, she still had no feeling that he took the concerns of girls that seriously. She wrote Marie Claire that her father was sick, then did not send the letter. She wrote in her notebook that Osman's eyes looked like holes, not eyes, but it scared her to see this in words and she crossed it out. She thought about talking to teachers and the girls at school. She even thought of trying to tell Miss Lefkowitz at Bloomingdale's or the Maddens that her father wasn't well. In the end, Sasha was the only one who would really understand what was upsetting her, and the one time she had tried to speak of her concern, she thought he would hit her. All night, she listened to Osman shuffle from his bed to his chair and back.

Then one afternoon at the end of October, he wasn't there and the apartment was wreathed in smoke. Not the smoke of cigarettes, but something more acrid, coming from the kitchen. In the sink were the charred remains of one of Danielle's albums. He had brought the others with him from the living room, but set fire to only one, the one brimming with pictures of their courtship and early married life in Paris, when they were so young and shy and Danielle's hair had been long and parted in the middle. The book was only partially damaged, Sophie saw as she leafed through the warped pages. Heat had blistered their faces and turned gray Paris a weird orange, and then he'd turned the water on it. Something had made him stop, but where he had gone?

She called the shop, but Nawang said that he hadn't been down. He hadn't called that day, either. Was everything all right? he asked in his careful English. "We're fine," Sophie said, just as carefully, knowing he did not believe her. By the time Sasha got back, Sophie was hopping and crying at the same time. "Where is he?" she kept saying. "Why did he do this?"

Sasha sat down at the kitchen table and touched the ruined photographs. Even though Sophie had opened all the windows, the whole apartment still smelled of doused fire. Then her brother put his head on the table and wept. He wept like an animal caught in a trap. He wept as though he were dying. He wept as if he would rather be dead. His shoulders shook, the sugar bowl shook, the entire table rattled. He did not raise his face. When he was done, he took a few enormous gulps of air.

They sat together as the evening fell. Sophie called the shop again, but there was no answer. Nawang had long since closed for the night. Sasha's eyes were streaked with red. He looked fully at her. "What should we do?" he asked, and to her surprise, Sophie knew. "We should go to the shop. He might be there." Sasha nodded, and she felt a stain of pleasure spread through her. He had listened.

They found an extra set of keys, then took a taxi that bumped over the potholed streets. The driver was skillful and fast and did not seem to think it strange to have two teenagers ask for an address in a part of the city that was mostly for merchants and Indian restaurants. He should have asked, Sophie thought. He should wonder how we are. But instead, he took their money and sped off around a corner.

The building was deserted, but the hall light was on and their feet echoed on the worn stone tile. When they opened the door to the shop, they saw him immediately. He was standing in one of the pair of tall, narrow windows at the end of the showroom. The sash was all the way open, and the wind that traveled through it smelled of the fall night and his cigarettes. His body filled the open space. A blackish, awkward star.

"Papa?" Sasha asked.

Osman said nothing, nor did he move.

They stood there. Sophie thought if they walked toward him at the wrong speed, they might by accident tilt him out the window. The slightest pressure and he would be gone. They would have to be so careful.

"What's wrong, Papa?" Sophie asked. He was still silent, but they could see him shaking his head. Something unfolded in Sophie then. She would never be able to say what it was exactly. Anger certainly, but anger with a fierce, specific purpose. She suddenly did not care if her father was going to leap. He was going to have to decide. She knew exactly what she wanted to do for the first time in months. A clear arrow of desire.

She walked to the end of the showroom where he stood and opened the other window. Her fingers bloomed orange in the streetlamps' glow. She opened the sash. Another swerve of wind stirred the cold air. She moved back from the window and leaned down to grab one of the folded rugs. It was heavy. A Bukhara, she thought in the dim light, but she could not say for sure. The night blurred its colors and patterns, and all she really felt was its stiff, awkward weight in her arms. She shoved it through the open window and watched it fall. It landed with a deep whump on the sidewalk. No one was passing. The streetlamps still sent out their pinkish light. The rug was still crumpled. It could have held a person in it. It could have been a person. A car passed. Nothing was different, except that one of her father's rugs lay in an angular C on the cracked pavement.

She waited for his body to follow the rug. But it didn't. She could hear him breathing. Sophie turned back to the pile of rugs and picked up the next one. Then Sasha was there, helping her. Together, their arms full of their father's carpets, they tossed one after another through the window. The rough underweave chafed their arms. They were breathing heavily. They did not care. Osman still watched. They set off an alarm when an especially heavy Kashgar hit the windshield of a parked sedan. A man with a shopping cart appeared. Several taxis stopped to see what was happening.

Sasha wondered what it must look like from below. The carpets didn't fly. They didn't catch the wind, they didn't soar. There was nothing leisurely or calm in their descent. They fell with a purpose, the way a hawk falls on prey. "Hey!" voices shouted up. He and Sophie, still working in silent tandem, aimed the rugs past the bystanders. Sasha paused, pulling New York's air into his lungs. He heard Sophie catching her breath, too. They had stirred up dust. Their arms ached. As they leaned out the window, they caught one last glimpse of the seven rugs they had launched, some still folded as they'd been thrown, some with a piece of their pattern exposed. They could not tell in the strange city night which one was which. "Take them," Sophie shouted down. "You can have them."

The taxi drivers moved slowly, assessing the danger. She wondered what they saw as they stared up, two dark heads, two slight bodies, two children getting rid of precious rugs. A man standing in the other window. Was it a dream or just another night for a cabby in New York? One man darted out, bundled the Kashgar into his trunk, and sped off, which seemed to release the others, who quickly shoved the rest of the carpets into their own cars. Manholes clanked as they pulled away from the curb. Their tires left the smell of skinned rubber; the smell of fast escape.

Osman came up behind them. He said nothing. He smelled of grief and tobacco. He smelled like their father. He touched them gently on their shoulder blades, one hand for each child. They stood there, letting themselves feel the faint pressure of his fingers. They almost didn't mean to, but they leaned backward. The smallest shifting of weight, the slightest relaxing of their bodies. They leaned into him and knew that he could bear it. If they needed this, he would stay here all night, his hands on their backs, watching the sky's color deepen and then slowly, almost unbelievably, grow light again.

 ACKNOWLEDGMENTS

I would like to thank Miss Porter's School for giving me the time and space to complete portions of this novel. Later, the Ucross Foundation offered me the quiet and beauty of Wyoming, where I finished the first draft.

My agent, Ginger Barber, also has my deep appreciation for her enthusiasm and good advice as the book took shape. Elisabeth Sifton's insight and acuity helped me enormously in polishing the final manuscript. I am very grateful for the elegance and care with which she edited my work.

Thanks are also due to my colleagues at the University of New Hampshire, who encouraged me as the novel unfolded.

Finally, I would like to thank Brad Choyt, whose support and patience make so much possible.